Stone Cold Dead

Stephen Puleston

ABOUT THE AUTHOR

Stephen Puleston was born and educated in Ynys Môn, North Wales. He graduated in theology before training as a lawyer. Stone Cold Dead is the eleventh novel in the Inspector Drake series.

www.stephenpuleston.co.uk
Facebook:stephenpulestoncrimewriter

OTHER NOVELS
Inspector Drake Mysteries

Brass in Pocket
Worse than Dead
Against the Tide
Dead on your Feet
A Time to Kill
Written in Blood
Nowhere to Hide
A Cold Dark Heart
Prequel Novella– Ebook only - Devil's Kitchen

Inspector Marco Novels

Speechless
Another Good Killing
Somebody Told Me
Times Like These
Dead of Night
Prequel Novella– Ebook only -Dead Smart

ISBN: 9798863034379

In memory of my mother
Gwenno Puleston

Chapter 1

Croquet hoops pinned to the pristine bowling green surface kept upright a piece of cardboard with the words "Welcome Jack" daubed in black ink on it. Jack Holt jerked his head up and scanned his surroundings. Lights from nearby houses cast a thin veil over the lawn as an ominous chill crawled up his spine.

This wasn't how it was supposed to be. The meeting was supposed to have been a civilised affair, prearranged to take place in comfortable surroundings with a glass of beer and enough time for them to talk. Jack peered into the darkness, his mind urging his eyes to see someone, to recognise a face. He walked over towards the middle of the bowling green, scooping up the cardboard sign as he did so. He wanted to feel safe and, in the middle of the green, he'd see anybody approaching and be prepared.

But the place was quiet. The sound of traffic passing on the road nearby drifted over. It reassured him that he wasn't alone despite the hour. He should have ignored the message when it reached his mobile asking him to meet at the bowling green. He should have realised it was an idiotic thing to do. He felt a fool. The possibility of that vital piece of information, that missing section of the jigsaw, had been enough to entice him there. And he wanted more than anything to silence his critics, but now, standing on the smooth grass surface not far from the croquet hoops, he just wanted to get home.

Ever since his schooldays he had hated croquet. It was a ridiculous upper-class game played by people with posh accents drinking Pimm's and lemonade. And it wasn't even a croquet lawn. It was a crown green bowling lawn. He let his gaze settle on the clubhouse, which was more of a large shed, that stood a few metres away from the edge of the turf.

He anxiously searched for any sign of activity. It was

probably where the members of the club kept their equipment. It might even have stored gardening machinery. From what he could tell the place was kept in excellent condition. He imagined the febrile atmosphere of elderly men and women competing against each other for some local cup.

Opposite the clubhouse was a small clump of trees and various benches and then an area where he imagined the youngsters of the town would play boules in the summer. He recalled playing the game on dusty park surfaces during childhood family holidays in France. The brief smile the recollection brought to his face quickly disappeared as he heard a noise and turned immediately towards the clubhouse. He spotted a light coming from around one corner. It was like the torch function on a mobile, but it was quickly extinguished. He opened his mouth, but dismissed the notion of calling out.

He needed to get out of the place. He'd reach out to his contact once again but next time he'd be far more careful about arranging meetings. He paced over towards the narrow steps leading onto the green. Quickly he was back on the gravelled path that led the way towards the exit.

He glanced over at the clubhouse. Now he saw a shadow, a movement around one side of the building and he paused for a moment. The only way he could exit the park was via the gravelled path in front of the building. He gritted his teeth and picked up his pace, walking briskly.

At the corner of the building, he saw a gate and then the road outside.

He broke into a jog but only managed a few steps before a figure stepped out onto the path in front of him.

'Welcome. I'm glad you made it.'

'What the hell do you think you're doing?'

'We need to talk.'

Jack felt his pulse hammering in his neck. 'Not here, not now.'

'I'm sorry you feel that way.'

He could see the head shaking in disbelief.

'I'm leaving now.'

More shaking of the head.

Then he heard movement behind him, a soft footfall on the fine gravel. He didn't turn round in time to see a face, just felt an excruciating pain as though nails had been driven into the back of his head.

He sensed his knees unable to keep the weight of his body upright. He raised his hands towards his head but couldn't touch it before another blow struck him. He closed his eyes and sensed his body falling, slowly at first and then crashing onto the gravel surface in front of him.

Chapter 2

Ian Drake indicated left off the A55, the main dual carriageway that runs along the North Wales coast. It would be a short journey through the morning traffic to his daughters' school. The weekend with Helen and Megan had passed too quickly. They were old enough now to entertain themselves, but still young enough to sometimes need his support and that of Annie, his partner.

Since announcing that he and Annie were going to get married, both his girls had seemed more mature. It pleased him that they enjoyed Annie's company, and their interest in the arrangements for the marriage pleased him even more.

Luckily his daughters were studious. Megan enjoyed music and the arts; Helen was good at sciences and had showed an interest in a career in medicine, just like her mother, but wanted to be a paediatrician. Single-mindedness was something she shared with her mother and her maternal grandmother. It had been one of the things Drake had found so attractive about his former wife, Sian, but with the long hours demanded by his job and the impact of his OCD their marriage hadn't survived.

He parked outside the school gates and watched as his daughters headed towards the main entrance. Idly he wondered what they'd be talking about – would they be discussing what he and Annie had been doing that weekend? Or what they were looking forward to doing at school?

Once his daughters had disappeared from view he drove away and drew up by a newsagent's shop, quickly popping inside to get what he needed. He returned and opened the newspaper at the sudoku page. He still couldn't discard the habit of completing the sudoku every morning in his favourite broadsheet.

He filled a few squares easily enough, knowing the ritual was going to help calm his mind and prepare him for the day ahead.

After completing four lines he discarded the newspaper on the passenger seat and made his way to headquarters. He was giving evidence later this week in a large burglary trial at the Crown Court in Mold. He would need to reread his witness statement before a meeting with the Crown prosecutor to review the case that was scheduled for two days' time.

There was an abundance of clear evidence the defendant was responsible and a conviction at the conclusion of the trial was likely to mean a lengthy prison sentence.

Until then he had annual appraisals for Detective Constable Gareth Winder and Detective Constable Luned Thomas to be completed. This was something he always thought should be undertaken by a trained HR professional. But there was no escaping the demands on his time to make certain the members of his team were up to date with everything. It was another part of policing that didn't feel like policing any longer.

He pulled into the car park at headquarters and spotted Superintendent Hobbs' Jaguar gleaming in the morning sunshine, parked in his usual reserved spot. There'd been rumours the superintendent had applied – unsuccessfully – for a promotion to Western Division. Gossip among the senior officers at Northern Division had concluded Hobbs would finish his career as a superintendent. Drake wasn't at all certain they could write off Hobbs' career that easily.

Drake made his way up to the Incident Room and pushed open the door. Two voices acknowledged his presence in unison, simultaneously announcing, 'Morning, boss.' Drake returned the greeting and made for his room.

Sara Morgan, the detective sergeant on his team, followed him in and stood in the doorway as he shrugged off his jacket before sitting at his desk, booting up his computer. He waved a hand at one of the visitor chairs and she sat down as he adjusted the photographs of his daughters by the phone on the desk. They had to be just so and adjusting them a few millimetres would satisfy his need for neatness.

A third photograph of Annie and his daughters completed the family unit.

'A civilian from the admin team called by first thing wondering whether you would be able to complete all the appraisals by tomorrow. She mumbled something about there being an inspection and that the paperwork was needed promptly.'

'Tomorrow!' Drake exclaimed. 'They've got to be joking.'

Sara made a serious face. 'She was an intense little woman. I got the impression that she didn't have any sense of humour at all.'

'I'll talk to them. It's completely unreasonable to expect us to complete these things so quickly.' Drake glanced at the emails populating his inbox. He was certain he saw one marked urgent from Superintendent Hobbs. Had the HR Department persuaded his superior officer to intervene about the appraisals?

'And Luned has a training course later today – something to do with first-aid.'

'I thought Luned had some medical qualification.'

'This is a refresher course.'

'I need to spend all day preparing for that trial at the end of the week. And with Gareth on a training course today appraisals will have to wait.'

Sara stood up and made to leave his office. He'd need to do an appraisal of his detective sergeant as well as the other two detective constables on his team. Her calm approach to policing was something he valued. She wasn't the impulsive sort that made decisions on the hoof only to regret them later.

He sensed his mind processing the disruption these appraisals were likely to create. He began to mentally compose the ticking off he'd give the civilian in HR. He was a detective inspector and there were more important things than box-ticking a personnel file form.

He scanned through his emails. He already deleted a few when his mobile rang.

'DI Drake.'

'Area control, Detective Inspector. We have a report of a dead body. You're needed at the crime scene.'

Chapter 3

'Sara, get in here,' Drake bellowed.

He got to his feet and grabbed his mobile from the desk. Then he stepped over to the coat stand and shrugged on his suit jacket. Seconds later Sara stood by the door to his room.

'Yes, boss.'

Drake read the postcode from the message on the screen of his handset.

'There is a report of a suspicious death at a park in town.'

'Do we have any more details?'

'I've got a postcode. Let's get going.'

He jogged out of headquarters, Sara behind him, and they headed down towards his vehicle. Once they were inside, he handed his mobile to Sara. 'Punch the details into the satnav, but I think I already know where the park is.'

The message from area control had been terse – a body had been found at the bowling green of a park in Colwyn Bay, not far from headquarters. He knew exactly where she meant. It had swings and children's play equipment and he had taken both his daughters there when they were younger. The place was popular with young families.

He accelerated hard out of the car park before taking a right turn. He ignored the instructions from the satnav but the disembodied voice irritated him.

'Switch the bloody thing off. I know where I'm going.'

Sara did as she was told.

Drake couldn't believe the amount of traffic that seemed to be dawdling more than necessary. When a car in front of him slowed at a zebra crossing, despite the absence of anybody waiting to cross, Drake's irritation erupted and he sounded the car horn. 'What's wrong with these people?'

The vehicle accelerated off and Drake followed, keeping far too close. A few minutes later Drake spotted several police cars and an ambulance parked outside the entrance to the park and he pulled up a little distance behind them.

Once he and Sara had left the car they marched over to the officer standing on duty by the gate. Drake flashed his warrant card at the officer, who nodded abruptly.

'Were you one of the first officers on the scene?' Drake stared at the officer's name badge which said Jameson.

'Yes, sir,' Jameson said. 'I was with another officer, PC Williams, who is over at the bowling green.' And he added as an afterthought, 'Our sergeant told me to stay here.'

'And is your sergeant with PC Williams?'

The young officer nodded and opened his mouth as though he was going to say something, but Drake had already walked away into the park. The gravel crunched loudly under his brogues. He had just cleaned them the night before and a brief spike of annoyance filled his mind that he would have to clean them again that evening after the dust and stones of the path.

Mulch covered the otherwise bare borders. In a few months, once the spring sunshine had worked its magic, the place would be a mass of colour, but for now every plant and blade of grass would be waiting for winter to finish. Drake spotted a uniformed sergeant talking animatedly to two paramedics. They blocked Drake's view of the bowling green behind them, but Drake could see a shed to his right. He guessed it stored playing equipment.

Drake scanned the surroundings and noticed two other uniformed officers strategically positioned to prevent any unwelcome members of the public gaining access. Some distance away there were properties and a road skirted away from the park towards the middle of the town.

The uniformed sergeant recognised Drake as he approached.

'I'm glad you got here so soon, sir.'

'Morning, Steve.' Drake had worked with Steve Turner on a previous case and was pleased he was in charge. It was so easy for inexperienced officers to contaminate a crime scene. 'You'd better show me where the body is.'

'This way.' Turner turned on his heel. He led them to a gap in the borders surrounding the bowling green and made for the steps leading onto the surface.

They walked over the grass to the body with its arms and legs splayed out.

Drake stared down. 'What the hell is that?'

'His arms and legs have been pinned to the surface by croquet hoops.'

'What?'

'It looks like some sort of ritual,' Sara said.

'A groundsman employed by the local council made the discovery.' Turner nodded his head towards a border nearby. 'He explained in graphic detail how he'd puked over the flowerbed.'

'We'll speak to him in due course,' Drake said without taking his eyes off the dead body a few feet away.

'He's waiting in his van outside. I warned him someone would take a statement from him.'

Drake mumbled an acknowledgement before walking slowly around the body. A hoop pinned each of the dead man's arms by the wrists and one more pinned each leg, just below the knee.

'Do we have any idea when the CSI team will arrive?' Drake looked up at Turner.

Before the uniformed sergeant could reply Drake heard two scientific support vehicles pulling up outside the park.

'Good, at least we can make some progress with the actual crime scene itself.'

Drake took the opportunity of staring at the dead man's face. He had a ghostly pallor. He wore faded, expensive-looking denims and a pair of tan Chelsea boots. A sweater underneath the thick navy jacket was a dark purple colour. Drake kneeled and spotted the gash at the back of the man's head and the blood pooled behind it. This answered a question that had arisen in his mind when he had first seen the body – whether or not the man had been dead when he had been pinned to the bowling green. It seemed unlikely, but the wound to the back of the head suggested the man had been overcome and perhaps even killed before being pinned to the lawn.

Was Sara right about this being a ritualistic killing? Drake had experienced strange killers in the past who had plumbed the depths of a depraved imagination. But he couldn't ignore the way in which the body had been set out. The killer was sending them a message, of that he was certain.

'Good morning, Ian.'

Drake recognised the voice of Mike Foulds so he looked up and over towards the senior crime scene manager as he approached. Another CSI followed him and deposited bags of equipment before the steps onto the green.

'What have we got here?' Foulds stared at the body.

'Well, it's certainly not a croquet game gone wrong,' Drake said.

'You never know. Croquet can be a vicious game.'

Foulds, already dressed in a one-piece white forensics suit, dragged on a pair of latex gloves and kneeled. Gently he moved the man's head to one side.

'There's a big gash on the back of his head. I suppose you want some sort of identification?'

Drake nodded.

Foulds dipped his hand into the pockets of the jacket. He pulled out a wallet and a mobile from inside. He placed the handset on the lawn by his side and began to flick through the wallet examining the contents of the various bank cards.

'His name is Jack Holt.'

'Is there a driving licence?' Drake said.

Before Foulds could reply they heard a voice and turned to see one of the crime scene investigators standing at the edge of a path surrounding the bowling green. 'Something you should see, Inspector.'

Drake led the way, and Sara followed, over the lawn towards the steps and then along a fine gravel path.

At the investigator's feet was a blood-smeared rock.

'I thought you should see this before I bag it up.'

'Good. Get it photographed and the blood tested as soon as possible.'

The investigator kneeled and began bagging up the stone.

Drake turned to Sara. 'Is there any sign of the pathologist?'

'I'll ask Sergeant Turner,' Sara said. She called over to the uniformed officer.

'He should be here any time.'

Drake retraced his steps to the bowling green lawn where he met Foulds, who had completed his examination of Holt's wallet. He had dropped his driving licence into a plastic evidence bag which he handed to Drake.

'Call area control and see if they can find any details about Holt,' Drake said to Sara. He read the address on the driving licence. Jack Holt lived a few miles away on the outskirts of Colwyn Bay so the bowling green would have been local to him.

His mind was alive with all the activity that had to be completed urgently.

House-to-house enquiries would need to be started. He needed a full team allocated.

Witnesses to any activity around the park the previous day and night spoken to.

He stood in the middle of the bowling green, Sara by his side.

'Why was he killed here?' Drake said.

'There might be some significance to the bowling green.'

Drake nodded at the prone figure. 'You don't just pin somebody to the ground with croquet hoops for no reason.'

Sara took a call on her mobile and Drake gazed over to

the shed-cum-sports pavilion-cum-clubhouse.

'That was area control,' Sara said. 'Jack Holt is a journalist, apparently, and he has a partner. But they haven't got a family liaison officer available until this afternoon.'

'Damn,' Drake said, knowing he and Sara would have to break the news to Holt's partner.

They still had to talk to the caretaker who discovered the body. Drake walked over to the building and, after checking, was satisfied there was no sign of a break-in, which suggested the croquet hoops hadn't been stolen from inside.

And that meant premeditation. Someone had brought the hoops with them. Deciding he couldn't delay any further, he began to walk for the entrance hoping the caretaker would still be sitting in his van. But his journey was interrupted when Dr Lee Kings bustled through the gate and down the path towards him.

'Good morning, Ian. What have we got here today?'

Kings carried on walking as Drake joined him, retracing his steps towards the scene. 'The body of Jack Holt was found this morning on the bowling green lawn. It looks as though his head was caved in and one of the crime scene investigators has found a large blood-splattered rock lying in a border.'

'So a murder weapon at a murder scene. I haven't had that for a long time. And you guess it was used to kill your man stone cold dead. Pardon the pun, I couldn't resist it.'

They paced over the lawn towards the dead body. After a cursory examination Kings got to his feet. 'I'll be able to make a better determination once I have the body in the mortuary, but it looks like he was killed late last night from a very rough estimate of the time of death.' He paused and peered at the croquet hoops pinning Jack Holt's body to the ground. 'What are the croquet hoops all about? Did his losing opponent in a game decide to get even?' Kings grinned.

'Let me know when you can do the post-mortem.'

'It'll be first thing tomorrow morning.'

Kings left them and Drake nodded at Foulds for him to finish their work.

He and Sara left the park and made for the uniformed officer at the gate. Jameson told them the park caretaker was waiting in the van parked a few metres away. Drake marched over and Geoff Norman left his van, painted in the livery of the local council, and stood with Drake and Sara on the pavement.

Drake flashed his warrant card at Norman. Sara did the same, but he didn't look at either. He was a man in his fifties with thinning hair and a paunch that pressed against his council-issue jacket. Finding a dead body was certainly not a regular occurrence by the tired, shocked look on his face.

'I need you to remember as much as you can about what happened this morning,' Drake said.

Sara continued, 'You were the person who found the body and we need to know everything about the circumstances as we are in charge of the murder inquiry.'

'Murder,' Norman drew a hand over his mouth.

'Look Mr Norman we could have this conversation down at the station headquarters if you prefer,' Drake said, glancing at his watch at the same time.

'He was there. Just like that. I thought it was a drunk at first. In the summer we get drunks sleeping rough. But I've never had a murder.'

'Was there anybody else in the park this morning?'

'No, nobody. I was going to work on one of the borders by the tennis courts. The boss told me he wanted it looking neat and tidy.'

'Was the park open when you arrived?'

'It's never locked.'

'And have you checked if the pavilion has been broken into?'

Norman stared up at Drake. 'No, of course not. I called the cops straightaway.'

'And you were on your own?'

'Yeah. Can I go now?'

'We'll need your address so that we can get a formal statement from you in due course.'

Norman nodded his understanding and stammered the details, which Sara jotted down in her notebook. He left Drake and Sara standing on the pavement.

'Let's go and talk to the next of kin.'

Chapter 4

Drake travelled the short distance to the address on Jack Holt's driving licence. It was a detached two-storey house in an estate of similar, older-style properties. A glistening, black-painted front door and matching dark grey windows gave the place a modern, clean look.

Drake never liked breaking the news of a bereavement. It was so much easier having trained family liaison officers, so he sat for a moment in his vehicle with Sara. He knew he shouldn't delay. A family had to be told. But those few seconds enabled him to drag from his memory the sort of words and emotion he should deploy to share the tragic news with Jack Holt's partner.

There might be children to grieve for a father, a parent traumatised by the loss of a son, siblings who'd mourn their loss.

'It's never easy is it, sir,' Sara said.

Drake nodded. 'There is no easy way to break bad news.'

Sara nodded.

Drake reached for the door handle. 'No time like the present.'

As he led Sara up the tarmacked drive to the front door, Drake straightened his tie, shrugged his jacket straight over his shoulder and composed his first two or three sentences.

The door was opened after a chime rang out through the ground floor. A man in his late forties appeared at the threshold. His hair had been trimmed neatly and he had a designer stubble of three days' growth on his chin. The sweater he wore complemented the one Drake had seen earlier, worn by Jack Holt.

'I'm Detective Inspector Drake and this is Detective Sergeant Morgan of the Wales Police Service. Are you David Ackland?'

'Thank God you're here. Yes, that's me, have you found

him?' A frown creased Ackland's forehead as worry filled his eyes.

'May we come in?'

'I reported Jack missing first thing this morning. I couldn't sleep, I tried texting and calling him and...'

Ackland stood there for a moment as though he were unable to move, unable to process Drake's request. Then he pushed open the door. Drake and Sara entered and followed him into a downstairs room at the front of the property.

The decoration was immaculate, and the furniture was set out in perfect symmetry, with scatter cushions of strong colours balancing the muted fabric of the sofa and chairs.

Ackland sat down; Drake and Sara, uninvited, did likewise.

It was as though Ackland knew somehow that two senior police officers on his doorstep could only mean the worst news.

'I'm afraid we have bad news, tragic news, Mr Ackland. The body of Jack Holt was found this morning.'

Ackland began to thread the fingers of both hands through each other. He looked between Drake and Sara with increasing incredulity.

'There must be some mistake.'

He searched for something in the faces of Drake and Sara to give him a glimmer of hope. Every strand of optimism faded from his eyes and he began to blink nervously.

'The body was found in the park in town, on the bowling green. I know this is an exceptionally difficult time, but I need to know everything you can tell me about where Mr Holt was going last night.' Drake could sense Sara's attention focusing entirely on the man sitting opposite them. He could be their primary suspect, after all. Members of the family needed to be eliminated from the inquiry so that they could focus on suspects with a genuine motive to kill the victim.

Ackland's eyes were awash with tears. 'Can I see him?'

'Of course, in due course, but we really need to know as much as you can tell us about Mr Holt's whereabouts last night.'

'He went out, early. I don't know when... I can't be certain. This is tragic.' Ackland stood up and walked to the window, staring blankly into the garden outside.

'Sara will make some tea or perhaps you'd like some water,' Drake said as Sara got up and left to find the kitchen.

Ackland mumbled his agreement. He retook his place on the chair he had left moments earlier and began scanning the various paintings and ornaments in the room. 'We bought all these together. What am I going to do now?'

'Did Jack have any family apart from yourself?'

'Why would you possibly want to know that?' Ackland retorted, a fraction too sharply.

'It's no more than standard protocol. We have to know as much as possible about every murder victim.'

'He doesn't have anything to do with his family,' Ackland continued.

Sara arrived with a teapot and three mugs on a tray. She poured the tea and placed a full mug on a coffee table next to Ackland.

'Why did you report Mr Holt as missing?' Drake asked, before taking his mug and drinking the tea. He hardly ever drank the stuff, but it was strong and wet.

'He hadn't come home last night.'

'Were you expecting him back?'

'Of course.'

'And where did Mr Holt go last night?'

'When can I see him? I mean, I want to see him, and I want to see him today.'

'I'm sure we can make arrangements for you to see him very shortly, but, Mr Ackland, I must ask you where Mr Holt went last night?'

'Jack's a journalist. He's working on this big story, has

been for years. It's about that cult with a place down the coast. He is completely obsessed by them.'

'Who do you mean?'

'It's the Peel Foundation. It was established by a man called Mervyn Peel and he basically seduces people into believing he's some sort of guru that can change their lives and make sense of all the difficulties and challenges everyday life can bring. He's a shyster.'

'Did you know who Jack was meeting yesterday?'

'He told me he was meeting Peel himself. He'd finally been able to persuade Peel to talk to him on the record about various things. He was going to meet up at some local hotel and buy him a beer and act as though they were old friends.'

'Do you know where that was?'

'That fancy place in town. The De Vere Royal.'

Drake recognised the name of the hotel. It was a grand old building that had been extended over the years.

'This is awful. Just awful. I cannot believe this has happened.' Ackland gripped his tea mug. 'It must have been Peel. It's the only thing Jack was working on which was ever dangerous.'

'Who did he work for?'

'He was independent but I'll give you the name of the magazine and website he was connected with.' Ackland's initial shock had dissipated.

'And what was your relationship like?'

'What are you trying to imply?' Ackland dumped his empty mug on the coffee table theatrically.

Sara took the initiative. 'It is standard protocol. I'm afraid there will be a number of difficult questions you will have to answer. But I'm sure it will be nothing compared to the difficulty you face in losing your partner. That is why we need to ask about your relationship.'

'Our relationship was extremely strong and healthy,' Ackland announced in a voice suggesting he wasn't going to be challenged. 'We were about to celebrate our eighth year together. We were planning a holiday in one of our favourite hotels in Corfu.'

'Does Mr Holt have a study or an office?'

Ackland nodded.

'We need to see the set up and any computer he has. Do you know if he keeps a diary on his PC?'

'I believe so. He was quite diligent about keeping proper records of people he was meeting.'

'Please show us.'

Ackland led them to an office attached to the rear of the garage outside the property. Books filled a cupboard against one wall and box files populated another next to it. Framed posters of the films *Casablanca* and *Roman Holiday* gave the room a certain bohemian air.

Holt's computer setup had a PC and two screens. A television hung from a bracket on the wall. Once Drake and Sara were alone, they rummaged through the desk drawers but there was no sign of any notebooks. Drake guessed Holt had most of his material stored digitally.

'Let's take the PC with us,' Drake said as he fiddled around the back of the PC unit on Holt's desk.

'Shouldn't we let the admin support guys collect everything?'

'I think we take it now. I don't trust David Ackland. And the tech guys can always sort out the passwords.'

They took a few more minutes to go through all of Holt's possessions and once Drake was satisfied they had everything of value they took the PC to the car.

When they returned to the property Ackland was standing by the door.

'I've got one further thing I need to ask you, Mr Ackland. It is only a matter of protocol, but we need to know where you were last night.'

'Oh, for Christ's sake. Do you really have to do this? This is like one idiotic cliché after another. I was at home, Detective Inspector. I had a meal, did some ironing and watched the television.'

Drake searched Ackland's face for any emotion. It only made him realise he'd need to dig a lot deeper into Jack Holt and David Ackland's personal life and relationship. 'Thank you, Mr Ackland. Officers will call tomorrow to collect the rest of Mr Holt's office possessions.' Drake handed him one of his cards. 'If there's anything else then please do not hesitate to contact me.'

Drake turned away and walked down the drive with Sara.

'What did you make of him, boss?'

'He really was playing to the gallery wasn't he?'

'Something wasn't right.'

They reached Drake's car. He bleeped it open with the remote control.

'I think we need to do a lot more digging into Mr Ackland.'

Chapter 5

Once two civilians had erected the board in the Incident Room, Inspector Drake seemed less on edge. Sara knew the absence of Gareth Winder would make him irritable. There was little point in dragging another detective constable to join their team when in the morning Gareth would get up to speed quickly.

Sara watched as Drake pinned an image of Jack Holt to the board. Luned had accessed the records of the DVLA, who kept images of everyone with a driving licence. She sat next to Sara who stared intently at Inspector Drake. Sara had worked with Luned on several investigations and had found the young detective constable to be competent, if a little intense and verging on geeky. Gareth Winder, Luned's colleague, was the same rank but he had been in the job far longer and naturally took the lead as her senior.

'Why the hell is Gareth on that course today?' Drake said.

His question didn't require an answer. Sara knew he wasn't expecting one.

'Jack Holt's body was discovered in the park in town this morning.' Drake pointed at the image on the board. 'So, we do the usual searches into his background. I want to know everything about him. And we'll need full details of his banking and financial history.'

Alongside Jack Holt's photograph Drake had pinned an A4 sheet of paper with the words "David Ackland" scribbled on it.

'Do you want us to do a full search against Ackland, too, boss?' Sara said.

'Yes, of course.' He looked over at Luned. 'He was Jack Holt's partner. We've just spoken to him and there was something odd, something out of place.'

'He had reported Holt missing,' Sara said.

'So he didn't seem surprised when we arrived. He

thought we were calling to tell him we'd found Holt. I wasn't comfortable with the replies he gave to some of our questions. When I asked him what he'd been doing last night he seemed to have his reply already packaged up – having a meal, ironing and watching television.'

'Maybe that's what he did,' Luned said, frowning.

'Do you want me to coordinate the house-to-house enquiries?' Sara said.

'Make certain the officers are fully briefed. The preliminary time of death is midnight but that might change.'

'What did Jack Holt do for a living?' Luned said.

'He was an investigative journalist. Apparently he was working on articles relating to the Peel Foundation which, according to him, is some sort of cult.' Drake nodded at Sara. 'We'll go and see the Peel Foundation later this afternoon. If Ackland was right and Holt met Mervyn Peel he might be the last person to have seen Holt alive.'

'Or he was the murderer.'

'Find out if there are any CCTV cameras in the local area. And establish with the DVLA what car Holt owned. He must have arrived at the park somehow.' Drake turned his attention to the board once again. 'Somebody wanted Jack Holt dead and we need to find out who and why. I'm going to do some digging into the background of the Peel Foundation. Sara, get started on some preliminary work on Jack Holt. Then we'll go and see Mervyn Peel and we'll do a final catch-up later this afternoon.'

Drake walked over to his office.

Sara enjoyed the buzz of the first few days of any inquiry. There was an energy about everything. The Incident Room felt alive with an urgency to track down the killer and bring him or her to justice. She lived for these moments, relishing the challenges she and her colleagues faced.

Sara sent Luned to the canteen for sandwiches and soft drinks as she began the work of setting up the records she needed to keep for every decision made. She had seen experienced detectives being cross-examined at length about poor record-keeping. It raised the unwelcome prospect of guilty defendants walking free. She knew every day from now on would be full on. She'd find time to run, as she did most days. But it meant the little social life she had would have to be put on hold until the inquiry was over.

She listened to Inspector Drake making various telephone calls. She guessed from the formal tone of his voice he was bringing Superintendent Hobbs up to date. Then she called the sergeant responsible for coordinating house-to-house enquiries.

'These murders take place at the most inconvenient time.' The officer sounded exasperated.

'We need a full team on house-to-house immediately. You know what it's like – the public must be reassured we are doing something.'

'Yes, of course, I know there is nothing like the sight of police officers tramping the streets. At least we won't have to have a mobile incident room – I'll use one of the ground floor reception rooms as a temporary drop-in centre for any concerned members of the public.'

'Good idea. And we're looking for any suspicious activity from six pm last night to first thing this morning when the council groundsman found the body.'

Sara settled down to some preliminary work on Jack Holt. A Google search brought up his name as the author of several articles. She skimmed through to page ten of the search results, impressed he had been so productive. One magazine that regularly featured his name was *The Examiner*. Sara clicked open the magazine's website. She scrolled through some of the articles and read the magazine's mission statement. It didn't seem to have a political angle. It was focused on making sure certain injustices were called out and that the human rights and dignity of individuals maintained.

Something that Jack Holt had done had led to his death.

Sara wondered if there was some article he had published that had offended someone. She guessed he was dogged and determined when he put his mind to an investigation. News was something that she paid scant attention to, occasionally watching the BBC news on television, but she consumed most of her current affairs from online apps and websites.

'There aren't any CCTV cameras near the park.' Luned's voice expressed her exasperation.

Sara looked over at the young officer. 'Doesn't surprise me. Not exactly an area likely to be the subject of regular crime.'

'I'll tell the house-to-house team to keep a lookout for CCTV cameras on properties.'

Sara got back to building a picture of Jack Holt and requisitioned the usual financial searches. Money could always be a motive for murder. Was she right to think Ackland's replies had felt forced and deliberate as though rehearsed? When asked about his relationship with Holt he had over-reacted, as though he were performing a role. Sara reminded herself that when things didn't feel right, they usually weren't. So she requested a full financial check on David Ackland, too.

She started to assemble a list of the articles Holt had written but she wondered if contacting *The Examiner* would be more constructive. Before she had a chance to do so, Inspector Drake left his office and announced, 'Let's get going to see what the Peel Foundation have to say.'

Drake walked briskly to his BMW X3. He pointed the remote at the car and it bleeped open. It had been years since he had owned a saloon car and occasionally he missed the thrill of the Alfa Romeo GT he had once owned.

He drove out of headquarters as Sara punched the postcode into the satnav.

'I found a glossy website for the Peel Foundation,' Drake said. 'They are all about self-help and assisting people on their journey in life and how self-learning and personal forgiveness is so important. But it doesn't say what they actually *do*.'

Drake pulled up at the junction by the busy main road and indicated left. He glanced at the satnav and headed in the direction of the property occupied by the Peel Foundation.

'I did some preliminary work on Jack Holt. He was quite a prolific journalist. He has investigated trafficking gangs bringing young women and children over from Europe. Most of his work is for a magazine and website called *The Examiner*.'

Holt's contact with the Peel Foundation was the only lead they had so far, and Drake was eager to find out exactly what the nature of his relationship with the business was.

'Was there anything about the Peel Foundation that made you suspicious, sir?' Sara said.

'It was a professional-looking brochure site. There wasn't a contact telephone number, but you could sign up for their newsletter.'

After a left-hand bend the road headed into the countryside. Drake slowed as the satnav announced he was reaching his destination. In the middle of a long straight stretch of road there was an entrance with a glossy sign nearby: "Peel Foundation – Private".

He pulled the car up to the gate and Sara spoke into the intercom. The gate buzzed open, and Drake drove through into a copse of mature trees. The road looked newly tarmacked and the ground under the trees carefully cultivated.

He reached the property at the end of the drive. It looked entirely out of character with the local area. It reminded Drake of a French country château with a tall roof and large ornate windows.

He pulled up outside the main door and as he did so a woman came out to greet them.

They left the car, and she gave them a professional

smile.

'May I see your warrant cards?'

At least she knew the correct name for their identification, Drake thought, despite the hint of a North American accent.

She gave both warrant cards an intense stare. Then she took a photograph of each with her mobile. She glanced at Drake, daring him to complain.

'How can I help you, Detective Inspector Drake?'

'We'd like to see Mr Mervyn Peel.'

'I am afraid he is very busy.'

'Perhaps I wasn't clear enough, Mrs…'

'Jane Quant.'

'Mrs Quant. This is official police business. We need to speak to Mr Peel now.'

Quant pouted and turned on her heel and went back inside the property. Drake and Sara followed and stood in a hallway as she disappeared into the rear of the building.

Large pieces of antique furniture filled the space. All far too big for any normal home.

Moments later she returned.

'Mr Peel has found time in his busy schedule. He has ten minutes.'

Now it was Drake's turn to give her professional smile whilst thinking, Peel will give me all the time I need.

She led them through a corridor passing various conference rooms where small groups of individuals huddled together. At the end she pushed open the door and waved for Drake and Sara to enter.

Three people stood by a conference table. The taller and older of the two men stepped over towards Drake.

He had piercing blue eyes and steel grey hair. His navy-blue suit was an immaculate fit and it put Drake's own off-the-peg variety to shame. He reached out a hand.

'Detective Inspector Drake.' Drake thought he heard the guttural vowels of a South African accent. 'I'm Mervyn

Peel, how can I help you?'

'We wanted to discuss a personal matter.' Drake looked over at the man and woman standing behind Peel.

'This is my wife, Martha, and Edward Murphy is our financial controller. We have no secrets here, Detective Inspector, that is the whole purpose of my foundation. We provide mutual support and respect.' He waved a hand at chairs at the table.

Peel, his wife and Edward sat down clearly expecting Drake and Sara to do likewise.

'What do you do here?' Drake said.

Peel gave him a patronising sigh. 'We help people achieve their full potential in life.'

Drake expected a little bit more detail. He frowned at Peel. 'And *how* do you do that?'

'It is a matter of realising a person's full abilities and focusing on how they can be used.'

Martha Peel butted in, 'There's no simple five-minute answer to your question, Detective Inspector. We often take weeks and months to be able to get people to master their skills and maximise their potential.'

'What do you want to speak to me about? I take it this isn't a social call,' Peel said.

'Where were you last night?'

'It's none of your business where I was last night.'

Drake narrowed his eyes and sensed his annoyance building. 'A Jack Holt was murdered last night. And your name has been mentioned as part of the inquiry. It would help us to eliminate you as a potential person of interest if you could confirm where you were between the hours of six pm and six am this morning.'

Drake didn't take his eyes off Peel as he repeated his request for information. The clear blue eyes were inscrutable. They just stared at Drake. There was no emotion, they were neutral, unfazed. He found it difficult to read the expression and make sense of exactly what lay behind the eyes.

'And where was Mr Jack Holt killed?' Edward said.

'His body was discovered pinned to the surface of a bowling green with croquet hoops by a groundsman this morning. We believe Mr Holt was killed from a blow to the head.'

Edward nodded as though it were entirely normal.

'Is it true Jack Holt was investigating your organisation?'

'I have no idea what Mr Holt was doing,' Peel said.

'Did he make contact with you?'

'I really don't see how this is at all relevant. He did reach out to one of my associates, as a matter of fact, but we don't speak to the press.'

'I'll ask you again, Mr Peel, where were you last evening?'

'And as I said, Detective Inspector, it is none of your business.'

Drake sensed his pulse beating a fraction too quickly. Very few people adopted this attitude towards the police. It fired off all sorts of alarm bells in Drake's mind.

'We believe Mr Holt was investigating your organisation.'

'And your question is?'

'I'm bound to say Mr Peel that your obduracy and failure to cooperate is noted.' Drake stood up. 'If we need to speak to you again, I shall be inviting you into Northern Division headquarters for a formal interview.'

Drake nodded at Sara and they left the room and headed back out to their car.

Drake sat in his car for a moment before starting the engine, allowing his annoyance to cool.

'He thinks he's cleverer than us,' Sara said.

Drake nodded. 'We need to be careful with that man. We'll need to do a full background search against Peel, his wife *and* their financial controller.'

Chapter 6

Drake had time on his journey from the Peel Foundation to gather his thoughts and calm his temper. Mervyn Peel was going to the top of the list of persons of interest. Even though they had no evidence other than David Ackland's belief his partner had met with Peel the evening before he was murdered.

A detour to visit the DeVere Royal Hotel where he had enquired about Jack Holt had met with shaking heads when Drake showed the reception staff the image of Holt.

After parking, they made their way back to the Incident Room, Sara detouring to the kitchen. Drake walked straight for the board where a photograph of David Ackland had been added underneath that of Jack Holt. Photographs of the crime scene from the CSIs were pinned to the other side.

Half a dozen images populated one corner of the board, each showing Jack Holt's body from various positions. It created the impression of activity and progress which all contributed to Drake's focus. He sat by one of the spare desks and looked over at Luned, recalling something about a course she was attending the following day.

'You'll have to cancel that training course tomorrow.'

Luned nodded her understanding. 'It was only a refresher course in any event.'

'We need you here. And Gareth should be back in the morning, too.'

'How did you get on at the Peel Foundation?'

'They were completely uncooperative. Mervyn Peel blanked all of my questions. He refused to confirm where he had been last night although he knew Holt was a journalist. He didn't give us any information.'

'That's a bit suspicious.'

'We need to dig into Mervyn Peel and his foundation in more detail.'

'I've started work on Holt's computer.'

'Anything?'

'There are drafts of articles and all the recent ones are about the Peel Foundation. I haven't had time to read them all, but he certainly had a fascination for the organisation. I found something in his notes about flying to South Africa to speak to Mervyn Peel's family there.'

'Good, excellent. But we need to find out where Holt went yesterday.'

Sara returned carrying a tray of mugs. Drake eyed the one she placed in front of him suspiciously as though she hadn't yet mastered the proper art of coffee making.

'What do we know so far?' Drake sipped on his coffee, not expecting an answer to his rhetorical question. 'Jack Holt left home late afternoon or early evening and had told his partner he was going to meet Mervyn Peel at the DeVere Royal Hotel. Peel is our number one person of interest.'

'The house-to-house inquiries might discover somebody who saw Jack Holt last evening,' Sara said.

Drake nodded, his mind still thinking about Mervyn Peel. 'I hate it when people refuse to cooperate. It just makes me super suspicious.'

'We should have his mobile from the CSIs by the morning. So we should be able to trace where he went last evening,' Luned said.

'In the meantime, let's begin our search against Mervyn Peel and the Peel Foundation. I want to know everything about them.' Drake got to his feet and took the half-finished mug of coffee with him back to his office.

He sat thinking about the priorities for the following morning. He texted Gareth telling the detective constable he was expected first thing. He thumbed out another message to Annie saying that he would be leaving shortly. He'd already warned her he might be late. Disciplining his mind to telling her what was happening had been a lesson he had learned from the difficulties in his marriage. Now he didn't allow his mind to force him to work late into the evening making certain every "t" had been crossed and "i" dotted. He had learned that much from the counselling he had received. If he was doing his best that was good enough.

But at the end of the first day of a new murder inquiry he had to have order in his mind. He began by making certain he had Post-it note reminders for all the tasks he needed to action. In the morning it would give him comfort to know he knew exactly what he was doing. It was another hour before he left, Sara and Luned already on their way home.

The traffic was light as he drove home, but the short days and long nights made his working day seem much longer. The volume of trucks crossing the A55 from the port of Holyhead to England and beyond never relented, but sections of the road had been widened and speeding restrictions removed which hastened the journey.

Soon he was indicating left onto the slip road for Felinheli. He parked on the drive behind Annie's car. She must have seen him on the video security camera he had recently installed because seconds later she opened the door.

He left the car and walked up to her and pulled her close kissing her on the lips.

'You're late, are you all right?' Annie said.

Drake nodded. 'It's been a full on day.'

After closing the door, they went upstairs to their open-plan kitchen and sitting room on the first floor.

'It's been all over the news.' Annie poured the contents of a kettle into a saucepan before filling it with pasta.

'The murder in Colwyn Bay?'

'Something about a bowling green in a park. Do you know the place?'

Drake sat at the kitchen table having draped his suit jacket over the back of a chair nearby. 'I've been there quite a few times with the girls over the years.'

'The news said the murdered man was a journalist.'

'He was a reporter working on a piece about the Peel Foundation.'

'Peel Foundation?' Annie said. 'I'm sure I've heard that name somewhere. There's been a documentary about them.'

'I saw Mr Peel himself this afternoon. He is a right specimen.'

'You should relax, try and switch off.'

Drake got up and helped himself to a bottle of lager from the fridge. He downed a mouthful and allowed the beer to work its magic. It had been a long hard day and he looked forward to spending a precious few hours with Annie. The previous weekend they'd been discussing the plans for their wedding, and she would know that at the end of the first day of the murder inquiry he wouldn't be in the mood to discuss guest lists and table settings.

She joined him at the table as he ate his Bolognese and finished off the bottle of lager.

'Dad has an appointment with the consultant at the end of the week.'

Annie had been worried for some time about her dad's health. Ever since he had retired from the civil service in Cardiff and moved to live near his daughter the angina and heart problems had worsened. More than anything she wanted him to give her away at her wedding and Drake knew how much it meant to her.

'I was hoping you might be able to be there as well. If it is bad news when he sees the consultant, then we'd both be there to support him after the appointment.'

'What time is the appointment?'

'It's early evening – apparently the consultants are working extra-long hours in order to catch up with the Covid backlog.'

Drake pushed his empty bowl to one side and smiled at Annie. 'Of course, I can be there.' He smothered the alarm bell ringing in his mind.

Annie beamed back.

Chapter 7

The following morning Drake slipped out of bed and left Annie sleeping whilst he showered and dressed as quietly as he could, hoping not to disturb her. He made coffee in the kitchen and ate a piece of toast before making Annie a mug of tea. The news on the radio carried a brief mention of Jack Holt's murder with the usual request for anybody with information to contact Northern Division headquarters.

Annie stirred briefly when he plonked the mug on her bedside table. He leaned down and kissed her. She turned over after thanking him for the tea which would probably be cold by the time she woke.

Once in the car, he adjusted the heating to its maximum setting before starting his journey. An early start gave him the opportunity to gather his thoughts and plan for the day. He was pleased Gareth Winder would be back. Winder was an integral part of his team, although he could be annoying at times. Officers like Winder, who would finish their careers as detective constables, were crucial for every investigation. He could be hard-working and lazy at the same time, all of which often frustrated Drake.

It felt as though he did the journey on autopilot, as if the car could drive itself on the regular routes he took.

The car park of the mortuary was empty, and he parked as near as possible to the entrance. He walked over and greeted the mortuary assistant.

'Good morning, Denver.' Drake smiled, knowing the man he was talking to had little personality or appetite for small talk.

Denver grunted back and pushed over one of the standard health and safety forms. Drake signed without reading, as he had done many times before.

Moments later Lee Kings, the pathologist, entered from the corridor leading to the mortuary.

'Good morning, Ian. I'm glad you're prompt. I need to

get on with this. Follow me – usual place.'

Drake followed Kings through into the mortuary. The temperature inside never seemed to vary much from one season to another. But now in the depths of winter it felt warmer than outside.

Kings finished checking the equipment just as Denver wheeled a trolley into the mortuary area. Kings gave him a nod of thanks once the trolley and the body covered in a sheet were in place.

Drake hadn't kept count of the post-mortems he'd attended. Nearly all had been conducted by Lee Kings. Drake could always rely on the pathologist to be professional and thorough.

When he had started as a detective he had never eaten or had a drink before a post-mortem. He hadn't wanted to tempt fate. But now things were different. Not even the smell could turn his stomach. He wasn't certain it was entirely healthy.

Kings pulled the sheet off the body of Jack Holt.

Drake looked over at the pathologist and saw the look in his eyes that he had seen at every post-mortem. A medical professional fascinated by the task at hand. Drake had often wondered why a doctor would want to qualify as a pathologist. Sian, his ex-wife, had always wanted to be a GP because it had meant regular hours with a good income and comfortable pension. Cutting up dead people was an entirely different proposition, Drake thought.

'At first glance he appears to be in good condition, apart from the fact that he is dead, of course.' Kings looked up at Drake, a smile playing in his eyes.

Drake didn't respond; humour and post-mortems were definitely incompatible.

Kings started his examination of Holt's feet and legs before turning to his arms and hands, all the time dictating his conclusions. There was nothing remarkable until he pushed Holt over onto one side and beckoned to Drake to join him.

There was a gaping wound at the back of Holt's head. If the rock the investigator had found yesterday was responsible, there must have been several blows Drake concluded from the extent of the injuries. Kings took several photographs before starting a formal explanation.

'As you can see, the skull has been badly damaged by several severe wounds. The blunt force trauma would have been more than sufficient to have caused catastrophic brain injury. But let's have a look inside and see if I'm correct.'

Kings spent time picking pieces of debris from the wounds, including what he described as gravel, shale or rocks. Detailed forensic analysis would compare those to the likely murder weapon.

Drake retook his position a few feet away from the trolley and watched as Kings found the saw that would slice off the top of Holt's skull. Ever since his first post-mortem, he had not been able to use a handheld grinder for doing DIY without thinking about Lee Kings.

It didn't take the pathologist more than a few minutes to go through this procedure and remove Jack Holt's brain, which he carefully placed in a stainless-steel tray.

The objectivity with which Kings handled various body parts always amazed Drake.

'There is severe trauma to the brain which suggests that Jack Holt was struck several times with a heavy object. Whoever did this wanted him dead.'

'Is there any sign he struggled?'

Kings took a moment to ponder the question. Then he made a further examination of Holt's arms and shoulders. 'There is a sign of bruising on the upper arms. It's difficult to be certain but it would suggest he was held from behind.'

'Or dragged?'

'Yes, that might be the case. Why do you ask?'

'If he was initially struck somewhere other than on the bowling green and then dragged to the position where we found him it would suggest more than one person was involved.'

Once Kings was finished, he turned to Drake.

'Jack Holt was a healthy, well-nourished individual. There don't seem to be any signs of underlying health issues and he was killed by several catastrophic severe blows to the head. I've removed fragments of rock and other organic material which suggests very strongly the bloodied rock your investigator found at the crime scene was the murder weapon.'

'The forensic results will provide confirmation about the murder weapon in due course.'

'And whether he was killed on the bowling green and then pinned to the surface or elsewhere is a matter of conjecture. All I can tell you is that there are signs of bruising consistent with him having been held antemortem.'

'And time of death?'

Kings pondered for a moment. 'As I said yesterday morning, I'd put the time of death between eleven pm and two am.'

'Send me the full report.'

Kings nodded his agreement and Drake left, retracing his steps out of the mortuary to the crisp winter morning air. If the pathologist was correct – that Holt had been killed late the evening before last – it meant they had to establish his movements for approximately six hours after he had left the house. Where had he gone and who had he been with?

As Drake reached his car his mobile rang. He didn't recognise the number.

'Is that Detective Inspector Drake? I understand you're in charge of the inquiry into the murder of Jack Holt. I'm the editor of *The Examiner*. I need to see you.'

Winder stood in front of the empty Incident Room board scarcely believing that the words "Peel Foundation" were printed on a sheet of A4 paper pinned under the image of Mervyn Peel. He guessed Inspector Drake would be attending the post-mortem, but Sara and Luned would be sure to arrive soon.

He stared at Peel's face. It was the face of a man who had caused Winder's family so much heartache. A first cousin had been seduced by Peel's foundation into giving him and his organisation all her money in the hope they could transform her life.

A substantial inheritance his cousin had received after the death of a close family member had all gone. His aunt and uncle had despaired when she had announced her intention to join the Peel Foundation. She had been a successful law student, taking a first-class degree in law from a prestigious university. Her parents had been thrilled at the prospect she could map out a career as a solicitor. But she had thrown all of that away when she had become entwined with the Peel Foundation.

He would have to tell his mum what was happening. And maybe even his aunt, her sister. Was his connection to the Peel Foundation enough to disqualify him from being involved in the inquiry? He'd need to tell Inspector Drake of the connection.

Sara was the first to arrive and Winder glanced over at her. She must have realised something was amiss from the look on his face.

'Morning, Gareth.' Sara's voice implied a question about his well-being.

'Morning.'

'Jack Holt, a journalist, was found dead yesterday morning pinned to the surface of the bowling green at the park in town.' She nodded at the image of Mervyn Peel. 'Apparently he was investigating the Peel Foundation.'

'I know.'

His reply must've mystified Sara because she came to stand by his side. He was still staring at the board. 'What's wrong?'

He realised Sara knew him well. 'A cousin of mine is

involved with the Peel Foundation. She's cut her ties with her family and it's caused a huge amount of family distress.'

'You need to tell the boss.'

'I know.'

Luned was the next to arrive, but she didn't read the signals from Winder. 'How did you get on in the course yesterday?' She shrugged off her jacket and sat at a desk booting up her computer.

'Okay, I suppose,' Winder said.

'Gareth has a personal connection to the Peel Foundation. A cousin of his is involved with them,' Sara said.

'Oh, I see. What's that about?'

'I'll tell the boss when he arrives.'

Winder took his seat by his desk and booted up his computer, but his mind kept focusing on his cousin, Phoebe. She'd been the clever one in the family. Her parents were always boasting about her academic successes, and it had made him feel second-rate. His own parents listened to Phoebe's family, who never seemed to take an interest in the achievements of anyone else and who had expected undiluted sympathy when she became involved with the Peel Foundation.

As his screen came to life, he glanced over at the board, wondering if Phoebe was still at the Foundation near the town or whether she was at one of their other properties. There had been talk that she might travel to South America or London but, as her family heard little from her, he knew nothing of her present circumstances.

He got up to speed by discussing with Luned and Sara what exactly was going on and what had been determined as priorities. He knew the sergeant in charge of the house-to-house enquiries, so volunteered to contact him. It was useful to speak to somebody outside the Incident Room, but his friend had nothing constructive to tell them about progress.

It had been made clear that establishing Holt's

whereabouts in the hours before his death was the priority. Winder took time to find a map of the town and eventually pinned it up on the board; a red pin showed where his body had been found. A yellow pin marked Holt's home with David Ackland. Inspector Drake always liked to have a map on the board. There was something visual about drawing a line between two points of interest.

When Inspector Drake arrived at the Incident Room Winder got to his feet unprompted.

'Glad you're back,' Drake said, as though Winder had been away on holiday.

'Morning, sir. There's something you should know.' Winder didn't want to waste any time.

Drake stopped mid-step and looked over at Winder. He must've seen an uncommon intensity in Winder's face. That was certainly how he felt. Drake frowned and he excused himself for a moment and returned coat-less. He walked over to the board and stood looking over at Winder.

'I think you should be aware, sir, that a first cousin of mine is involved with the Peel Foundation.'

Drake continued to frown. 'Go on.'

'She was taken in by all their bullshit. It's caused an immense amount of grief to the family. My cousin Phoebe gave the Peel Foundation a lot of money she'd inherited.'

'When did you see her last?'

'She hasn't spoken to her parents for a long time. She hasn't been to any family celebrations for... I can't remember. Christ, I just can't remember... it's as though she doesn't exist any longer. Everything is about the Peel Foundation and what it can do for her and for the future.'

'But what do they do?'

Winder looked confused. 'It's all this wellness crap and getting in tune with your inner self and potential. They took advantage of Phoebe when she was at a low ebb after a long-term relationship broke up. She was a bright kid, but she was naïve and impressionable.'

Luned made her first contribution that morning. 'Is there anything religious about them?'

Winder shook his head.

Drake picked up the thread. 'From the website I visited there was no suggestion of any religious connotation to what they were doing.'

'Maybe they just dupe people for money,' Sara said.

'Thanks for telling me, Gareth. Prepare me a detailed memorandum with full details about your cousin and her family. For now you continue as a member of this team. We keep an open mind about the Peel Foundation. We need to find who killed Jack Holt – that's our priority.'

Drake outlined the tasks in hand, but Winder barely registered that he should be liaising with the house-to-house team. Their focus was establishing Jack Holt's movements in the hours after he left his home to when he was killed, but all Winder could think about was how this case felt much closer to home.

Chapter 8

Drake sat at the table at the conference room on the ground floor of headquarters, Sara by his side, the editor of *The Examiner* magazine opposite. The tone of Alex Normanton's brief conversation with Drake had left no room for ambiguity – he had something important to share.

'Thank you for seeing me, Detective Inspector,' Normanton said.

Drake nodded. 'How well did you know Jack Holt?'

'Very well, I mean on a professional basis. I can't say I knew him socially or personally. Occasionally if he was working in our offices we'd go out for a meal or a beer.'

'I thought all journalists were fond of socialising.'

Normanton ignored Drake's comment. 'He was a dedicated and determined journalist. He was old-fashioned in many ways. He had a strong sense of natural justice and he hated if he came across a story where people were being taken advantage of.'

'You've driven a long way, Mr Normanton. Why do you want to speak to us?'

Normanton reached into a bag at his feet and drew out several folders which he deposited on the table in front of him.

'These are papers relating to Jack's investigations over the past five years, since he has been working with us.'

'Thank you.' Drake glanced at the documentation. 'Is there anything in these papers you think might assist us?'

'One of the big stories Jack had been working on was the Peel Foundation. It's run by a Mervyn Peel. It's basically a scam to get people to part with their money for no real gain. He persuades people to give him thousands of pounds in return for participation in his foundation which supports them with courses and talks and lectures. In reality it takes advantage of vulnerable people.'

'Can you tell us if Jack ever mentioned meeting Mervyn

Peel?'

Normanton paused for a moment. 'We had published articles Jack had written about the Peel Foundation in the past – none of them complimentary. He contacted me last week and told me he thought he'd made a breakthrough with a big story about the Peel Foundation.'

'Did he give you details?'

'He had discovered that a charity associated with the Peel Foundation had been acting illegally. The consequences for the charity and for the Peel Foundation could have been serious. And he also mentioned he was in contact with the family of a person Peel had scammed who had reported the Foundation to the economic crime unit of the Metropolitan Police.'

'Did he mention anything to suggest he was in direct contact with Mervyn Peel?'

'On the journey over here I kept trawling through my memory to see if I could pinpoint any comments he made that might help, but that's all he said. I told him to be careful.'

'What did you mean specifically?'

'Mervyn Peel can be dangerous when he puts his mind to it. He has a history of unprovoked violence. Let me show you.'

Normanton picked up his mobile and after finishing scrolling he pressed play on the video. 'You should watch this. Peel wasn't aware he was being filmed. It was taken near the central London property used by the Foundation as their base.'

Sara leaned on the table and Drake shared the screen with her. The person filming was some distance away from the entrance to a sleek looking office building. Drake recognised the face of Jack Holt; he had a satchel over his shoulder and a handheld recorder in one hand.

Drake zoomed in and although the quality of the image was poor Drake recognised Mervyn Peel emerging from the door. He gave Holt an angry look and stepped over towards the journalist. Holt held up his hand as though he were inviting Peel to answer a question.

Two of Peel's minders stood either side of him. It was clear from his body language and the way he stabbed a finger into Holt's chest that he was furious. Holt backed away, clearly startled by the physical intimidation.

Although the recording was being made from many metres away, Peel's raised voice was audible. What he said wasn't clear but there was no doubt he was launching a verbal tirade against Holt.

'When was this taken?' Drake said.

Sara continued to stare at the screen.

'Three months ago when Jack Holt was in London.'

When Peel and his minders walked away, Jack Holt followed them. It amazed Drake that he did so. It was a foolish thing to do. Once Peel's bodyguards realised what was happening they turned and confronted Holt. Holt circled around jogging to where he could continue his questioning of Peel hoping, no doubt, that he was protected by being in a public place.

It wasn't the safeguard he hoped for, as Peel ran off and both his minders set upon Holt, taking turns to push him away until eventually they pushed him to the ground. They shouted abuse and threats. Holt got up and followed them, only to be confronted again.

This time one of the men punched him in the face. Drake could see Holt putting a hand to his nose, clearly in pain. Both men left Holt, sprinting away, presumably to rejoin Mervyn Peel who wasn't anywhere to be seen.

'Did Jack Holt report this assault?'

'No, I don't think so.'

'This video is more than enough evidence to present to a court for a case of common assault. Do you know the names of these two goons who were helping Mervyn Peel?'

'Sorry, Inspector. I have no idea.'

'What was Jack Holt doing in London?'

'I believe he was trying to interview Mervyn Peel.'

Drake turned to Normanton. 'I need a copy of this footage.'

'Of course.'

'And if there's anything else you think might be relevant you must contact us without delay.'

Normanton nodded. Drake brought the meeting to a close and showed Normanton to reception. He watched the journalist leave the building as his mobile rang. He recognised Mike Foulds' number.

'We're finishing here at the park. Something I want to show you.'

Luned had never seen Winder so quiet. It unnerved her that the Peel Foundation had had such an impact on his family. So, she suggested to Winder they both go to the DeVere Royal Hotel and find out if there was any member of staff who saw Jack Holt visiting the evening before his body was found.

Uncharacteristically, Winder showed little interest in leaving the Incident Room. 'Yes, I suppose.'

Suitably bundled up in their coats against the winter air they left headquarters. Luned drove, Winder sat in the passenger seat.

'The boss is meeting the editor of one of the publications Jack Holt worked closely with. Hopefully he'll have something helpful to contribute,' Luned said, pulling up at the junction at the main road before indicating right.

'People like Mervyn Peel are dangerous.' Winder's voice was full of authority.

Luned decided to probe some more. 'I can't imagine what it must have been like for your aunt and uncle when Phoebe got involved with them.'

Winder didn't reply immediately: he stared out through the windscreen. 'It was a sad time for them. Still is, I suppose. She was their only child.'

'Did you do a lot with her when you were younger?'

Winder nodded. 'We'd go on holiday together, camping and caravanning. We were very close for a while until we were teenagers. She was the clever one and we grew apart.'

The hotel came into view and Luned pulled into the car park. After leaving the car they walked over to the main reception area and flashed their warrant cards at the staff.

'We are part of the team investigating the murder of Jack Holt. We believe he might have been here the night before last. We need a list of all staff members who were on duty from six pm until midnight.'

The receptionist gave them a worried look. Her high cheekbones and deep-set eyes gave her an Eastern European look but the accent was Rochdale, not Romania.

'I'll speak to the manager.'

She left Luned and Winder standing in reception but moments later returned with a man in his sixties with a glistening shaved head. 'What's all this about?'

'Is there anywhere we can discuss this in private?' Luned said.

'Follow me.'

The manager led them to his office where he stood by his desk.

'I'm Detective Constable Luned Thomas and this is Detective Constable Gareth Winder. We are part of the team investigating the death of Jack Holt. We have information to suggest he may have been here the evening he was killed.'

'I don't believe it. We've never been involved in something like this.'

'He may have been meeting someone. Do you have CCTV in the hotel?'

'Yes, of course we have.'

'We'll need all the footage from six pm to two am the night before last.'

'It might take me some time.'

'This is a murder inquiry. You don't have *some time*. We need it by the end of today.' Luned gave the manager her card with her contact details.

Winder made his first contribution, 'Do you have a list of the staff on duty the night before last?'

The manager nodded and sat at his desk clicking into his computer. Moments later a printer purred into life. A single sheet of A4 was spewed out. He handed it to Winder who asked, 'How many of these people are working now?'

The manager peered at the monitor on his desk. He rattled off the names of half a dozen employees.

'We will need to speak to them all.'

It pleased Luned that Gareth seemed to be back to his usual self. She knew he enjoyed the practical side of day-to-day policing. Interviewing witnesses, establishing evidence. He wasn't so good on the supporting paperwork.

The manager took them into the main bar area, announcing that three members of staff working the evening before last were preparing for their shift. He disappeared behind the bar area and eventually led out three women, who sat on stools near a small table requisitioned by Luned and Winder.

Luned showed an image of Jack Holt on the screen of her mobile. 'Did you see him here the night before last?' They stared intently at the face but shook their heads. They returned to work, whispering to each other as they did so.

As the manager took them through to reception and the restaurant to speak to the other three members of staff who had been on duty, Luned spotted a CCTV camera high up on a wall. 'Is that the only camera covering reception and the bar area?'

'Yes, that's right. And there's a camera covering the entrance to the car park at the rear.'

'We'll need footage from that camera too.'

The receptionist they had met earlier frowned at the image Luned showed her as though her very life depended on it, then she looked up at Luned and then at Winder. And then back at the image. It was only then she shook her head. 'I've never seen him before.'

The staff working in the restaurant reacted in a similar vein.

They returned to reception and a woman in her twenties stood chatting with the receptionist. The manager beckoned her to join them.

'This is Kirsty Williams. She was working in the bar when you believe your victim may have visited.'

Luned showed her Holt's image and she nodded. 'He wasn't here long and he came in through the entrance from the car park. It was about six and the bar was quiet.'

'How long did he stay for?'

'Maybe half an hour. I can't be certain.'

'And did you see him with anyone?'

'I don't think so. I got the impression he was waiting for someone because he kept looking up whenever guests arrived.'

'Thank you.'

It pleased Luned that at least they had some success with Kirsty, who had rejoined her friend at reception. It felt like progress and the footage might be more helpful.

Luned turned to the manager and used her most officious voice.

'I'll expect the footage later today.'

They left the manager standing in reception with a terrified look on his face, and headed back for their car.

Chapter 9

Drake and Sara took the short journey to the recreation park. Drake pulled up behind the last of four scientific support vehicles. Yellow crime scene tapes fluttered in the gentle breeze marking the outer perimeter. It was too cold for officers to stand guard at the gate but, as soon as Drake and Sara approached, a uniformed constable emerged from a vehicle. He relaxed when he saw both senior officers.

'The crime scene manager is expecting you, sir.'

Drake and Sara ducked down under the tape held high by the young officer and headed over into the park.

Mike Foulds walked over to join them.

'I've had my team complete a thorough investigation. Let me show you,' Mike Foulds said. He led them over towards the corner of the pavilion where he began an explanation. He pointed at the outline of the footpaths around the perimeter of the bowling green. Drake noticed the dark stain on the surface caused by Holt's blood.

'We've treated everything from the path on the far side of the green to where we are standing now and the pavilion and all the borders and pathways we can see as the crime scene. It's meant a hell of a lot of work I can tell you, Ian.'

'Thanks, Mike, I know what these sort of crime scenes can be like.'

'Come with me.' Foulds led them down a path along one side of the bowling green. It was between the playing surface, and narrowed after a wide section near the pavilion. Foulds stopped and stood to one side, gesturing for Drake and Sara to do the same. Then he pointed at the gravel surface at their feet. Drake could see where it had been clearly marked for the purposes of having photographs taken.

'There are blood spots leading towards the steps onto the bowling green.'

Drake looked over and saw a line of white circles

indicating the existence of blood residue.

'It is my belief that Jack Holt was first struck approximately here. There is a trail of blood leading along the path towards the entrance to the bowling green. And you can see where the gravel has been disturbed. He probably fell here if he was struck from behind.'

'And then he must have been dragged or carried,' Drake said.

'That's right. And there is evidence of something being pulled over the surface.'

Drake scanned the rutted surface of the path. 'But they don't go the whole distance to the bowling green.'

'Top of the class, Detective Inspector. He was killed by several blows to the head. Then his body was probably dragged and then carried on to the lawn where it was dumped and then the croquet hoops pinned into place.'

'And that means two people were responsible.'

'That's a reasonable conclusion. But one person could have been responsible.'

'Any other evidence?'

Foulds gestured for Drake and Sara to follow him. They skirted around the bowling green where he stopped and pointed down into a border. 'There are four different footprints in the various borders. Two of them belong to work boots that match those the council issue to the groundsmen. But two others are trainers of some sort. We haven't been able to identify the make or size at the moment.'

'If they did belong to the killer or killers why would they be walking in the borders?' Sara said.

Foulds shrugged. His job was to gather the evidence: the detectives had to decide how everything fitted together.

Drake looked over at the pavilion, noticing the open door.

'Anything in that building?' He nodded over towards it.

'I was half expecting to find a croquet set with its hoops

missing,' Foulds said. 'But we've been through all the contents and there isn't anything.' He walked over towards the pavilion. Drake and Sara followed.

An investigator was still working inside. He left when Foulds told him they needed to check the contents.

'Was there any sign of a forced entry?' Drake said.

Foulds stepped into the pavilion with Drake and Sara. The air was stale and thick with dust.

Some outdoor tables and chairs were stacked against one corner and in another Drake could see beyond a door a makeshift kitchen worktop. Boxes and bags of bowling equipment filled the place.

'There are two windows to the rear but they were all securely closed and locked. There was no sign of any break-in through the doors. We've taken the precaution of making certain we record everything here.'

'And no sign of any croquet sets?'

'None, Ian, I think you need to look elsewhere.'

They retraced their steps to the outside and they stood for a moment on the gravelled area. Drake looked over to his right where Foulds believed Holt had first been assaulted. 'That path must have taken him towards the gate leaving the park.'

'None of them are locked at night. It is a bit surprising really,' Foulds said.

'And did you find anything in Holt's car?'

'Nothing. It was clean and tidy with a tank full of petrol. We've recovered two sets of fingerprints but I would guess that one belongs to Holt and the other to his partner or wife.'

Drake nodded. 'Partner, a man called David Ackland.'

'You might get his fingerprints for the purposes of elimination.'

Sara piped up, 'What I can't understand is why on earth was he here?'

'Is there any significance to this place in his life?' Foulds said.

'I don't think he's local.' Drake stared over at the children's playground behind the bowling green. He had visited here with Helen and Megan on numerous occasions when they were younger. It had been quality time he had spent with his daughters. Now it would always be tainted with death.

He hoped their preliminary enquiries into Jack Holt's background would give them something to suggest a link to the park or the town. It might be completely random. The killer or killers had lured Holt to the park and made a spectacle of pinning him to the bowling green.

'Using croquet hoops to pin the body to the surface is certainly an odd thing to do,' Foulds said.

Sara picked up the thread, Drake still staring into the distance and at the playground. 'There must be some significance to using the croquet hoops in this way. We must find out what it is.'

'We'll probably be finished by later today. I'll let you have our full report in due course.'

'I guess the bowling green is going to be out of action for a while.'

'Somebody from the council called by wanting to know about progress. The chairman of the bowling club was with him. They'll cut out a section of the turf which is badly stained and replace it. The bowling club chairman was most upset at the prospect their precious lawn had been damaged. Apparently it takes years to build the bowling green to the right standard.'

Drake joined the conversation, 'Hardly the stuff to be concerned about, surely. A man was murdered here – doesn't that mean anything to these people?'

'You know what people are like, Ian, they just think of themselves.'

Drake paced over to the edge of the path and then down onto the bowling green. Apart from the occasional spot of discoloured turf the lawn looked remarkably well maintained with a smooth, level finish. Then he walked over to where the body of Jack Holt had been found and stared down at the bloodstain.

Why was he here and why the croquet hoops? It was one of several questions he would need to answer during the course of the inquiry.

As they arrived back at headquarters a message reached Drake's mobile from Luned telling him they would be back within a few minutes from their visit to the DeVere Royal Hotel. It gave him time to gather his thoughts in preparation for a catch-up session with the rest of the team, prior to his meeting with Superintendent Hobbs.

He detoured to the kitchen near the Incident Room with Sara and she flicked on the kettle. He measured the exact amount of coffee grounds to be dropped into the small cafetière and once the kettle had boiled, he set his watch for the right interval, before pouring the hot liquid over the coffee. It was important the water wasn't too hot. Sara seemed perfectly content with instant. He took the cafetière through into his room and glanced over at the board as he did so.

He sat by his desk and when the timer on his mobile rang he knew the coffee was ready so he plunged the filter on the cafetière and filled his mug. A golden cream-coloured skin formed on top of the liquid and he took his first sip. He scanned through the Post-it notes arranged on his desk, content he hadn't missed anything significant on his to-do list.

The first email he read was confirmation from the crime scene investigators that the blood on the rock recovered at the scene belonged to Jack Holt. At least they now had a murder weapon.

From his computer he downloaded the financial reports on Jack Holt. He had considerable savings with various institutions, as well as a healthy current account. There were no credit card debts or loans or overdrafts and Drake wondered if the same were true for David Ackland. He couldn't find the results for the search against Ackland but there were details on Mervyn Peel.

It amazed Drake that someone would keep almost as much as his own annual salary in his current account. Peel had other accounts and no doubt in due course there'd be investments to match the considerable cash deposits he held. He took another mouthful of the black coffee and scribbled on one of his Post-it notes that the finances for Ackland would need to be chased up, as well as ensuring they had all the details for Mervyn Peel.

Money could always be an unambiguous motive for murder. He heard Luned's voice greeting Sara, so he took the unfinished mug of coffee out into the Incident Room. Winder made an entrance with a tray with a drink for himself and for Luned.

Drake walked up to the board and put his mug down on a desk nearby. 'How did you get on at the DeVere Royal Hotel?'

Luned replied, 'We spoke to one of the bar staff who recalled seeing Jack Holt. It was about six pm and he sat in the bar as though he were waiting for someone.'

'Excellent. At least we can place him in the hotel. All we have to do now is find out where he went for the rest of the evening. How long did he stay at the hotel?'

'She couldn't be certain but she thought it was about half an hour. I've asked the hotel manager to send us the footage from the CCTV cameras that cover the main reception as well as the entrance from the car park.'

'And the member of staff couldn't recall him being with anybody?'

Luned shook her head.

'Sara and I have just been to the crime scene with Mike Foulds. He talked us through what he believed might have happened. Holt was attacked on a path leading to a gate. His car was parked nearby. So it would make sense to believe he gained access through that gate and was leaving the same way.'

Drake drank the last of his coffee and then moved nearer the board. 'Why the croquet hoops?'

'They must have some significance,' Luned answered.

'I agree,' Drake turned to the team. 'There might be something in Holt's past about croquet. But we could waste hours looking for a connection.'

He looked at the board and tapped a finger on the image of the bloodied rock. 'I had confirmation earlier that the blood on the rock belongs to Jack Holt so this is definitely the murder weapon. He was struck a number of times and it's likely his body was then carried from the path onto the bowling green.'

'That must have taken two people,' Winder said.

'We keep an open mind. I don't suppose it's completely beyond the realms of possibility that one person could have moved the body.'

'There is a trail of blood along one path onto the bowling green surface,' Sara said.

'There's also footage of Jack Holt being assaulted outside the offices of the Peel Foundation in London which I'll circulate in due course,' Drake said. 'We don't know the names of the two men who were with Mervyn Peel at the time, but I guess it wouldn't be too difficult to establish their identities. And Holt believed he had a breakthrough with his investigation into the Peel Foundation. We start going through the documentation the editor of *The Examiner* left, as well as Holt's computer. I'll start on the paperwork. I want you, Sara and Luned working on Holt's computer. We're looking for any contact with solicitors about a trust and officers of the Met as well as the Charity Commission.'

Deep lines creased Winder's forehead.

'Gareth, somebody has seen Jack Holt from the time he left home before he arrived at the park. Make contact with the officers on the house-to-house enquiries. Somebody would have seen something. And there has to be some CCTV of him driving around late the night he was killed.'

Drake stared at Jack Holt's image. 'Somebody knows where he was for those few hours.'

Drake returned to his office and adjusted the photographs of his daughters by the telephone on his desk. He moved the Post-it notes that he had assembled tidily on his desk onto the top of a cupboard knowing he needed the workspace for the files Alex Normanton had left. There was an urgency in identifying if Normanton had been right that Jack Holt had made a breakthrough in his investigation into the Peel Foundation.

The first folder he opened had various press cuttings relating to a people-trafficking ring that operated in Eastern Europe. Drake didn't waste time reading the articles, but he did scan through the notebooks Holt had kept, hoping for some reference to the Peel Foundation.

Several folders were filled with documents and notebooks relating to other investigations Holt had conducted. None related to the Peel Foundation and Drake quickly got into the rhythm of identifying if there was anything of relevance and then discarding the folder onto the pile on one corner of his desk.

Drake read the words "Peel Charity" on the outside flap of a folder and his mind focused. He began to read the notebooks Holt had kept, which included contacts with officers from the Charity Commission as well as professional firms who specialised in undertaking work for charities. There was a three-page letter from a chartered accountant advising Jack Holt about the alleged impropriety that seemed to be undertaken by the charity run by the Peel Foundation. Drake scribbled its name – the St Agnes Charity – in his own notebook, deciding he'd google the name once the task in hand had been completed.

Drake read several letters from a firm of solicitors, each

of whom suggested that the activity Holt outlined was clearly illegal and likely to be a breach of charity law. Drake wondered exactly what Holt had hoped to achieve – was there going to be some massive exposé? Would the Charity Commission investigate the St Agnes Charity and its link to the Peel Foundation? If there was any possibility of adverse publicity or consequences from illegality, he concluded Mervyn Peel and his eponymous foundation wouldn't relish Holt publishing.

Holt kept the names of two contacts anonymous, referring to them in his notebook as A1 and A2. Drake read the contemporaneous notes Holt had made of his meeting with both people which he'd recorded on a piece of paper he'd headed "Confidential Source". From the comments he read Drake could see clearly that there was every possibility A1 and A2 had damning evidence about impropriety.

There was even a section in Holt's latest notepad, "contact with PF", that Drake took to be shorthand for the Peel Foundation. It was ominously blank.

Drake made a mental note that he needed to include reference to this material in his briefing with Superintendent Hobbs later. Then Sara appeared in his doorway. 'We found some material on his computer, boss.'

Drake waved her inside and pointed at one of the visitor chairs. Winder and Luned stood by the threshold to his office.

'We haven't been able to find any contact with the Metropolitan Police but there is a folder of materials on his computer with contact that he made with the trustees of a wealthy trust from the south of England. One of the family members got involved with the Peel Foundation and promised to give them some money but it was all tied up in a trust. The trust advanced some money subject to various documentation being prepared.'

'And of course nothing transpired.'

'That's right, boss. And we're talking about a lot of

money – almost half a million pounds.'

Winder added, 'And there's a clear suggestion in some of the paperwork that all the money had been sent to Mervyn Peel and Martha Peel's personal bank account.'

Sara continued, 'And that would have been completely contrary to the agreement the trust was making with the Peel Foundation. Jack Holt spent a huge amount of time talking with the family members and with these solicitors about what had happened, and he had prepared a draft article exposing the fraud and misappropriation of funds by Mervyn Peel.'

'That gives him one hell of a motive.' Winder again.

Drake nodded.

Sara added. 'I've found a copy of Jack Holt's will in his papers. It was prepared by local solicitors and it leaves everything to Ackland.'

'Call the lawyers and ask them if it's been changed.'

'Yes, boss.'

Drake looked at the time on his computer, knowing that he needed to speak to Superintendent Hobbs before the end of the day. 'I've also found some stuff relating to a St Agnes Charity the Peel Foundation is connected with. It's all in here.' Drake put a hand on the paperwork on his desk.

'We'll need to contact the trustees you mentioned in the morning. And there's reference to two anonymous sources in relation to the St Agnes Charity. Let's see if we can find out who they are.'

Disappointment at being turned down for preferment to a chief superintendent role had eaten away at Superintendent Hobbs' mind for days since he had received the decision. He had been able to make his way up the career ladder of the Wales Police Service reasonably smoothly when he was in Southern Division. And he had been content to seek promotion to Northern Division, but now he had begun to regret the move if it was going to stymie his prospects. He had even considered a role in one of the English police forces. Perhaps he should take up the opportunity of discussing his future with the assistant chief constable who had given him the news that he had been turned down for the chief superintendent role.

He had ignored his wife's urging to put it behind him. This was his life, for Christ's sake. Perhaps he needed to be more hands-on with the investigations under his command. He had instigated so many positive reforms since his appointment, including making certain information was correctly provided to him in standard report formats.

And still the appointments panel had turned him down!

When his secretary rang to announce that Inspector Drake had arrived, he realised he had forgotten all about the meeting. Hurriedly he found Drake's email with the initial briefing about the death of Jack Holt. He skimmed it quickly before asking his secretary to send Drake in.

Hobbs didn't get up from his desk and watched as Drake walked over towards one of the visitor chairs. Hobbs was rather jealous of the way Drake wore a suit well. Hobbs' wife had always chided him that he needed to lose weight if he was going to buy the best designer suits. Hobbs wasn't convinced it was as simple as that.

'Are you making progress with this Holt case?' Hobbs said, once Drake had sat down.

'A rock one of the investigators found at the scene has been identified as the murder weapon. Holt was investigating the Peel Foundation at the time of his death.'

'Who?'

'The Peel Foundation. It's an organisation run by a man called Mervyn Peel. They run courses supporting people on their journey in life, assisting them to realise their full potential.'

'Sounds like a cult of some sort.'

'We've spoken with Mervyn Peel and he was particularly obstructive.'

Hobbs frowned.

'So we're treating him as a person of interest.'

'I saw from your preliminary memorandum that Holt was an investigative journalist.'

'That's correct, sir, he was freelance, but did a lot of work for a magazine and website called *The Examiner*. And he was building a big story that the editor believes could have been very damaging for the Foundation and Mervyn Peel.'

'They're high-profile aren't they? I'm sure they've been on the television news.'

'Yes, sir,'

'I might sit in on one of your team briefings in due course. You never know I might be able to contribute something constructive.' Hobbs gave Drake a brief, insincere smile.

The Inspector left moments later, and Hobbs sensed there was every likelihood the death of Jack Holt would generate publicity. And that was something he could take advantage of: it would require his input as a senior officer. It would do no harm at all for his face to be in front of the television cameras, which could only be a reminder for the senior officers who would interview him when his next job opportunity arose.

Chapter 10

'There's somebody here you should see, boss.' There was an urgency to Winder's voice.

It was early the following morning and Drake had barely hung his coat on the stand in his room. He had scanned the office, content that everything was just so and in place.

He took the stairs back down to reception and made for the conference room requisitioned as a mobile incident room. Drake wasn't certain it would be effective in that role, as the public couldn't simply drop in if they were passing the park. It would mean a specific journey to headquarters, a short but significant distance. He had always been unenthusiastic about the merits of a mobile incident room. If someone had information they could always call the helpline.

It was the smell that struck Drake when he entered. Skin cells and sweat and other bodily fluids contributed to the dank musty odour that attacked his nostrils. The man responsible sat on a chair in one corner, hungrily eating a sandwich from the canteen. A steaming mug of tea was on the table by his side.

'This is Danny,' Winder said.

Drake nodded.

'Danny might have some information about Jack Holt, but he wanted to speak to you in person.'

Drake dragged over one of the visitor chairs but didn't extend the usual courtesy of offering his hand for Danny to shake it. Had he done so, he'd have been in the bathroom scrubbing his hands clean moments later.

'I'm Detective Inspector Drake. I'm in charge of the team investigating the death of Jack Holt. Do you have information that might be of assistance?' Drake even managed the barest smile.

'Yeah. I quite often sleep in the park.'

He took another mouthful of the sandwich and

simultaneously washed it down with a slug of tea.

'I see, are you sleeping rough, Danny?'

There was a brisk nod of the head. Danny's dank hair was draped over his shoulder. A razor hadn't seen his chin for months. He had tired, bloodshot eyes. Black dirt was caked under his fingernails and a coat thin with age was piled up on the floor by his feet.

'When did you sleep in the park last?'

A terrified look filled his eyes, as though by sharing details of his sleeping location he was somehow inviting Drake into his world.

'I can't remember. It's cold this time of year and I get a meal from the church in town.'

'So you were in the park on Sunday night?'

'I was outside. Sometimes I've kipped behind that big shed. Good place to put my head down.'

'And did you see anybody near the park? Or maybe somebody sitting in a car or walking or maybe cycling.' Drake looked at the empty sandwich carton on the man's lap. 'Would you like another?' Drake smiled.

'Yeah, thanks. And another tea, three sugars.'

A young uniformed officer on duty was dispatched to the canteen.

'We'd really appreciate all the details that you can remember.'

Danny looked over at Winder who nodded his encouragement.

'I saw a couple in a car. When they saw me, they drove away.'

'What time was this?'

'How would I know, I don't have a watch.'

'But you remember them in the car – why was that?'

'I saw them again later. Walking by the entrance to the park. I was sitting in the doorway of that closed launderette. I used to pinch old clothes from that place. They'd throw stuff out into a skip at the back. Shame it closed.'

'How long were they there?'

Danny shrugged and looked over at the door, a hungry look on his face. 'I can't tell you. A few minutes maybe. Time doesn't mean much to me anymore. But they were two women. I could tell from the hair and that.'

'And what sort of car was it?'

'Dunno – silver maybe. But there was a red car too. You don't see many red cars. You see lots of silver and black cars and white cars. But not many red cars. Maybe it was a Ferrari. They do red cars don't they?'

Drake glanced over at Winder who had a serious look on his face. It wasn't the usual Winder.

'I'm going to show you an image of Jack Holt, who was killed at the park. I'd like you to tell me if you saw him on Sunday night.'

Danny peered at the screen for far longer than necessary. It made Drake almost believe he had seen him. Then he shook his head. 'Never seen him. How did he die?'

'Mr Holt owned a 3 Series BMW which was parked near one of the entrances of the park. It was a grey car – do you remember seeing it?'

Danny frowned and took time to think. 'Which gate was that?'

Drake explained it was the one nearest the pavilion.

'I can't say I did.'

'And you've no idea when you saw the two people in the maybe-silver car?'

Danny shook his head.

'But you're certain though they were the same people you saw walking near the park?'

The young officer returned with another pack of sandwiches and a mug of tea. The prospect of more food brightened Danny's face.

Once he had taken a mouthful of the sandwich, he turned to Drake. 'They were the same right enough.'

'And are you still not certain when you saw these

people?'

Danny finished chewing. Drake wanted to avert his gaze but he watched Danny wash down the food with another large glug of tea.

'A cop car went past me. You could ask them.'

Drake thanked Danny and left Winder with instructions to trace the police car on duty the night Holt was killed, and returned to the Incident Room. And they needed to trace the red car and the people Danny had seen in case his evidence might prove important. Sara got to her feet. 'We've just had the police national computer search on David Ackland. You won't believe this.'

Drake gestured for her to follow him into his office where he sat down and she did likewise.

'The PNC searches came back and David Ackland has a number of convictions for dishonesty, fraud and forgery.'

'When was that?' Drake replied, his mind beginning to compute the implications. White-collar crime may not have been the same as having a conviction for violence, but it meant they would need to pay him far more attention.

'It was six years ago. He spent ten months inside, mostly in an open prison.'

'And we know Ackland and Jack Holt have been an item for eight years. Which means they met before Ackland was sentenced.'

'I made some preliminary enquiries and I've spoken with Jack Holt's parents who are in their seventies. I've made arrangements to go and see them.'

'Where do they live?'

'Cheshire'

Drake drove through Tarporley while Sara read aloud from an issue of Cheshire Life describing the village as the most glamorous Cheshire village. Georgian townhouses lined the high street and the satnav directed Drake to an elegant estate of detached properties on the outskirts.

'Do you know anything about Mr and Mrs Holt?' Drake said.

'Sorry, boss, nothing. I expressed our condolences of course.'

Drake switched off the satnav and pulled up at the kerb outside number twelve. He looked over at the bay windows on the ground and first floors. A tasteful red facing brick had been used on the external elevation of the property and the light grey windows and door suited them perfectly.

'Swanky sort of place,' Sara said.

'Let's see what Mr and Mrs Holt have to say.' Drake read the time. It was barely late morning, as the journey to Tarporley had been quicker than the satnav had anticipated. It meant he could be back at headquarters in good time. 'What did you say their names were?'

'Vivian and Charles Holt.'

They left the car and walked up to the front door, Sara fumbling for her warrant card as she did so.

Drake pressed the doorbell and a slim woman with expensive-looking clothes and well-kept silver hair brushing the collar of her blouse opened the door.

'Mrs Holt? I'm Detective Inspector Ian Drake of the Wales Police Service and this is Detective Sergeant Sara Morgan.'

'It's Reverend, actually.'

The accent was clear and well educated.

'I'm sorry, Reverend Holt. I'm in charge of the inquiry into your son's death. My condolences for your loss.' Drake didn't use the word "murder" – he wasn't going to remind her of the tragic circumstances of his death. 'May we come in?'

'Of course, how rude of me.' She pushed the door open and invited Drake and Sara inside. 'My husband is in the kitchen at the rear.'

Reverend Holt led Drake and Sara through a corridor into a kitchen that looked over a well-maintained garden. It had an ornamental fountain not far from the patio doors, as well as netting over a pond.

A tall man with a head of thick dark hair got up from the chair by the window and walked over towards them. He was wearing a chunky crewneck sweater and red corduroy trousers.

'Good morning, Mr Holt. I'm Detective Inspector Drake.'

'Reverend Charles Holt, actually.'

The first reverend must've realised Drake's confusion. She piped up, 'We were both vicars in the Church of England, Detective Inspector. Although we are retired we do take services occasionally.'

Charles Holt encouraged Drake and Sara to sit by the log burner that filled the room with a crisp dry warmth. There was something unnatural about a child dying before his parents. Drake had never been able to find the right words to offer condolences with the right sincerity. It was why family liaison officers broke bad news. And it pleased him that Sara took the initiative.

'We are trying to build a picture of your son's life. When I spoke to you earlier you thought you might be able to assist us.'

'Jack was a very determined young boy and he carried those traits with him into adulthood,' Charles Holt began.

'When did he contact you last?'

Charles Holt shared a look with his wife that Drake found difficult to read. She replied. 'Whenever he was away from North Wales and out of the clutches of that man Ackland.'

'How often was that?'

'It varied of course. He'd been in Liverpool for a few days a couple of weeks ago and spoke to us regularly. And before that, he called in to see us about a month ago when he was driving home from Birmingham.'

'Have you met Mr Ackland?'

'Once only. And that was more than enough,' Charles Holt replied.

'You may think us un-Christian, Detective Sergeant, but we were convinced David Ackland simply wanted to sponge off our son. We are lucky that our families are reasonably well off and we were able to provide for him. We gave him a great start in life, and it distressed us enormously he chose to take up with Ackland.'

Drake picked up the thread of the conversation. 'Did you disapprove of your son's sexuality?'

Averted eye contact and a lowering of heads gave Drake his answer. He wondered how they'd have felt if Jack Holt had been in a relationship with a woman.

'Jack had previous relationships with women, and it surprised us when he… had a boyfriend,' Vivian Holt replied. 'In fact, we got on very well with one of his girlfriends years ago. They were well suited, and we believed they would be a long-term match for each other.'

'Is there anything in particular you believe we should be aware of in our investigation?' Drake didn't want to be sidetracked any longer than was necessary by Jack Holt's parents.

'Jack inherited a substantial amount of money a few months ago from my late brother,' Charles Holt said. 'He had been a very successful businessman, working for an international oil company. He had never married and had no children, so he left most of his estate to Jack.'

'And do you think the fact your son inherited money might have played a part in his death?'

'All I can tell you is that since Jack's involvement with David Ackland his relationship with us changed – he wouldn't come to any family celebrations and rarely talked about Ackland, as one would if the relationship was healthy and normal. We understand Ackland has been to prison – but you probably know that already. He has an unsavoury past.'

Drake looked over at Vivian Holt. She was blinking

rapidly. 'David Ackland hasn't been in contact with us. If he had any caring bone in his body, he would have at least picked up the telephone to extend his condolences to us as a family. We've lost a son after all, our only child.'

Charles Holt placed a hand on his wife's and turned to give her a brief, reassuring smile. 'You probably think us vindictive and indeed that may well be the case, but we wanted you to be aware of our concerns.'

Drake and Sara left shortly afterwards, returning to their car and heading back to headquarters. Speaking to Holt's parents had confirmed they needed to treat David Ackland as a person of interest – he had a complex background and perhaps there was more to his relationship with Jack Holt than simply romance.

'It must be terrible to lose a child – especially when you are in your seventies. After all, a parent would expect to die before them.'

Drake didn't have time to reply as his mobile connected to the car rang. Winder's voice filled the cabin. 'You need to get back here, sir. There's a demonstration outside the entrance to the Peel Foundation.'

Chapter 11

Luned opened Holt's folder on the charitable trust Inspector Drake had referred to, determined to establish what Holt had been investigating. In addition, they had to work out if there was any way to identify the anonymous sources providing Holt with information about the St Agnes Charity. Once Gareth was available, he could assist, but in the meantime Luned got on with the work in hand.

Luned read through the notes Jack Holt had made of his meetings and telephone calls with the trustees. They were detailed and comprehensive. He had been sent copies of emails from Mervyn Peel to the beneficiary of the trust who had been persuaded to lean on the trustees to advance them money. Holt had also been sent copies of correspondence from the trust's solicitors and Luned spent time reading the heavy legalistic language. In the final few sentences, the lawyers advised in the clearest possible terms that money should not be advanced unless there was more clarity about the entire transaction.

The relationship between the trustees and Peel had rapidly deteriorated, with lawyers emailing him asking for more details which he had simply failed to provide. Angry letters had been written by the beneficiary to the trustees alleging they were failing in their duties to abide by his wishes. They in turn eventually advanced money to the beneficiary, who in turn sent the money to Mervyn Peel's personal account.

One of the trustees had contacted Jack Holt which had led to the journalist meeting the trustees with a view to writing an exposé of Mervyn Peel's activities. Luned read through the draft article Holt had prepared. It had damning and explosive language, far removed from the previous dull article he had written for *The Examiner*.

It was mid-morning when she decided to call one of the trustees.

'I'm one of the detectives on the team investigating the death of Jack Holt, the journalist,' Luned said, after introducing herself.

'I had heard. It is desperately sad.'

'We have read Jack Holt's file of papers in relation to your dispute with Mervyn Peel.'

'Dispute? It was fraud pure and simple. He made certain promises to the beneficiary of the trust and to us and when it came to it nothing materialised.'

'Have you been to the police?'

'Jack Holt told us to wait. He wanted to write the story and see what response he'd get from Peel. Jack was salivating at the prospect of publishing an article about Mervyn Peel. He said it would be catastrophic for them.'

It didn't surprise Luned that Jack Holt had advised them not to make a complaint to the police. Had they done so it would have prevented him publishing anything and she guessed he was more interested in building his own career than protecting a wealthy trust.

'With Mr Holt dead will you now make a formal complaint?'

'It's something I'll need to discuss with the other trustees.'

Luned ended the call as Winder returned to the Incident Room.

'Good timing, Gareth. We need to find the name of the anonymous sources in relation to the St Agnes Charity.'

It was late morning by the time Luned and Winder had made progress. She had decided to spend time getting more background on the St Agnes Charity. It quickly became clear from the documentation she read in Holt's files that financial irregularities were apparent in the charity's record-keeping. Documents from auditors suggested irregular payments were being made to Mervyn Peel and there was some question about the charity's fundraising activities.

Winder announced he had to leave for a personal matter

at lunchtime, but he offered no reason for his absence. 'I've gone through all the paperwork and Holt's computer. There's nothing to identify who A1 or A2 might be. Holt had a lot of stuff on Mervyn Peel and his organisation.'

Luned nodded. 'It gives Mervyn Peel one hell of a motive to get him out of the way.'

Detective Inspector Drake always reminded the team that money was a substantial motive. So Luned wasted no time after Winder had left assembling a picture of the finances of Jack Holt and that of his partner David Ackland. All the information about both men had arrived and building detailed spreadsheets was something Luned enjoyed.

She began with the various investments in Jack Holt's name. He certainly had no financial worries and it made Luned ponder why on earth he kept on working. But having savings wasn't the same as an income and the job satisfaction that being gainfully employed gave a person.

The property where both men lived was in Jack Holt's sole name and had been purchased several years previously. There was no mortgage and he had no loans or overdrafts or outstanding credit cards.

David Ackland's position was much less rosy. Substantial credit card debt had been paid off at about the time he and Holt had met. Luned spent time analysing Holt's finances, realising he had paid off all of Ackland's liabilities.

But Ackland's finances had deteriorated again over the past three years and it didn't take Luned long to establish that the payments had all been made to online gambling websites. She took a moment to double-check she had established the position correctly. Inspector Drake would want to be certain there was no doubt about Ackland's financial predicament.

And that gave him a motive.

It was early afternoon when the telephone on her desk rang. It was reception. 'There's someone here who wants to speak to a detective on the Holt case. You're the only one available.'

Luned made her way downstairs. The woman she'd spoken to moments earlier pointed at an elderly pair sitting on reception chairs. 'It's Mr and Mrs Wakeling and they can talk the hind legs off a donkey,' she whispered.

Luned walked over and smiled at the visitors. 'I'm Detective Constable Luned Thomas. I'm a member of the team investigating the murder of Jack Holt.' She gestured for the couple to join her as she led them to one of the ground floor conference rooms.

'How can I help?' Luned said once they were sitting at the table.

'It's about Jack Holt,' Mr Wakeling said. 'We live next door to him and his…'

'Partner,' his wife said. 'That's what they call them these days. People who live together and they're not married.'

'Anyway,' Mr Wakeling resumed, his accent a cultured version of the Liverpool accent common along the North Wales coast, 'we wanted to make absolutely certain you knew about him and David Ackland.'

'I don't know what you mean.'

'Well, they are… You know—'

'What my husband is trying to say is that Jack Holt and David Ackland are gay. He finds it a bit difficult to accept that fact.'

Wakeling gave his wife a startled, patronising look. She continued, 'There were arguments. We heard them shouting at each other very often.'

'Do you know what they were arguing about?' Luned jotted the details in her notebook suspecting Mr and Mrs Wakeling revelled in their role as nosy neighbours.

'We couldn't hear everything, of course, but it was often about money and how much Ackland was spending. Mr Ackland could be very aggressive and impolite. I didn't like it one little bit.'

Mr Wakeling continued, 'He was downright rude to my

wife. I was tempted to give him a piece of my mind. But you know nothing good comes out of that sort of thing and he was the sort of man who would give as good as he got. So we kept out of their way.'

'That sounds very sensible, Mr Wakeling,' Luned said. 'Now I'll need a little bit more detail from you. Perhaps we can start with some dates and times.' She smiled over the table at Mr and Mrs Wakeling, who settled down to recount everything they knew.

Winder couldn't help but mention to his mother that Jack Holt's case pointed to the involvement of the Peel Foundation. And when he had suggested he meet her and her sister, Phoebe's mother, over lunch he wanted to believe it would benefit the inquiry.

He relegated any reservations to a distant corner in his mind. He arrived at his mum's home at the same time as his aunt pulled into the drive.

'I'm so glad to see you, Gareth,' Auntie Gwen said as they met outside the front door.

Winder kissed her on the cheek and smiled. 'It's good to see you too, Auntie Gwen.'

Winder's mum opened the door and gave them both a serious look before ushering them inside. It was an odd feeling, sitting around the kitchen table in his mum's home at lunchtime during the week. Family gatherings were usually at the weekends.

Sandwiches and bottles of soft drink were already laid out on the table. Gwen sat down opposite Winder, and he looked over at his aunt, convinced she looked older and thinner than when he had seen her last. His mum was organising tea, but Winder declined, opening one of the bottles and pouring himself a glass.

He wasn't certain how he was going to start the conversation. It all seemed like a good idea when he first thought about it but actually talking about the case with his mum and Auntie Gwen felt strange now. And he began to regret the decision – would Detective Inspector Drake criticise him for discussing the Peel Foundation with his mum and her sister?

His mum brought a pot of tea and two mugs to the table. He had to be in charge, he had to take the lead.

'We are investigating the death of the reporter whose body was found in the park at the beginning of the week.'

His mum and Auntie Gwen nodded seriously.

'He was an investigative journalist. He'd been looking at a story about the Peel Foundation. Apparently that was all he was doing at the moment.'

'It's about time somebody did something about them.' Auntie Gwen had her fingers wrapped around a mug as though the warmth was giving her comfort.

Winder took the opportunity to munch on a sandwich.

'What do you know about them?'

'They are evil, all of them. They got their claws into Phoebe years ago after she finished with Philip. She was at a low point and went to a couple of their meetings. Then they flew her to America and then to South Africa for a month. She came back and she was all excited about what the Peel Foundation did and how they made a real difference to people's lives.'

Gwen paused and took another mouthful of tea. She shook her head when her sister suggested she eat something.

'But after every visit Phoebe seemed to become more and more insular. When she came back from a month in South Africa she could barely talk to us about what she had done. The Peel Foundation was going to redirect her life and she was going to inspire others to do the same.'

Winder's mum added, 'She always wanted to help others.'

'But not like this. Not when it's cost her everything.'

'What do you know about the Foundation?' Winder had finished one sandwich and was eyeing another.

'Everything is so glossy and too good to be true,' Gwen said. 'We were invited to a family presentation. I can see now it was all part of a grand scheme to fool us all.'

'What happened?' Winder said.

'Mervyn Peel was there. He is a real smooth operator, made my skin crawl. But his wife is the real danger. I was standing talking to her for about half an hour. She's got these dark eyes and I got the impression her soul was empty.'

'Why did Phoebe get involved with them?'

'She met this man after she broke up with Philip. He was one of them and she went along to some of the meetings and then eventually got sucked in completely.'

'Have you been in contact recently or heard from her?'

Gwen shook her head, her eyes filling with tears. Winder's mum found a box of tissues and yanked a couple out.

'We haven't seen her for thirteen months. It was at the funeral of a school friend. So we made a point of being there. We said hello and we exchanged a few words and we offered to take her for a meal,' Gwen stared at the sandwiches on the table, 'but she said that she was too busy.'

'Do you know anything more about what the Foundation does?'

'They trap impressionable people like Phoebe who have capital. The money is given to the Foundation and it's used to fund the whole setup. They run courses to encourage people to fulfil their own potential. And then those that are seen as good candidates get caught up in the scam like Phoebe.'

'You think somebody in the Peel Foundation killed Jack Holt?' Winder's mother asked.

It was the question he hoped he wouldn't have been asked. But he had an answer ready.

'All I can tell you is that we are looking at Holt's work into the Peel Foundation.'

Gwen stared at Winder and spat out her next few words.

'I hope they're responsible. I hope you catch them and I hope the whole Peel Foundation comes crumbling down. Can you help get my Phoebe back?'

Chapter 12

Drake powered the car out of Tarporley and headed towards the A55. When he reached the dual carriageway, he accelerated into the outside lane heading back for Colwyn Bay and the premises of the Peel Foundation.

He delegated Sara to discover more about the demonstration. Details were difficult to come by and Drake's frustration spilled over with the contradictory messages she shared. 'Why the hell can't area control find some basic information?'

'There's a uniformed inspector on the scene and apparently Mervyn Peel has made a formal complaint that the protesters are causing a public nuisance.' Her mobile rang with another call. Drake listened to the brief one-sided conversation before Sara turned to him. 'That was the solicitors who wrote Jack Holt's will. They confirmed it hasn't been changed, by them at least.'

'Good, it gives Ackland a motive.' Drake flashed the headlights at cars dawdling in front of him. 'Better warn the traffic officers we're not going to keep to the speed limits.'

Sara called the traffic department warning them that if there were unmarked police vehicles on the road ahead of them they should leave them well alone.

Drake relaxed the nearer he got to Colwyn Bay. He left the A55 and followed the road towards the sprawling estate the Foundation owned. In the distance he saw the lights of a patrol car and two motorcycle officers. He parked and they marched over to the main entrance.

There were twenty, maybe more, individuals carrying placards and shouting a chorus of 'Stop The Foundation' 'Stop The Thieves'. It was all intended for the consumption of the television cameras situated on the opposite side of the road. Drake could imagine the headlines all over the evening news. It would be more unwelcome attention for the Peel Foundation.

A uniformed inspector spotted Drake and Sara and came over to them. 'What the hell are you doing here, Ian?'

Drake drew the lapels of his jacket up to his neck against the cold. 'Professional interest. I'm the SIO on the Jack Holt murder and he was investigating the Peel Foundation.'

'Well, I've given these protesters long enough. I'm going to have to give them an ultimatum to disperse pretty soon.'

'Who are they?' Drake said, scanning the various individuals involved. Was it just coincidence that this protest was taking place so soon after Jack Holt's murder?

'The leader of the protest is that woman in the far corner by the gate.' The inspector nodded his head towards a woman with long curls and a thin face.

'Have there ever been protests here before?'

'Not that I know of.'

Drake stared over at the woman. Years of policing told him that coincidences like this didn't just happen. He wondered what connection the woman had to the Peel Foundation. But walking over to her and trying to engage in polite conversation was completely impractical.

He pondered how best to approach her and as he did so a hooter sounded from the Foundation building. Then the gates slowly opened and from inside another half a dozen protesters emerged. They encouraged the others standing outside to join them and they ran into the premises.

Now Drake could hear three different voices on megaphones. He realised this had been carefully planned. He doubted that anyone from the Peel Foundation had invited them, which meant a complaint of burglary and criminal damage was imminent.

'Bloody hell.' The uniformed inspector turned to Drake. 'That's the last thing we want. It looks like someone has broken in and has been able to get the gate open. I'll talk to Mr Peel. He's already been on the phone a dozen times.'

Drake stood by his side and listened to the one-sided

conversation with Mervyn Peel. The inspector turned to Drake, rolling his eyes despairingly. Once he had finished, he announced to the uniformed officers, 'The owners are happy for us to have access to the property. There's been a formal complaint of criminal damage and burglary.'

Drake glanced at his watch, knowing he needed to be back at headquarters. He turned to Sara. 'We'll wait. Let's see exactly what happens.'

He tapped out a message to Annie in the meantime as the uniformed inspector gathered his officers together before marching over to the entrance. *Going to be late tonight. Sorry. I'll text you later X*

Drake followed the officers into the premises. Most of the protesters had peacefully sat on the tarmac outside, disappointed the television crews hadn't followed them through the gates. From a first-floor room Drake heard a commotion and shouts of protest. A few moments later officers escorted three individuals out of the building, one of whom was the woman the uniformed inspector had pointed out previously. She glared at Drake, frowning as she did so.

The three individuals were escorted down the drive. The inspector joined Drake. 'We've arrested those three on suspicion of burglary and criminal damage. We'll interview them later.'

'Any objection if I tag along? I'd like to speak to the ringleader.'

The uniformed inspector gave Drake a seriously troubled look, as though he were completely surprised and wrongfooted by the request. 'You'll need to check it out with the custody sergeant.'

After a short journey to the area custody suite, Drake and Sara followed the officers inside. It was the specialist centre that handled all prisoners arrested in the area immediately surrounding headquarters. There would be other similar custody suites throughout North Wales and Drake was well accustomed to the setup and luckily he knew the custody sergeant.

'I'm the SIO on the Jack Holt murder enquiry. He was investigating the Peel Foundation and Mervyn Peel is a person of interest. It's too much of a coincidence these protesters were outside tonight. I need to talk to the ringleader. Off the record, no tapes.'

The custody sergeant paused. It was an unusual request. Drake expected him to say it was totally out of order. The sergeant was responsible for all the prisoners in the custody suite and the rules governing his procedures didn't accommodate something like this.

'I don't know, Ian… This is a bit irregular.'

'It's only for a few minutes. I just want to talk to her. If she refuses, fine… Sara will be with me,' Drake said, nodding his head at Sara, including her in his plans.

A convoluted look crossed the custody sergeant's face. He couldn't quite make up his mind whether to agree to Drake's request. 'I'll ask. And if she's okay you can use one of the interview rooms. There are no tapes. And she is not under caution.'

Drake nodded. 'Like I said – off the record.'

The sergeant returned a few moments later. 'She's in interview room three. She was as intrigued as I am. So I guess that's why she's happy to talk to you.'

'Thanks.'

Drake turned to Sara. 'Let's go and talk to her and then we'll go back to headquarters.'

Zoe Lloyd introduced herself as soon as Drake entered the room. She pushed out a hand towards Drake and then at Sara. 'The sergeant said you wanted to talk to me, off the record. It all sounds very Jason Bourne.'

'I'm the senior investigating officer in charge of the inquiry into the murder of Jack Holt.' Drake waited for a response but didn't get one. So he continued. 'We believe Mr Holt was investigating the Peel Foundation. It's not a state secret that he had written articles about the organisation that weren't complimentary.'

'And you think the protest this evening is somehow connected with his murder?'

Drake should have known that an off-the-record approach was going to turn the tables on him. Lloyd was asking the questions now, not him.

'Coincidences always make me feel nervous, Zoe. There's never been a protest outside the Peel Foundation premises in the past. And now a couple of days after Jack Holt is killed you've organised one. I take it you are the ringleader.'

'It's not as though there's one person in charge of this. We've all been damaged by the Peel Foundation.'

'Tell me how they've affected you?'

'My brother got ensnared with them several years ago. He was married with kids. He borrowed money to give to Mervyn Peel. His wife was distraught, and the kids never had a proper home. Then she tried to divorce him, but he tied her up in knots for years.'

'What happened?' Sara said.

'She just ran out of hope. She just couldn't fight any more. She killed herself.'

A terrifying silence occupied the space between Zoe Lloyd, Drake and Sara.

'So how did you know Jack Holt?' Drake said.

'I knew what he was working on. He was a good guy. He was going to expose all their lies and deceit.'

'We'll need to talk to you again.'

'Have you found out who killed him? Was it Mervyn Peel? Was it Martha Peel – she is a real witch. You need to be really careful with her.'

There was a knock on the interview room door and the uniformed inspector that Drake had seen earlier entered. 'We need to formally interview Ms Lloyd now. There are serious complaints she needs to answer.'

Once Lloyd had left, Drake turned to Sara. 'Let's get

back to headquarters. I want to hear about Winder and Luned's day.'

Drake sat at the table in the Incident Room, facing the other officers on his team. Winder had been dispatched to organise coffee and as he did so Drake texted Annie, telling her he was back at headquarters and that he wouldn't be long. Winder returned with a tray of four mugs and a plate of biscuits.

'Good coffee, Gareth,' Drake said, taking his first sip. 'Let's get up to date.'

Drake pointed at the image of Jack Holt on the board. 'We've been to speak to his parents in Tarporley, Cheshire. They didn't know much about his life as a journalist apart from the fact that he was professional and dedicated. But they certainly didn't like his partner, David Ackland.'

Drake looked over to Luned who was nodding her head seriously.

'Holt's parents mentioned a substantial inheritance he'd received from his uncle recently.'

'There was a big financial disparity between Jack Holt and David Ackland,' Luned said.

'But they were living together and there's nothing to suggest that Ackland had a motive to murder Jack Holt.'

'I spoke to one of the trustees who Holt had spoken to about Peel defrauding them. He was clear that Holt's proposed article could have created major adverse publicity for Peel.'

Drake nodded. 'Any luck with those anonymous sources?'

Winder shook his head. 'Nothing, boss.'

Luned added, 'I googled death by croquet hoops, sir, and I discovered an episode of Midsomer Murders featured a victim pinned to the ground using them. Then he was pelted with wine bottles.'

'So we're looking for a fan of Midsomer Murders now?'

Winder sounded cynical.

Luned persevered. 'I'm just telling you what I discovered.'

'Thanks, Luned. But this isn't some cosy mystery.'

'Nothing cosy about some of the deaths in Midsomer Murders,' Sara said. 'My mother loves that series.'

Luned raised her voice as though she were afraid no one would pay her any attention. 'I spoke to a Mr and Mrs Wakeling today. They live next door to Jack Holt and David Ackland. They had heard arguments between both men taking place in the house. They gave me lots of detail.'

'Really? I think we should speak to David Ackland again. He is clearly a person of interest. Before we do so let's find out what car he owns. And have we been able to trace the police car and the officers driving in the vicinity of the park on the night Holt was killed?'

'I've sent a request through,' Winder said. 'It might take a bit of time to get the information we need.'

'Put a bomb under them. It must be easy to identify the officers on duty that night.'

Sara made her first contribution: 'I think we need to be careful about relying on any evidence from that homeless man.'

'We treat Danny's evidence as importantly as anyone else's until it's proved otherwise,' Drake snapped. It had been a long day and the last thing he wanted was obstacles and cynicism, especially from Sara. 'And we need to find a red car driving near the park on the night Holt was killed.'

'I spoke to my mum and my Auntie Gwen, Phoebe's mother, today about my cousin and her involvement with the Peel Foundation. She really hates them for what they've done to their family. She went to a presentation when Phoebe started to get involved, but then once Phoebe got sucked in she cut all contact. Auntie Gwen is utterly devastated. It's as though her whole life has been ripped apart.'

There was a brief moment of silence that recognised the impact on Winder's family.

'Auntie Gwen described Mervyn Peel making her skin crawl. And she thought Mrs Peel was an evil influence.'

'It must be very difficult for your aunt,' Luned said. 'I can't imagine what it must be like.'

Drake stood up and walked over to the board. He peered at the map pinned to it. 'We know Jack Holt was in the DeVere Royal Hotel for about half an hour from six pm. And we know he was killed very late in the evening or in the early hours of the following day. We need to find out exactly where he had been for those missing hours.'

'What happened at that demonstration at the Peel Foundation?' Winder said.

Drake looked over at the detective constable. 'A bunch of people organised a protest outside the main entrance but at the same time some of them broke in. They are facing burglary and criminal damage charges. I spoke off the record to a Zoe Lloyd, one of the ringleaders. She knew about Jack Holt. I can't help feeling there's more going on there than we know about yet.'

Drake glanced over at the clock on the wall. It was late, they all needed to be home getting some precious few hours away from the Incident Room. He walked over to his office, tapping out a message to Annie as he did so. *Just leaving. See you soon X*

Then he dragged on his coat and headed out for his car.

Chapter 13

When Drake arrived home, he felt his body dragged down with fatigue. Annie kissed him warmly and he held her close but, when she had enquired about his day, from the troubled look on her face he realised he'd mumbled something incoherent.

'I'm sorry. It's been a long day. I've been over to Tarporley in Cheshire to speak to Jack Holt's parents.'

'That must have been difficult.' Annie led the way up to the open-plan kitchen and living room on the first floor.

After a meal Drake fell asleep in front of the evening news, only to be awoken with a start by Annie insisting he get to bed. He didn't recall undressing or visiting the bathroom and he certainly didn't remember his head hitting the pillow. He woke the following morning to see Annie emerging from the en suite bathroom, a bath towel draped over her body.

Drake gave her a welcoming smile.

'I've got an early start,' Annie said. 'You'd better get up and shower.' She disrobed and threw the damp towel at Drake. She started to dress as he made for the shower. He smiled to himself as he let the hot water stream over his body. The image of her entering the bedroom would stay with him all day, enabling him to add colour in his own mind to the rest of the day.

'I spoke to someone at the university about the Peel Foundation,' Annie said, as they sat at the breakfast table. 'They offered to deliver lectures and run courses but the lecturer at the psychology department began to feel uncomfortable. She did some digging around into the organisation and found comments on a blog post. They're not very nice people are they?'

'Did I tell you that Gareth Winder's cousin is involved with them?'

Annie shook her head. Drake finished the last of his

toast. 'She was a promising law student. She inherited a big chunk of money and gave it all to the Foundation when she got involved with them.'

'I've read the articles Jack Holt wrote for *The Examiner* magazine. I got the impression he knew more but couldn't include it.'

'I spoke to his parents yesterday – they were both vicars in the Church of England. They really didn't like his partner.'

'How are you getting on with the investigation? I did show interest last night but…'

'I was so tired I couldn't think straight.'

'And you won't forget Dad's hospital appointment tomorrow night?'

'Of course not.'

Drake finished his coffee and left Annie, promising to be home at a reasonable hour. She rolled her eyes, telling Drake she knew how unlikely that was.

Drake's thoughts on the journey into headquarters were dominated by the Peel Foundation and David Ackland in equal measure. Mervyn Peel had the perfect motive for murdering Jack Holt. But there was more to the Peel Foundation than simply Mr Peel. Perhaps Mervyn Peel wasn't the sort to get his hands dirty by personally being responsible for the death of Jack Holt. If there were two people involved, it could well have been two of the bodyguards who assaulted Holt as he attempted to interview Peel outside the Foundation's offices in London.

Drake pulled into a parking slot at headquarters and made his way to the Incident Room. He headed for his office and after booting up the computer he adjusted the photographs of his daughters, as he did every morning. Then he checked his Post-it notes and moved to the urgent column marked Peel Foundation – Mrs Peel and others.

He heard voices in the Incident Room and called out Sara's name.

She appeared in his doorway moments later.

'Morning, boss.'

'Let's go and see the Peel Foundation again today. But first I want an update on the burglary and public order incident from yesterday.'

'I'll chase the inspector in charge of that inquiry.'

Drake nodded. 'Once you're done, we'll go and talk to Mrs Peel and all the other employees there. Let's see if anybody fits the description of the two men we saw on the footage.'

'They won't be happy.'

'To hell with that. We can always get them into area control for formal interview under caution.'

Drake spent a few moments replying to various emails and completing an up-to-date report for Superintendent Hobbs, using his standard reporting template. He printed out a blurry version of the two men from the video Jack Holt's editor had provided.

Why had Zoe Lloyd and her friends decided to stage that protest? There had never been issues of public order at the premises before and Drake's only conclusion was that it had been timed to draw attention to the Peel Foundation. He suspected she knew far more than she had told him yesterday, and he wondered what her motives were.

Sara rapped a knuckle on the door into his room and he waved her in.

'I've just spoken with the inspector we saw last night. He's finished the interviews. All the protesters went "No comment" about their involvement in breaking into the property.'

'Was anything damaged? Or stolen?'

Sara shook her head. 'He's going to be putting a file together and making a referral to the Crown Prosecution Service. He's letting them decide about whether or not to prosecute.'

Drake nodded. It wasn't unusual and it meant a delay

before a decision on prosecution. He wondered how Zoe Lloyd would feel about that.

Drake got to his feet. 'Let's go and pay the Peel Foundation another visit.'

It didn't take long for Drake's BMW to warm up as they left headquarters and headed out of town. It only took them a few minutes to reach the entrance gate, where Sara pressed the intercom. Despite announcing who they were there was a long delay before the gate opened.

Drake drove up to the front of the building. The same young woman appeared but she'd dropped the officious air. This time she said simply, 'Follow me.'

Drake and Sara were led down a corridor, the doors to the offices off it firmly closed. At the end they reached the door with "Mervyn Peel – Peel Foundation" in large letters on a sign pinned to it. The woman knocked a couple of times and pushed the door open.

'I do hope this is a visit to confirm the Wales Police Service will be bringing the entire weight of the criminal law to bear against the protesters who broke into our premises last evening,' Peel said as he stood up from behind the large mahogany topped desk.

'You'll need to speak to the inspector in charge of that inquiry for details of progress,' Drake said making himself comfortable in one of the visitor chairs, Sara by his side doing likewise. Peel sat down. He gestured for the woman to leave them and turned to Drake.

'What the hell is this about?'

'We'd like to speak to all members of your staff.'

'What!' Peel exclaimed. 'And why the hell would you want to do that?'

'It's all part of our ongoing enquiries.' Drake smiled insincerely at Peel. 'We'd like a list of all your employees.'

'This is preposterous. I mean you can't just come in here demanding lists of people who are employed by the Foundation.'

'Of course I can. I'm the senior investigating officer in a murder inquiry. And if you're not prepared to agree voluntarily, I could quite easily apply for a warrant and bring a full team including specially trained search officers. Now I'm sure you want to cooperate, particularly as you have an outstanding complaint with the Wales Police Service in relation to last night.'

Peel shot a look of complete disdain and contempt, first at Drake and then at Sara. He opened his mouth a couple of times as though he were gasping for breath. Then he found a piece of A4 paper from a drawer in his desk and scribbled the names of the members of staff present. He pushed it over to Drake.

'We'll need somewhere where we can interview everyone in turn.' Drake turned to the list. 'And that will include your wife who is not on this list.'

'Martha! And why on earth would you want to be speaking to her?'

'Is she an important part of the Peel Foundation?'

'Of course she is. This is outrageous. I thought we were living in a civilised country.'

Drake wanted to respond with some pithy comment about the activities of the Peel Foundation but decided against it.

Drake stared at Peel, who must have realised there was little to gain by being obstructive. He got to his feet and without ceremony announced, 'You'd better come with me.'

As Peel walked down the corridor Drake said, 'Once we've spoken to every member of staff, I'll need to speak to you again, Mr Peel.'

Peel grunted an acknowledgement and led them to the conference room they had visited on the first occasion. The room was cool, and Drake noticed the bland abstract paintings on the wall, wondering if they were part of the Peel Foundation's psychological programming for participants sitting around the table. The young woman they had met earlier joined them as they entered.

'This is Katie. I'm sure she can assist you with your interviews,' Peel said neutrally. Katie nodded formally at Drake and Sara.

'Detective Inspector Drake wants to interview all the members of staff. I've given him a list. I'm sure you can assist him.'

Peel left, leaving Drake and Sara with Katie.

'Please sit down,' Drake said, deciding he would begin with Katie.

Sara deposited her file of papers and a laptop on the floor by her chair. Then she opened her notebook on the table. Once Sara was ready, Drake turned to Katie. 'How long have you worked here?'

'Four years.'

'And what did you do previously?'

'How is that relevant?'

'We'll get on much better if you answer my questions,' Drake smiled.

Katie pouted. 'I was a secretary at an accountancy firm in Manchester.'

'I'd like you to tell me where you were Sunday night?'

'You don't think I had anything to do with the murder of Jack Holt, do you?'

'Just answer the question, Katie.'

'I was over visiting my parents, if you must know. They live in the Wirral and as we didn't have any activity planned I took the opportunity of going to see them. We had dinner, we talked a bit and I returned here about eleven-thirty pm when I went straight to bed.'

'We'll need their full names and contact details.'

'Oh really, this is quite absurd,' Katie said, before volunteering the information.

'Thank you, Katie.' Drake looked at the list of staff members, telling her who he'd like to see next.

Katie left and Sara turned to Drake. 'You didn't ask

about the image of the two men on the footage from London?'

'Let's wait and see if any of them are on the staff already.'

Sara nodded and fidgeted in her bag for the two images which she placed into the notepad on the table in front of them.

'What did you make of her?'

'She's a bit officious. If Peel is behind the murder, he probably wouldn't have chosen her to assist him.'

Katie pushed open the door and a tall man with a head of thick wavy hair marched in. The shirt collar hugged his neck and the light blue pattern tie was knotted perfectly.

'This is Martin Swan,' Katie said before leaving.

Drake gestured at the young man who sat giving Drake an expressionless gaze. Sara raised the cover of the notepad sharing with Drake the blurry image of Swan. It was clearly one of the men from the footage although his hair was longer now – drawn into a tight ponytail. Drake nodded slowly at Sara, gathering his thoughts.

They established quite quickly he had worked for the Foundation for over ten years and that previously he had been a golf professional. Swan sounded professional and cooperative when he answered Drake's questions, as though the meeting was entirely reasonable. He didn't express any surprise when Drake asked about his whereabouts on the night Jack Holt was killed. 'I was conducting an online Zoom course. There were delegates from five different countries. We do a lot of these courses in the evening because of the time differences.'

'Did you know Jack Holt?'

'I knew of him.'

'Had you ever met him?'

'No, I don't believe I had.'

Drake took the image of Swan from the notepad and slid it over the table.

'This is a screenshot from footage of you assaulting Jack Holt outside the London offices of the Peel Foundation. Why did you lie to me about not having met Holt?'

Swan stared at the image as though he couldn't believe he'd been caught out. Then his face hardened. He pushed it back at Drake and his lips flattened but he said nothing.

'There's enough evidence on this footage to justify arresting you for assault and interviewing you under caution in the area custody suite. Would you prefer that?'

Gone was the constructive tone from Swan's voice. He spat out a reply: 'No comment.'

'What do you have to hide?'

Swan continued to stare.

'Do you make a habit of assaulting men in the street?'

Swan remained silent.

'The murder inquiry takes precedence to investigating an assault charge, but your lack of cooperation doesn't look good.'

Swan got up. 'This meeting is at an end.' He walked over to the door and yanked it open.

Katie returned, having been standing in the corridor waiting for further instructions. Drake read out the name of the next member of staff. She nodded her agreement and left.

'What did you make of Swan, boss?'

'I hate it when people pretend to be reasonable and then refuse to cooperate. We'll pin his image onto the board as a person of interest.'

Katie returned with a man called John who was quite clearly not the other man who'd assaulted Jack Holt. He was thin and wiry and into his fifties, judging by his complexion and the wrinkles around his eyes. He quickly confirmed his status at the Foundation and that on the evening in question he had been at a seminar in Manchester and had stayed overnight. He gave Drake and Sara the details of the hotel and the other member of staff with him, who was the next person they requested Katie to bring to them. Without prompting, the details John had given were confirmed.

Two more members of staff were interviewed, and all provided confirmation they had been at the Foundation on the evening in question relaxing and watching television. As both were women, they didn't fit the description of the two men from London.

The second bodyguard from the video footage wasn't a member of staff at the Foundation – or certainly not those present that day – and Drake had to be satisfied with further bland interviews. He asked Katie to fetch Mrs Peel.

Katie duly obliged.

'It is always a pleasure to assist the Wales Police Service,' Martha Peel said, once she had sat down.

Martha had straight black hair parted in the middle, which curtained her round face. Her upper lip protruded slightly but she had a strong mouth and dark, fierce eyes.

'As you know we are investigating the murder of Jack Holt. You must be pleased he is not a nuisance to your organisation any longer.' Drake said, aiming to irritate Martha as soon as he could.

'He was a journalist. It's a free country, but what he was trying to do was completely wrong.'

'What do you mean?'

'He had no concept of what was right and wrong. He was just interested in himself and making a story.'

'Are you pleased he is dead?'

There was the barest hint of a smile playing on her lips. 'You cannot catch me out that easily.'

'Where were you on Sunday night?'

'I was here of course, where else would I be?'

'And were you with anybody? Can anyone account for your movements?'

'Unless you think I'm a suspect in your inquiry then I'm not going to answer any of your questions.'

'I was really hoping you would be prepared to cooperate, Martha,' Drake smiled. 'Because I'm sure you can appreciate Jack Holt's interest in your organisation gives everyone in the Foundation a motive for his death.'

'Do you have any more questions?' Martha stood up.

Drake shook his head. He wanted to add 'for now at least.'

Drake finished the list of staff members and organised for Katie to show them back to Mervyn Peel's office. As he did so Sara whispered. 'We haven't seen the accountant. He wasn't on the list.'

Mervyn Peel was still working on documents, looking important and dedicated and highly professional as he did so. He jerked a hand at the chairs, and they sat down.

'There is an accountant or financial officer who works in the organisation based here but we haven't seen him,' Sara said.

Peel nodded an explanation. 'Ted is away. He should be back tomorrow.'

'Everyone has been most cooperative,' Drake exaggerated. 'I was hoping you would be prepared to be so too. When we initially spoke, you refused to confirm details of your whereabouts on the evening Jack Holt was killed.'

Peel sighed.

'In order for us to eliminate you from our inquiry we need you to provide full details of where you were on the evening Jack Holt was killed.'

'I think it's preposterous you should be pursuing your interest in me as a possible culprit when you're doing nothing about these lawbreakers and terrorists who broke into our property without justification. They created an almighty disturbance outside my property yesterday and they broke in – surely that's burglary or breaking and entry or whatever you call it in Wales.'

'That matter is being investigated. As indeed is the murder of Jack Holt, which concerns me. Now Mr Peel please confirm where you were on the evening he was killed.'

Peel looked down at his desk and picked up a ballpoint, which he turned through his fingers. 'If you must know I was with an investor. Someone who is prepared to see the value of what we are doing here and make a financial commitment towards its future.'

'I shall need full details of where I can contact this person.'

Peel gave another irritated sigh before reaching for his mobile.

Chapter 14

Once Inspector Drake and Sara had left, Luned got straight down to working on Jack Holt's mobile, which had arrived late the previous afternoon from the forensic department.

Winder, sitting opposite at his desk in the Incident Room, was trawling through the reports from the house-to-house enquiries with little of his usual enthusiasm. Having an officer on the enquiry team with such a close family connection to the Peel Foundation was only likely to cause problems. Luned thought it was inevitable Winder would have to be replaced and a new detective allocated. After all, how could he possibly have enough objectivity to be an effective member of the team.

For now, she was going to do her best to include him in everything she was undertaking. His experience could contribute significantly to the management of the inquiry.

Once she had set in motion a request for a triangulation on Holt's mobile for the evening he was killed she looked over at Winder. 'I think we should go and try and find the two uniformed officers in that patrol car Danny said he saw passing the park.'

Winder paused before looking over at her.

'Let's call at the DeVere Royal Hotel again. We didn't talk to all the members of staff working the night Jack Holt visited.'

'Let's do both. Have you had the footage from the hotel?'

Realising she hadn't checked that morning she opened her emails. 'It's here. I'll send it to you.'

A few moments later they each stared at their monitor screens. Luned clicked at five thirty pm and fast-forwarded the recording until the image of Jack Holt's car came into the screen. She recognised the BMW as it parked. Then Holt left the car, a small briefcase in hand, and headed into the hotel via the rear door. After pausing that footage Sara opened the second lot of recordings the manager had sent. She found the time on the footage from the camera inside the hotel and hit play. She fast-forwarded to the exact time Holt entered from the rear of the premises. She watched as he walked into the bar area.

She continued to play the footage for a few minutes. Jack Holt was clearly preparing for a meeting. She guessed the work of a journalist could mean odd hours, interviewing people willing to talk to him in the evening in a bar. Who could that person be?

'Nothing much there,' Winder said. 'It just looks like he's going for a drink in the bar.'

'He had a briefcase with him.'

'Maybe he was just doing some work. Catching up with things.'

'His partner made clear he thought he was meeting Mervyn Peel.'

'I'll put his number plates through the ANPR system. It might bring up something, but if he wasn't driving along any of the major routes there won't be any results.'

'Let's hope the triangulation of his mobile will be more productive.' Luned got up and announced, 'Let's go to admin support. We need to track down the police car Danny saw.'

Luned and Winder spent an hour being sent from one office to another. It amazed her how difficult it was to establish which officers were on duty the night Holt was killed and what car they were driving. Identifying the police car without a registration number might take some time, but she had the location and the time of day so she hoped it would be straightforward to pinpoint the names of the officers.

Eventually one of the civilians suggested they contact the police station covering Colwyn Bay. 'It's probably one of theirs. But you never know, it could have come from Rhyl or Bangor.' The young civilian gave her a positive, encouraging sort of smile which was quite the opposite to how she felt.

They left headquarters and travelled the short journey to the De Vere Royal Hotel. Luckily all the members of staff that had been working on the night Holt called at the bar were present. Nobody recognised Holt. Luned left the hotel feeling despondent as they made for their car.

'It's got to be a car from the station in town. It's more likely to be one of theirs,' Winder said.

Luned nodded. At least it wasn't raining as the forecast had promised, but it was still cold and she shivered sitting in the car – it would take ages to get properly warmed up. Luckily it was a short drive to the police station responsible for Colwyn Bay. They parked and made their way inside through the usual security protocols.

They found a sergeant eating an enormous Danish pastry and drinking from a massive mug of tea. Luned recognised the name as the same officer who had been present at the crime scene when Inspector Drake and Sara had initially been called.

'DC Luned Thomas and this is DC Gareth Winder,' Luned said.

'Hello Gareth,' Sergeant Turner replied. 'We go back a long time. It's good to meet you, Luned.'

Luned started to flush but quickly regained her composure and sat by the officer's desk. 'We're trying to trace two officers who were in a marked police car driving near the park on the evening Holt was killed.'

'First I've heard of it.'

'We've got an eyewitness, a homeless man who has given us some information we need to check out.'

'It's not Danny, is it?'

Luned nodded.

'You need to be careful with him.' Turner sounded cautious. 'I wouldn't describe him as an ideal witness.'

'We need to check it out nevertheless.'

Turner clicked into his computer and scanned the screen for a few moments. 'Nope, nothing to do with us. You might try one of the other stations. The officers from Llandudno or Rhyl often come over here.'

Luned and Winder thanked the sergeant and left.

'I think we should go over to Llandudno. I don't think the officers from Rhyl would come over here,' Luned said.

'Yeah, okay, but we detour on the way. I'm starving.'

Luned reckoned that Winder spying the Danish pastry on the sergeant's table had been enough to trigger his hunger pains. He was back to his normal old self. She felt quite pleased.

They stopped at a bakery on the journey from Colwyn Bay and Winder munched his way enthusiastically through a Danish pastry before slurping the coffee he bought.

It was a short journey to the police station in Llandudno and they repeated the security requirements to enter the station itself. The woman on reception notified them that an inspector was on duty.

They found his office easily enough and announced their arrival.

'Good morning, sir,' Luned had her warrant card in hand, but he waved it away once she and Winder had introduced themselves.

'What can I do to help?'

'We're part of the team investigating the murder of Jack Holt. He was killed in a park in Colwyn Bay four nights ago. An eyewitness has told us he spotted a police vehicle was in the area that evening. We've been to the station in Colwyn Bay and they have no record of any officers being called out at that time.'

'And you're wondering if any officers from this area were over there.' The inspector leaned over his desk and clicked into his computer at the same time. 'Let me check.' It took a few moments until he nodded. 'Two officers were over there following up a lead on a domestic violence complaint.'

'We need to talk to them.'

The inspector stared at his screen. 'You're in luck, they're both here today.'

He scooped up the handset of the telephone on his desk. He chased down both officers and asked them to attend in his room without delay. Both looked surprised when they saw Luned and Winder.

'Detective Constables Thomas and Winder are part of the team investigating that murder in Colwyn Bay at the beginning of the week.' The inspector nodded at Luned. 'We have an eyewitness who says he saw a patrol car near the park where Holt was killed that evening.'

Both officers nodded. 'We just drove through. We didn't stop. The satnav must have taken us nearby as we had an address for a suspect we needed to talk to.'

'Do you remember a red car or a silver 3 Series BMW loitering around the place. Or anything at all suspicious?'

Both officers looked blankly at each other. Then they shook their heads.

'We did have a dashcam, so that might help?'

'We'll need the footage.'

The inspector replied, 'I'll get it sent over.' Then he thanked both officers, who left the room.

Luned spoke first. 'Thank you, sir.'

'I hope you find your killer.'

'I certainly hope so too.'

Drake parked a little distance from the home Jack Holt had shared with David Ackland. Sara pointed at the property. 'The evidence Mr and Mrs Wakeling gave Luned was that they heard frequent arguments between Holt and Ackland.'

'Couples do argue.'

'The neighbours reckoned there was more to it than simply a disagreement. They would be shouting abuse at each other.'

'Let's see what he says. I want to hear what he has to say about the financial disparity and about his gambling habit, too. You take the lead,' Drake said to Sara.

She nodded her understanding, pleased she would do the questioning. Drake could be brusque, particularly if he felt witnesses were being unhelpful, and she wondered if he felt the feminine touch might be more appropriate with David Ackland.

'Sure thing, boss.'

They left the car and walked over to the front door. David Ackland gave them a surprised look when he saw them outside. 'Any developments?'

'We'd like to speak to you in more detail,' Sara said.

Now Ackland frowned. He hesitated for a moment before inviting them inside. They entered the same room they had visited when they had broken the news about Jack Holt's death. Sara scanned her memory for anything that suggested insincerity or an artificial response at the time. He certainly had a theatrical streak. But was that enough to be suspicious of his motives?

Ackland looked disappointed when Drake and Sara declined the offer of coffee. They weren't there on a social call.

'We wanted to ask you about your relationship with Jack,' Sara said. 'How would you describe it?'

'Perfectly normal.'

'Any arguments?'

'I don't know what you mean.'

'We have evidence from your neighbours that they had heard blazing rows between you and Jack on several occasions.'

'Mr and Mrs Wakeling next door are bigots. And more than that they are homophobic bigots. I don't think you should rely on anything they say, at all, ever.'

'I appreciate that in every relationship there are disagreements, arguments even, but they overheard regular slanging matches between you and Jack. If that's true we'd like to know what the disagreements were about.'

'Am I a suspect in Jack's murder? Do I need a solicitor? I can't believe this is happening.'

'I'm sure you appreciate that we have to examine every aspect of Jack's life as part of the investigation. And that means looking into your relationship with him.' Sara sounded her most reasonable best.

It seemed to do the trick, as Ackland mellowed. 'Of course, we had arguments like every couple, but our bond was strong enough to survive.'

Nice smooth answer, Sara thought. 'Can you tell me what you argued about?'

She wanted to see how honest David Ackland was really going to be.

'All the usual things, holidays, housekeeping, family, you know...'

'No, I don't think I do know, Mr Ackland. Perhaps you can clarify.'

'His parents were obnoxious. And they wanted nothing to do with me at all and made it perfectly clear to Jack.'

'Did you argue about money?'

'Sometimes, but nothing serious. And, you know, most couples argue about money at some point, don't they?'

Sara could detect Drake fidgeting by her side. Ackland was doing his best to downplay the arguments.

'As part of our enquiries, we have conducted a detailed financial background check into Mr Holt and you, Mr Ackland.' Sara looked straight at Ackland, who blinked nervously.

'And it's come to our attention that Jack paid off a credit card debt you owed some years ago.'

Ackland nodded and, if he had had any sense, he could have seen what the next question was going to be.

'And we are aware that since then you have incurred substantial debts to an online gaming company. Was that the source of your arguments with Jack?'

Ackland didn't reply.

'Had Jack refused to pay your new debts? If he had, that must've been a source of some embarrassment.'

Ackland folded his arms and pulled tight against his chest.

'And we know Jack Holt had left a will making you his only beneficiary. You are likely to inherit a large amount of money.'

Ackland got to his feet. He spat out a reply. 'I think it's time you left now.'

Drake and Sara paused but once they realised Ackland was deadly serious they got up and left.

Once inside the car, Sara let out a long lungful of breath. 'I don't like him. I don't trust him. I think we should get him in for a formal interview under caution.'

Drake nodded and as he did so his mobile rang. He pushed the handset to his ear and Sara listened to his side of the conversation.

'Superintendent Hobbs wants me back at headquarters.'

Chapter 15

Superintendent Hobbs hated any situation where he wasn't in control. And the circumstances outlined by the public relations officer sitting in his office that afternoon needed to be managed carefully.

'Superintendent, this isn't a journalist reporting for a local rag. This is a reporter from one of the major news outlets.'

Hobbs appreciated the civilian officer using his rank. So many of them didn't bother and that irked him. Although they weren't directly answerable to him as they had their own chain of command, he was the senior officer after all.

'Run that past me again.'

'The reporter has been asking very specific questions about the inquiry into the death of Jack Holt. Holt was obviously well connected with high-powered journalists in London. He has been digging around into Holt's past and into the work he was doing.'

'I suppose he considers Holt's murder as the death of one of their own.'

'Exactly – Holt was highly regarded.'

'So what do you suggest we do?'

'I want to talk to Detective Inspector Drake so that I can formulate a proper response.'

Hobbs nodded. 'I'll get him back here as soon as I can.'

The public relations officer left immediately, with Hobbs promising to notify him when Drake had arrived. It gave Hobbs time to review all of Drake's memoranda. The inspector's OCD had meant every single section of the reporting template had been completed accurately. It didn't give Hobbs any way of criticising Drake's record-keeping.

He rang Drake, who promised to be back within a few minutes. So far they had issued a press release inviting anyone with relevant information to contact the hotline. There had been the usual time-wasters and others where uniformed officers had spoken to the callers, but nothing substantive had arisen.

He didn't have to wait long for Detective Inspector Drake to arrive. His secretary ushered Drake inside and followed moments later with coffee and three cups and saucers.

'I've invited John Westcott from the public relations department to join us,' Hobbs said, without explaining any further.

Drake nodded.

'Is there any significance to the croquet hoops?'

'The croquet hoops are baffling, sir. We cannot find any link to Holt as yet. But clearly they were of relevance for the killer, as why else use them?'

'And otherwise, how are you getting on with the inquiry?'

'We are still focusing on Jack Holt's interest in the Peel Foundation. And we've also been looking at his relationship with David Ackland, his partner. Holt had inherited a large capital sum recently. Ackland has debts which we believe caused serious arguments between them.'

'So are you treating Ackland as your main person of interest?'

'There is certainly every reason to suspect he had a motive. But the circumstances of Jack Holt's death suggest there were two people responsible.'

'But it's not inconceivable a single individual was responsible?'

'No, of course not.'

Drake sipped on the coffee which was always excellent when Hobbs' secretary prepared it. John Westcott joined them soon afterwards. Drake had worked with him in the past and knew him to be dependable.

'Hello, John, good to see you,'

'And you Ian. How are the family?'

'Good, thanks.'

Hobbs got back to business; he wasn't going to allow both men to hijack his meeting for their personal catch-up. 'John, please share your update with Inspector Drake.'

'We've had contact from a Brian Powell – he's a journalist from one of the major agencies in London. I get the impression he knew Jack Holt very well. They worked together and also with the BBC for a few years. He is beginning to ask some seriously awkward questions.'

'I don't want him interfering with the inquiry in any way,' Hobbs said.

'We can either ignore him or we can try and manage the situation by organising a press conference to which he would be invited. If we begin to give him special treatment then he's going to smell a rat.'

'What is special treatment?' Drake said.

'He asked to speak to you, Ian.'

'I wouldn't want that to happen.' Hobbs frowned.

'It wouldn't satisfy Powell and he would only dig further.'

Hobbs turned to Drake. 'What do you reckon about a press conference?'

'We've already issued a press release. I'm not certain we'd benefit from a press conference at the moment.'

'Agreed, for now. I suggest we review again at the end of the week.'

Wescott added. 'Don't leave it longer than that. By then Powell will have a team digging for all it's worth.'

The prospect of a press conference troubled Drake. They rarely achieved anything, and he had a suspicion most of them fuelled uncontrolled press interest. But the possibility of some hotshot reporter interfering with his investigation was a worry too. He threaded his way through the corridors of headquarters to the Incident Room.

Sara and the two detective constables were sitting around the table. Drake nodded a greeting and glanced over at the board. Something had changed and Drake realised a pin had been added, its location confirming where two officers had driven near the park on the evening Jack Holt was killed.

'Holt's mobile has been released by the CSIs and I've checked his calls on the night he was murdered. There were three incoming calls from burners,' Luned said.

Drake nodded. It was hardly a surprise Holt's killer had used an untraceable handset.

Luned continued. 'We managed to track down two officers from Llandudno station who were investigating a domestic abuse case.'

'So Danny's evidence is correct,' Drake said.

'Did they see anything else?' Sara said.

Winder shook his head. 'We've asked them to get back to us if they can recall anything. And they're going to send us their dashcam footage.'

'And we spoke to members of staff from the DeVere Royal Hotel who were working the evening Jack Holt was present. It didn't take us any further. Only one member of staff could recall him in the bar and that person didn't see him with anybody else.'

'I've requisitioned a search of the ANPR cameras for David Ackland's vehicle as well as Jack Holt's BMW,' Luned said.

'I want images of Martha Peel and Martin Swan, one of Mervyn Peel's two minders on the board. Do searches for vehicles owned by them. We might then be able to place them near the park. We still need to identify the second minder.'

'They probably parked well out of the way,' Winder said.

'But people make mistakes.'

Drake turned back to the board and started to rearrange the photographs. He placed Jack Holt's in the middle and on the left-hand side pinned an image of David Ackland and then to his right that of Mervyn Peel. He left a gap under Peel for Martha's photograph before adding the grainy image of the minder they had interviewed earlier.

'Mervyn Peel said he was meeting an investor on the evening Jack Holt was killed.' Drake glance at the time on his watch. 'I'll call to see him on the way home. In the meantime, chase the ANPR results and revisit the house-to-house enquiry reports. Somebody must have seen something.'

Drake fiddled with his phone and found the album from Kelly Jones' new band – Far From Saints – and set it to play through the sound system in his vehicle. Although he was driving in the direction of his home he was still working and his mind hadn't switched off from the course of the inquiry. He drove down to the A55 and accelerated into the outside lane.

He started to think about Jack Holt's professional and private life. The shadowy Peel Foundation clearly had a motive for his death. He resolved to work through more of Holt's papers in due course. The attention he had paid the documentation Alex Normanton had given him had been perfunctory so far and whilst he wasn't going to unearth a specific clue from the paperwork it might well steer him in the right direction.

The journalist's home life troubled Drake. But was a troubled relationship between Holt and Ackland enough to make Ackland a murderer? If he had asked the question of Holt's parents they would probably have replied in the affirmative.

More than anything, they needed to establish where Jack Holt had been for the hours after he had been sitting aimlessly in the bar at the DeVere Royal Hotel until he had met his death in the park beside the bowling green.

He reached the tunnel under the Conwy estuary and emerged moments later on the western side. He hadn't been to Conwy for years and he resolved to take the children to visit the castle and for a walk around the ancient town walls and the other historical sites in the middle of the town.

He hurried on towards the tunnel through the mountain and then for Penmaenmawr. The satnav directed him to a substantial detached property, high above the town. He pulled into the drive and parked alongside a Range Rover. It meant he could take in the view and to his left he made out the shimmering lights of Beaumaris in the distance. A couple of lights bobbed up and down on the Irish Sea, brave sailors indeed going out at this time of year, and he guessed they were heading for the marina at Conwy.

He got out of the car and walked over to the property. Leonard Ferrier was waiting for him at the front door. He was a man in his fifties with confident, enquiring eyes and a clear, healthy complexion. There wasn't a brand logo on the blue Bengal stripe shirt, but it looked expensive. Ferrier reached out a hand. They shook.

'I saw you arriving.' Ferrier nodded at the CCTV camera above his head.

Drake gave Ferrier enough time to examine his warrant card but he showed little interest.

'Come in.'

Drake followed Ferrier inside.

'Would you like something to drink, Detective Inspector?'

'Water, thanks.'

Ferrier deposited Drake in a large study on the ground floor that had a substantial bookcase with textbooks and a large selection of fiction. Novels had been ordered by the surnames of the authors. Drake noticed what appeared to be complete collections of hardback novels by Patricia Cornwell, Michael Connelly and Ian Rankin.

Drake regretted he rarely had time to read for pleasure. Ferrier returned with a glass of water and a bottle of beer for himself.

'How can I help, Detective Inspector?' Ferrier sat on a leather upholstered chair. It matched the sofa Drake sat on.

'I'm in charge of the investigation into the murder of Jack Holt, an investigative journalist.'

Ferrier said nothing, just looked at Drake.

'I understand you have an involvement with the Peel Foundation and that you met Mervyn Peel on Sunday evening, which was the night Jack Holt was murdered.'

'Do you suspect Mervyn Peel may have been responsible for his murder?'

'I'm sure you can appreciate that's not the sort of detail I could discuss.'

Ferrier nodded.

'Can you tell me the nature of your relationship with Mervyn Peel?'

Ferrier took a glug of his beer and put the bottle down on a table. 'I'm a business improvement specialist. I work with companies looking for finance or expertise in order to take advantage of their assets and the current market conditions.'

Ferrier handed Drake a card.

'What exactly were you doing with Mervyn Peel and the Peel Foundation?'

'The Peel Foundation owns a substantial tract of land which they acquired some years ago. It has considerable planning potential but it requires work to realise its full market value. That's where I come in. I've been discussing with Mervyn and Martha Peel the prospect of a joint venture company that would take advantage of the potential value of the land. I'm very well connected with several property companies that would consider the possibility of purchasing the land for commercial development.'

'Where is this land?'

'It's part of their property holdings in North Wales.'

'And why doesn't the Peel Foundation do all this work themselves?'

'Things are never that easy. The complexity of this sort

of situation requires expertise.'

'How long have you been working on this project?'

'A few months.'

'And how many meetings have you had with Mervyn Peel?'

'Quite a few. I can provide you with a detailed list if you require it. But most of the meetings were with Martha Peel. She seems to be the one driving the proposal. And she has a confident grasp of all the details.'

'Was Martha Peel with you on Sunday evening?' At least this was one way to check her alibi.

'No, she wasn't. And there are matters she needs to address before we can really move forward.'

Drake's question had established that Martha Peel was heavily involved in the project. He slotted the information into the back of his mind. 'How much money are we talking about?'

'I'm making a substantial investment of approximately half a million pounds, but the possible value of the land is several million.'

'Is the transaction guaranteed to succeed?'

Ferrier took another drink from the bottle of beer while Drake sipped on his water. The business improvement specialist was clearly gathering his thoughts, judging how much he really could share.

'There are a number of companies I am aware of who would be very interested in the property. Our discussions with the relevant authorities are going well. So, to answer your question, I am confident matters would proceed satisfactorily.'

'I guess you wouldn't have invested half a million unless you thought there was a guarantee of return.'

Ferrier didn't reply but he gave Drake a self-satisfied smile.

Drake continued, 'Do you visit the Peel Foundation very often?'

'Yes.'

'And have you met the accountant at the Peel Foundation?'

'I have. But the land isn't owned directly by the Peel Foundation but by Mervyn and Martha Peel in their names. I can't tell you how that came about.'

'Let me go back to your meeting with Mervyn Peel. I need the details of when the meeting started and when you finished.'

Ferrier took another mouthful of his beer. 'I met Mervyn at the Foundation at seven pm and we continued until ten pm. There was a break in the middle for something to eat and drink and I was home here by ten thirty.'

'Do you often have meetings on Sunday evenings with potential business partners?'

'It's not commonplace, I suppose, but not exceptional either.'

'And how did you get on with Mrs Peel?'

'She's a very determined individual. She is confident and most able. Mervyn wouldn't make decisions without her input.'

Drake finished his water and thanked Leonard Ferrier who showed Drake to the front door. 'If there's anything else I can assist with, Detective Inspector, please do not hesitate to contact me.'

Drake turned to Ferrier. 'Were you aware of Jack Holt?'

'I knew of him, but we had never met.'

Drake nodded. A businessman would simply assess the likelihood of a profitable transaction. He wouldn't be looking at the morals of the people behind the Peel Foundation or the ownership of the land. Business wasn't about that, after all. He looked over at Ferrier. 'Thank you, Mr Ferrier.' He walked over to his car. The two yachts he had seen previously were nowhere to be seen. Ferrier struck him as trustworthy and honest. Martha Peel certainly featured prominently, and it reminded him that Holt had focused more on Mervyn Peel. He wondered why that was the case. Then he started the car – it was only a short journey back home now, enough time to finish listening to the album he had started when he had left headquarters.

Chapter 16

Drake kissed Annie warmly on the lips as he left the following morning. She had reminded him when they had eaten breakfast about her father's hospital appointment later that day and he had nodded his confirmation that he wouldn't be late.

'I'll be there on time.'

As he passed Penmaenmawr he brought to his memory his discussion with Leonard Ferrier. Martha Peel had taken the driving seat with Leonard Ferrier in the development of the property. Drake couldn't suppress a nagging feeling she was an important part of the Peel Foundation despite the bluster and bravado her husband revelled in. And they had still to talk to the accountant and identify his exact whereabouts on the evening of Jack Holt's death.

Drake arrived at headquarters and headed for his office and the Incident Room. Winder stood by the board, pinning to it photographs of the Peel Foundation members of staff.

'Get a photograph of Martin Swan pinned up there too. He was one of the Peel thugs who assaulted Holt.'

'Yes, boss,' Winder said.

'Maybe we should show some of these images to Danny, sir,' Luned said.

'I agree. But be careful with him.'

'We've had the dashcam footage from the police car driving through Colwyn Bay on the night Holt was killed.'

'Excellent, make that a priority and then talk to Danny again.'

Both detective constables replied in unison, 'Yes, boss.'

Winder added, 'I've also had the results of the triangulation on Jack Holt's mobile for the night he was murdered.'

'Get that over to Sara.' Drake turned as he heard his detective sergeant entering. 'I've just asked Gareth to send you the report on the triangulation for Jack Holt's mobile.'

Sara nodded and after she shrugged off her coat she sat down at a desk and booted up her computer. Drake made for his office where he found the file of papers Alex Normanton had left him and began working his way through the documentation. In addition, there was an external hard drive full of further material.

Building a picture of a murder victim was always a macabre activity. It meant collecting information, cold, clear and unemotional data. Jack Holt had been educated privately at Fremantle High public school in Dorset. It was one of many private schools in that area and had been established to serve principally children of Church of England clergy, but since the numbers had declined the school had been forced to cast its net further afield. The fees were substantial and even on two regular salaries Drake doubted most ordinary people would be able to afford such schooling unless there were trust funds and monies from grandparents available. The school's website referred to its traditions and its commitment to preparing its pupils for the modern world.

After reading English at Cambridge University, Holt had studied at Cardiff University for a postgraduate diploma in journalism. The curriculum vitae Alex Normanton had prepared contained scant details after his graduation. A simple one-line entry related to where he had begun his journalistic career and how it had progressed.

For the past ten years he had been an investigative journalist working independently on stories for websites and magazines and, occasionally, independent television production companies.

Drake had barely started working on the articles Jack Holt had prepared when he heard Sara's voice. 'I've got something, boss.'

Drake got to his feet and left his office, joining Sara at her desk.

'I've been able to track Jack Holt's mobile to an area around Denbigh on the night in question. He was there for about four hours.'

'Four hours! What the hell was he doing there?'

'I can place the mobile in the approximate position of two housing estates north of Denbigh itself.'

'Where are Gareth and Luned?'

'They've gone to that homeless shelter in town to see if they can track down Danny again.'

'And no doubt he will enjoy our generous hospitality and the wonderful sandwiches from the canteen. In the meantime, we can wear out some shoe leather. I haven't been to Denbigh for years.'

It was a short journey to St Asaph and then south towards Denbigh. Drake indicated right off the roundabout where the bypass would take traffic to the east and then south for Ruthin. He had decided they would spend a couple of hours, no more, on the house-to-house enquiries to see if they could identify anyone who could recall Jack Holt's vehicle or even his face.

If they drew a blank, a full team of officers would need to canvas the whole town.

'This is about the best location I have,' Sara said pointing to a junction for a housing estate.

Drake pulled up. He checked that Sara had the details of Holt's silver BMW on her mobile, as well as his image. She nodded her understanding, and they left the vehicle.

An hour later they stood together at the far end of the estate. Sara shook her head gently as he approached.

'Nothing, boss.'

'I was the same. Let's do some more and then if we don't have any luck, I'll have to get a full house-to-house team organised.'

They retraced their steps to Drake's BMW and he drove to another estate nearer the middle of town.

He parked and they set out to repeat the same exercise. After calling at many empty properties, Drake decided it was a job more properly undertaken by a house-to-house team.

He would just have to overcome any obstacles Superintendent Hobbs placed in his way – budgetary constraints would have to go to hell. This was a murder inquiry.

He spotted Sara in the distance talking to a householder as he walked down a path towards a detached property at the end of the estate.

The doorbell rang out and the door opened as though the person inside must have been standing right by it. A man in his sixties glared at Drake.

'What do you want?'

Drake decided his demeanour deserved a warrant card to be pushed in this face. When the man realised a detective inspector was at his doorstep his body language relaxed.

'I'm looking for any information about a Mr Jack Holt.' Drake showed the image of Holt on his mobile.

He stared at it then looked up at Drake.

'Yeah, I've seen him. What's wrong, what's he done?'

'He was killed this week. There's a murder inquiry. Haven't you seen the news?'

'Don't watch the news, mate. I just watch Sky Sports and Netflix.'

'So tell me what you know about him?'

'He was a real pain,' the man jerked a finger at the road outside. 'He parked his BMW there all times: day and night. I complained that it was an obstruction. He just smiled at me and told me he wouldn't do it again. But he did do it again.'

'Did you see him here last Sunday evening?'

'Yeah, come to think of it. I'd been walking the dog and he was parked up here when I came back. Before you ask, the time would have been about seven thirty.'

'Thank you,' Drake said before getting the man's full details.

He turned and could still see Sara deep in conversation as he walked over to her. 'This is Trish,' Sara said, 'and she thinks she can help us with our inquiry.'

'I've seen that bloke in the car lots. He's always parking and blocking the pavement. I told him, we've all told him, all the neighbours. Like I said he spent hours with his girlfriend.'

'Girlfriend?' Drake said. 'Are you certain you've got the right man?' He glanced at Sara who gave him a perplexed look.

'Yeah, of course. She lives down the road in one of the terraces. They've got no place to park the car and he just parked here as though it was perfectly normal. We complained to your lot once, but nobody ever came round. Fat lot of good the police are these days.'

'You've been very helpful, Trish,' Sara said. 'But we do really need to know the exact address for Jack Holt's girlfriend.'

'It's number five, or it used to be called number five, but she's put a house name on it now. And instead of one of the old Welsh names she's called it The Hollies, can you believe it?'

'Thank you, Trish,' Drake said, nodding at Sara for her to leave.

Drake almost sprinted down the road and, in the distance, he could see a line of terraced properties. It didn't take them long to find one in the middle with a piece of slate screwed to the outside wall with "The Hollies" on it. They rang the doorbell and waited. There was no sound from inside and Drake was sorely tempted to form a fist and thump the door. But it opened moments later, and a thin woman stood there. When she saw Drake and Sara it was as though she guessed who they were as a sense of relief washed over her. Drake guessed from her pasty complexion and tired-looking eyes she was nursing her grief painfully.

'I'm Detective Inspector Ian Drake of the Wales Police Service and this is my colleague Sergeant Sara Morgan. We'd like to speak to you about Jack Holt.' They both held up their warrant cards. The woman stood there for a moment giving them both blank looks. She didn't express surprise at seeing two detectives standing at her door.

She pushed the door open and motioned them inside.

Once the door was safely closed, she led them to the rear kitchen. The warming smell of basil and oregano filled the room and she pointed to a battered round pine table. Drake and Sara pulled out a chair each and sat down. Sara opened her notebook on the table.

'Can I have your full name?' Drake said as the woman sat down.

'Teresa Ostler.'

'And how do you know Jack Holt?'

'We've been friends for some years. I worked with him a few years ago when he was based in London. We had a brief relationship then before he got involved with...'

'We are aware he was in a relationship with a David Ackland,' Sara said.

'We've been seeing each other for about a year. He realised his relationship with David wasn't what he thought it was going to be.'

'Can you tell me what exactly he meant by that?' Drake said.

'I can only tell you what Jack told me. David had a gambling habit and he was an extremely controlling and jealous individual. He prevented Jack from seeing his parents.'

'We have spoken with Jack's parents.'

Teresa looked pleased with Drake's comment. 'They're decent people, I'm sure.'

'We are trying to trace Jack's movements on the evening he was killed. Was he here that evening?'

Teresa nodded. Then she paused. 'He got here about seven. I was so glad to see him.'

'And when did he leave?'

'He left at about eleven o'clock. He knew it was late and he guessed Ackland would be angry. Probably even driving around looking for him, but he didn't care. We were planning our future together. He was going to tell David Ackland their relationship was at an end.'

'Did he tell you anything about his work?'

'Only that he was working on some big story in relation to the Peel Foundation. He'd been completely obsessed with it for months.'

'Did he mention anything else? We believe he was meeting somebody earlier that evening before he came here. Do you know anything that might help us?'

'There were a couple of telephone calls whilst he was here. They were all very brief and it was about meeting someone after he'd left.'

'Did he say who it was?'

Teresa shook her head.

Chapter 17

Winder began viewing the dashcam footage sent over from the Llandudno area inspector. It surprised him that Inspector Drake hadn't made a fuss about the two officers failing to realise they should have reported their presence near a crime scene. There'd been a murder in a park nearby, for Christ's sake.

There were CCTV cameras everywhere these days: on public buildings to dissuade disorderly behaviour, on house doorbells, on floodlights attached to properties and on police vehicles. Some officers even wore cameras on their uniform. It certainly made for certainty if ever there was a complaint about an officer's conduct and more than anything it gave detectives the chance of gathering evidence.

Watching video footage suited Winder perfectly. Winder wasn't convinced that relying on the testimony of a homeless man was going to help them. He could hear the Crown prosecution lawyers howling in disbelief if the case relied on Danny. It was all very well Detective Inspector Drake saying they had to value everyone's evidence. All Danny thought about was where his next meal was coming from and where he'd be sleeping that night.

Winder opened a map on a tab on his monitor. Then he started to play the footage, establishing exactly where the marked police vehicle had turned off the A55 as it made its way into Colwyn Bay. He paused the video when he couldn't place where the vehicle had gone on the map. Once he knew which road they were on he was able to track them carefully. They pulled up and the officer in the passenger seat got out and Winder could just make her out as she hammered on a front door nearby.

Moments later she looked at her colleague in the car and shook her head. After returning to the vehicle, they continued their journey. They were travelling at a snail's pace, which confirmed the reason for their visit to the town.

They had no luck tracking down the culprit they were looking for as they stopped on two more occasions. On each, one of the officers left the vehicle and returned empty-handed.

Once they were back onto the main road Winder's attention refocused as he realised they were nearing the park. Winder recognised a café he had once visited.

Winder paused the footage again. Satisfied he knew exactly where they were, he pressed play.

Almost immediately he was rewarded with the image of Danny shuffling along the pavement on the passenger side. Winder jotted down the time. The car proceeded in the direction of the park. Winder's pulse pounded in his neck, hoping he'd see Mervyn Peel walking on the pavement and entering the park. He wanted so much to be able to tell Auntie Gwen they had arrested Mervyn Peel for murder. She'd probably do a jig to celebrate, hoping that without him the Foundation would simply fold and that she'd get Phoebe back again.

A vehicle some distance ahead of the police car indicated right into the same road. Winder paid little attention until the police car had passed it. Then he realised how stupid he'd been and, annoyed with himself, he pressed replay until the vehicle came into view for the first time.

What grabbed Winder's interest was its colour – red.

Then he cursed as there was no way he could read the number plate. If only there was a dashcam recording from the rear window that might have captured the details as the car turned after the police had passed.

He called out to Luned, 'You won't believe this.'

Luned raised her head and looked over at Winder.

'That homeless bloke Danny was right. The dashcam footage from the two officers in Llandudno records a red car near the park.'

'Were there many vehicles around?'

'No, the road near the park was quiet.'

'It confirms Danny is a reliable witness then.'

Winder nodded confirmation but he was thinking about the possibility there could be CCTV cameras somewhere on the street leading up to the junction that might have recorded the red car. And that the footage might give them a number plate.

'Have you finished?' Winder said.

'Yes, why do you ask?'

'We need to go and find Danny and I want to do a brief detour en route.'

They buttoned up their coats as they took the stairs down to reception and then out to Winder's vehicle. 'I think it's got colder.' He shivered.

'Forecast is for snow over the weekend.'

It was a short journey to the middle of town and Winder turned the heater to maximum. He wasn't one to suffer the cold.

Winder found slots to park on the side street. They both left the vehicle and Luned joined him on the pavement. On either side there were shops and cafés. He pointed at the junction at the top of the road. 'The car came up this road and stopped at the junction. If there is any CCTV in any of these properties there's a chance they might have recorded the registration number.'

Luned nodded. 'I'll take one side, you take the other.'

Winder trotted over the road and started with a café on one corner. The manageress gave him a blank look when he enquired about CCTV cameras. The next three properties were all shops where the staff gave him the same quizzical look. A charity shop manager pointed to the CCTV cameras high up inside the premises explaining they didn't cover the pavement.

Winder retreated outside and spotted Luned. She shrugged noncommittally. He continued towards the junction and found another café on the corner. He darted inside and scanned the walls for any sign of a discreetly placed camera.

He ignored the strange looks from the half dozen or so customers.

A spike of excitement quickened his pulse when he saw a camera high up on a wall but pointing down at the tables. He quickly assessed it also covered the window, looking out over the pavement and street outside.

He flashed his warrant card at the manageress. Then he pointed at the CCTV camera. 'I need all the footage from that camera for last Sunday evening.' He hoped and prayed the camera was kept permanently in operation.

'I don't think... Give me a minute.'

Winder turned to look out of the window and saw Luned standing outside. He beckoned in. 'They've got CCTV,' Winder whispered when she joined him.

The manageress returned. 'The owner says you have to formally request it in writing.'

'This is a murder investigation,' Winder hissed.

The gasps from the nearest customers told him he had failed to keep the details private.

'I'll need your full name and I'll need the full name of the owner.'

'I don't know about that...' The manageress stammered before she gave him the information he'd requested.

Winder handed her one of his cards. 'Tell the owner to contact me.'

Winder turned on his heel and marched out with Luned.

They stood on the pavement, Winder's pulse gradually returning to normal.

'Why do we have to put up with these people?' He turned to Luned. 'Did you have any luck?'

'No, a couple of the shops have CCTV covering the inside but nothing recording the pavement or road.'

'We could extend the search.'

'But we don't know if the red car is important or relevant, Gareth. Let's go and find Danny and then once we're back at the Incident Room the boss will be there. He can decide.'

Winder nodded. They marched back to the car. Winder pulled into traffic and accelerated up towards the same junction he had seen the red car leaving on the footage.

It was a short journey to the homeless shelter and Winder turned into the makeshift car park at the church. The church hall, no longer used by the shrunken congregation, doubled up as a dormitory for the homeless community. Two women were cleaning up in a toilet area by the front door. The air was rich with the smell of dirty bodies.

Both women gave Winder and Luned's warrant cards a disinterested glance, as though they saw police officers every day.

'We are looking for Danny,' Winder said.

'He was here last night, right enough. He smells bad at the moment. He refused a shower.'

'Any idea where he might be?'

Both women shook their heads. Then one suggested. 'You might try the shopping centre. It's nice and warm in there and sometimes the security guards can't be bothered to kick them out.'

On the way, Winder detoured around the middle of town just in case he spotted Danny dossing down in a doorway. He didn't, so he parked near the centre and they made their way inside. Guards prowled around making their presence felt, speaking into microphones on their lapels like special agents in a thriller movie, but there was no sign of Danny.

They left the building only to spot Danny making his way up towards the middle of town. His ancient coat dragged on the pavement and the plastic carrier bag he held in one hand bulged almost to the point of bursting, threatening to disgorge its contents.

Winder sprinted over to him and even from a few metres away he could judge the woman at the homeless shelter was right. Danny stank.

'Danny,' Winder said, standing in front of him.

Danny gave him a puzzled look as though he couldn't quite make out who Winder was. Everything about him seemed to have decayed since they had seen him last. His skin was darker, his eyes wearier. It made Winder feel sad that Danny's life had come to this.

'It's Detective Constable Gareth Winder. We need to speak to you. I want you to come with us back to headquarters.' Winder added quickly, 'You're not in any trouble.'

Danny followed Winder back to his car. Luned wrinkled her nose at the smell as Danny climbed into the back. Winder shrugged his shoulders and wordlessly communicated there was nothing he could do if they wanted Danny to cooperate.

Sara followed Drake as they returned to his vehicle. She hadn't realised how cold it was until she left Teresa's property. Drake started the engine, and she turned to him. 'What did you make of that, boss?'

'The information about Holt's intention to finish his relationship with Ackland is significant. She came across as completely genuine and authentic. And she's obviously been grieving.'

'I suppose it chimes with what we were told by Jack Holt's parents about the nature of his relationship with David Ackland.

Drake drove out onto the main road and headed north for St Asaph. 'At least we know where Jack Holt was until eleven pm on the night he was killed.'

'So now all we have to do is find out who lured him to the park. It's a shame he didn't give Teresa any more details about who he was meeting.'

'All the evidence suggests that he was meeting someone important.'

'Do you think it was Mervyn Peel and his henchmen?'

'Hopefully by the time we get back Gareth and Luned

will have made more progress.'

Sara had worked with Drake long enough to realise he was pondering everything they knew so far.

'I've got to leave promptly tonight,' Drake said as he parked the car at headquarters. 'Annie's father has a hospital appointment this evening.'

'This evening?' Sara sounded surprised.

'They're working overtime to catch up with the backlog.'

Sara nodded. Drake had mentioned his forthcoming wedding to Annie. His relationship with her had certainly had a positive effect on him. The obsessive behaviour she had seen had mellowed and he was less brusque.

'I hope he's okay.'

They left the car and headed for the Incident Room.

They exchanged the usual pleasantries with Gareth and Luned, and Sara sat at her desk. Drake walked over to the board.

'We've just spoken to a Teresa Ostler who was having a relationship with Jack Holt. He was with her until eleven pm on the evening he was killed.'

'But I thought Holt was gay?' Winder said.

Luned just frowned.

'They were planning a life together, apparently,' Sara said.

Drake turned to the board and pointed at the image of David Ackland. 'And that means that if he found out then the red mist might have descended. He could have been consumed with jealousy and rage.'

'But why pin Jack Holt to the bowling green lawn?' Luned continued to frown.

'Once we find that out, we can make more sense of this case,' Drake said.

'The dashcam footage from the police car records a red car, just as Danny described.' Winder said.

'So his evidence is accurate.'

'And we've found a café near a junction where the red car was spotted that had CCTV pointing at the outside. Hopefully we'll be able to identify the registration number.'

Luned continued, 'And we've gone through the images of all the staff members at the Peel Foundation with Danny and he didn't recognise any of them.'

Drake looked at the time.

'Hopefully by tomorrow you will have that CCTV footage and we need to work on the papers Alex Normanton left me.' Drake turned to the board. 'Somewhere amongst all these players is someone who wanted Jack Holt dead. All we have to do is work out why and find that person.'

Chapter 18

Drake found a parking slot easily enough that evening at the hospital. On previous occasions when he hadn't found a space quickly he'd parked on the pavement and placed the *On Police Business/Heddlu Swyddogol* sign on the dashboard. Nobody would challenge him then.

It pleased him that that wasn't going to be necessary and once he'd found a free space he made for the entrance. As he walked over he texted Annie: *Just parked on my way in X*

She replied quickly enough: *Ask for the cardiology outpatients X*

The woman behind the reception desk gave him details of where to find the clinic and he negotiated his way through the corridors until eventually he spotted Annie and her parents in a waiting area.

Roland Jenkins looked more shrivelled than he had done in the past. Drake recalled how healthy he had once looked, even with his heart problems. Now the skin on his face seemed to cling to his skull. Even so, he looked up, saw Drake and smiled.

'I'm glad you could make it,' Roland said.

Drake sat next to Annie, and kissed her lightly on the cheek. Her mother, Rebecca Jenkins, looked over at Drake and nodded her appreciation that he was present.

It was lucky hospital consultants were working additional hours in order to catch up with the backlog of treatment caused by the Covid-19 pandemic. Problems with the health board contributed to the difficulties in delivering proper healthcare. One of Roland's oldest friends who still lived in Cardiff had even suggested he return to the capital city for his healthcare treatment. Roland had repeated his friend's unflattering comments about the dire state of health care in North Wales. It couldn't get much worse so Drake had to hope Roland would get good care from now on.

'Is it still cold outside?' Rebecca attempted small talk.

At least she had the good sense not to ask Drake how his week had been. Discussing his working life with family and friends was virtually impossible apart from the normal day-to-day routine of office politics. His job was unlike any other. And with other patients within earshot, he doubted anyone would want to hear about the nitty-gritty of a murder investigation.

He smiled at Rebecca. 'It was beginning to freeze when I parked.'

'Apparently there's going to be some snow over the weekend.'

Roland Jenkins didn't have to wait too long for the nurse to call him through and Rebecca went with her husband. Annie turned to Drake and whispered, 'I really thought you were going to be late. Dad is really pleased you're here.'

'It's been busy this week. But I made certain I could get here on time.'

'I've made us all something to eat once he's finished.'

Drake nodded. It meant he could relax over a decent meal and a glass of wine for the first time since the inquiry began.

After twenty minutes, Annie gave Drake a worried look. 'What do you think has happened?'

He shrugged. 'He's just taking his time. You know what doctors are like.'

Another ten minutes elapsed before Roland and Rebecca emerged from the consulting room, sharing their thanks with the doctor and rejoining Annie and Drake in the now empty waiting room.

'Roland has to be careful. No rich fatty foods. And the consultant is going to monitor his cholesterol and heart function over the next couple of months,' Rebecca said.

'But I can have the occasional glass of wine,' Roland winked at Drake.

'Only in moderation,' Rebecca sounded a warning shot.

'Moderation, of course.'

'And Roland is going to be doing a lot more exercise.'

The look on Roland's face suggested he wasn't looking forward to that at all.

Drake expected Annie to interrogate her parents in far more detail once they were back home. She would want to know every scrap of advice the consultant had given, what the prognosis was and what she could do to help in any way.

But she would leave that until they were home. They walked out of the hospital and Drake was convinced the temperature had fallen by a degree or two. He walked them to their car and watched as they left the car park as he walked to his BMW.

When Drake arrived home, he found a bottle of lager in the fridge and then joined Roland in the sitting area, where a glass of sparkling water was sitting on the table. Normally it would have been a gin and tonic, so he was giving the water an unenthusiastic look. Annie announced that their meal would be ready shortly, so it gave Drake time to chat to Roland.

A lifetime working in the civil service in Cardiff had given Roland Jenkins a breadth of experience about public life and an interesting take on most functions of government. Drake regretted he hadn't spent more time learning about Roland's past. There never seemed to be enough time for that sort of mundane activity.

He regretted that his own father had died before he had had the opportunity of meeting Roland. Although they were from different backgrounds, he was certain both men would have got on well with each other.

Drake sat in a chair next to Roland.

'How are you feeling?'

'I'd prefer a gin and tonic.'

Drake grinned. 'I will organise a glass of wine for you with the meal.' Roland's face lit up. Roland enjoyed a decent claret with his Sunday lunch, and any other meal given half a chance.

'Are you in charge of this latest murder?'

'Yes, and I've got the usual team helping me.'

'There hasn't been a press conference yet. I like watching those. Isn't it the case there have been press conferences where family members have been recorded sobbing and crying while all along they were guilty of murdering their loved ones?'

Drake nodded. 'People can be complicated.'

'Rebecca tells me that the plans for the wedding are coming along well.' Roland's face lit up. 'She's organised for me to be measured for a suit. Can you believe it, at my age?'

'Annie is very well organised.'

'She was like that as a child. Bossing people around.' Roland smiled. 'At least the consultant doesn't think I'm going to kick the bucket in the next few months so I'm going to be around for your wedding, Inspector Drake. I hope you'll take care of my one and only daughter.'

'I certainly plan to.'

There was a shout that their meal was ready. Both men walked over to the table and once Roland was safely seated Drake found a bottle of wine which he opened and filled everyone's glasses from. The glare Roland gave his sparkling water soon evaporated as he smelled the wine.

Winter temperatures suited the hearty beef stew which Annie produced, together with mashed potatoes and a selection of green vegetables. Rebecca didn't notice when Drake refilled Roland's glass or perhaps she purposefully ignored it. They shared their experiences of the health system as they sat chatting around the dinner table. Roland commented on the state of the local health board from first-hand personal experience and from his work in the central government in Cardiff.

After a pudding of apple crumble – Roland's usual version which was drowned in custard was pared back significantly – Rebecca announced she was taking her husband home for an early night. They thanked Annie and Drake for all the help and left soon afterwards.

Drake began to feel the waves of tiredness smothering his enthusiasm for washing up. After filling the dishwasher and once the kitchen was reasonably neat and tidy he turned to Annie. 'I think we should have an early night too.'

Annie smiled.

They walked down the stairs to the bedroom on the ground floor.

'Your father asked me if I was going to take care of you.' Drake pulled her close. Then he started to unbutton her blouse. 'I thought I might start now.'

Annie kissed him on the lips. 'What did you have in mind, Inspector?'

Drake reached over and pushed the door closed.

Chapter 19

Annie joined Drake, who was sitting at the kitchen table the following morning. She kissed him warmly. 'It's a Saturday, you should wear something a little less formal than a suit.'

'Force of habit,' Drake said. He had paired a double-cuffed white shirt with a dark navy tie, its discreet purple stripes barely visible. He hadn't chosen his best suit, the one he reserved for court appearances, but the dark grey version had recently been dry cleaned.

'Are you going to be back at a reasonable time – don't forget we are supposed to be meeting Colin and his new girlfriend for dinner.'

Drake had forgotten. Annie often organised some social event for the weekends when he didn't have the children staying. And one of her colleagues had started a relationship with a lecturer in the psychology department. He had been keen for Annie and Drake to meet her. It was the worst possible timing for the first Saturday in a murder inquiry.

'It should be okay. I'll call you later.'

Soon afterwards Drake left the house and made his way to the A55 before flooring the accelerator. If he had to work on a Saturday morning, he wasn't going to waste any time reaching headquarters.

The car park wasn't as busy as usual, so Drake found a slot near the entrance. Reception was quiet when he entered and headed for the stairs to the Incident Room. As he opened the door and noticed Sara looking up from her computer, his mobile rang just as she greeted him.

Drake pushed the handset to his ear. 'DI Drake.'

'Area control. You're needed at the scene of a suspicious death.'

'Send me the details.' Drake looked over at Sara. 'Get your coat.'

After flinging the broadsheet with the first lines of the sudoku puzzle completed onto a spare desk Drake trotted out of the Incident Room; Sara followed immediately.

'There's a suspicious death,' Drake said as he took the stairs to reception two at a time. 'I'll drive, you get the details from area control.' All the usual imperatives flooded his mind – securing the scene, establishing an identity, liaising with the CSIs and pathologist and notifying the family.

They sprinted over to Drake's BMW and seconds later he was accelerating for the junction to the main road. Sara punched in the postcode he'd been given, and they didn't have to wait long for the journey to appear on the screen. Drake indicated left and noticed the route took them inland to one of the villages to the south of Colwyn Bay.

Drake hurried through the town, finally taking the satnav's directions out into the countryside. After twenty minutes Drake saw a marked police vehicle parked in a layby outside the property, its garden perimeter lined with a thick hedge. He caught a glimpse of the Arts and Crafts house with its attractive dormers.

He pulled up behind the police vehicle and looked around for a sign of any scientific support vehicles, but there were none to be seen. It meant he and Sara were the first at the scene.

A uniformed officer stood at the gate. When he recognised Drake, he came to attention and ushered both senior officers into the property. Another officer stood by an old-fashioned patio of differently shaped flat rocks. 'I'm glad you got here so quickly, sir.'

Drake nodded – it was the same young officer who had been present at the scene of Jack Holt's murder.

'Who reported the circumstances?'

'A gardener arrived for work about half an hour or so ago. He spends every Saturday here over the winter, weather permitting, getting the garden ready for spring.'

'And he found the body?'

'Yes, sir, but he'd been moving tools from his van, so he

hadn't noticed that the homeowner wasn't around when he first arrived.'

'And where is this gardener now?'

'He's sitting in his van parked up the road. I told him you'd need to speak to him.'

Drake turned to Sara. 'Get an ETA for the crime scene investigators. And the pathologist, while you're at it.'

'Yes, boss.' Sara dialled the number and held the mobile to her ear.

Drake nodded to the young officer. 'Show me the scene.' He listened to Sara as they walked to the bottom of the garden. All the carefully pruned shrubs and trees and plants laid out in the borders would clearly justify a gardener for at least one day a week over the summer.

The owner certainly had deep pockets, Drake guessed, and must have enjoyed the garden. Drake saw pristine-looking tables and chairs on a decking area stacked up inside a summer house surrounded by decking.

'Was the gardener able to identify the dead man?' Drake said as the officer led him towards a shed and an area of lawn.

As he neared the body, prone on the grass, a dark sense of foreboding filled his chest when he realised the body had been pinned to the turf with croquet hoops.

'He identified the man as a Mr Murphy.'

Drake stood staring at the body at their feet.

He heard Sara finishing her call with area control as she joined them.

'You won't believe this, sir,' Sara said. Then she saw the dead man. 'Jesus Christ, it's just like Jack Holt.'

'What's the update from the CSIs?'

'A full team is en route and should be here in minutes. The pathologist has been called to attend.'

'What were you saying about something I wouldn't believe?'

'The owner of the house is Edward Murphy. He is the

accountant for the Peel Foundation.'

'Bloody hell.' Drake looked down at Murphy. The questions he wanted to ask the accountant would go unanswered. There'd be another visit to Mervyn Peel and Martha Peel soon enough, Drake concluded. It put the Peel Foundation right in the middle of the inquiry.

'Who the hell would want him dead?' Sara said.

'From the croquet hoops it's the same killer or someone wanting us to believe it is.'

Drake pulled the lapel of his jacket up to his neck. The high hedges and shrubs were no barrier against the biting cold wind.

'Let's go and have a look inside the house.' Drake wasn't going to stand around outside in the cold waiting for the crime scene investigators to arrive. The two uniformed officers could do that. It would be character-building stuff.

He told the officer to stay where he was and make certain nothing interfered with the crime scene before he led Sara back through the garden to the house. Drake pushed open the rear stable door, painted a garish red.

Everything was in place in the kitchen, nothing had been disturbed. There wasn't a dirty mug on a draining board or dishcloth hanging from the oven handle. The only implement visible was an electric kettle, its green colour matching the tiles surrounding the worktop.

'Wow, that's tidy,' Sara said.

Neither officer touched any of the surfaces, and they walked through into a hallway. Drake stood and marvelled at the sideboard and wall lights that seemed to match the decor of the kitchen perfectly.

'Is this Arts and Crafts style?' Sara said.

'Yes, and very expensive.'

A dining room off the hallway had a highly polished octagonal table and chairs. The walls had been lined with timber panels and above the picture rail was a shelf adorned with various glass mugs and jugs.

The sitting room opposite was equally precisely furnished. Drake admired the attention to detail and the sheer obsession Murphy must have had for collecting this sort of furniture. Drake heard a shout from the kitchen.

'Ian, where are you?'

He recognised Mike Foulds' voice so he retreated back and greeted the crime scene manager at the threshold of the rear door.

'Nothing's been disturbed inside. And we haven't touched anything,' Drake said.

'Good, glad to hear it. Now you'd better show me where the body is.'

Once Drake emerged outside he rebuttoned his jacket, which he had loosened inside. Discarding the latex gloves, he thrust his hands into warm, fleece-lined leather ones.

He nodded towards the bottom of the garden. 'He's by the shed at the back.' Foulds followed Drake and Sara; another investigator began lugging boxes of equipment.

When they reached Murphy's body Foulds stared at the scene and then up at Drake. 'It's like Jack Holt. So what connects them? And why the bloody croquet hoops? You've got a weird one here.'

'I know, Mike, and we're still working on the croquet angle.'

Foulds kneeled. He moved Murphy's head to one side and it exposed a bloody wound.

'We know his name is Edward Murphy. And he works for the Peel Foundation. So there is a link to Jack Holt, as he was investigating the organisation.'

'Any sign of the pathologist?'

Foulds didn't have to wait for a reply as he heard the booming voice of Dr Lee Kings approaching. 'My God, it's cold. Couldn't this have waited until Monday. Murderers are so inconsiderate.'

Drake had known Kings long enough to realise his tongue was very firmly in his cheek.

'Good morning to you too, Lee.'

'Detective Inspector Drake and Detective Sergeant Morgan. How nice to see you again.' He looked down at the body. 'So our croquet fanatic has been busy again. Have you been interviewing all the members of croquet clubs in North Wales?'

'Come off it, Lee,' Foulds said. 'Nobody plays croquet in North Wales. It's a posh person's game, played in the public schools of England.'

'You'd be surprised,' Sara contributed. 'It's more popular than you think.'

'Much as I like all this engaging small talk can we please get on,' Drake said.

It took a moment for Kings to formally pronounce life was extinct. He stood up and turned to Drake. 'It looks like a similar injury to the one that killed Jack Holt.'

'And time of death?'

Kings scanned the body and its immediate surroundings. 'What's the temperature?'

'It was two degrees on the dashboard of the car when we were driving down.'

'So it must have frozen last night. Time of death is probably going to be within the last 12 to 15 hours. I'll be more precise at the post-mortem tomorrow.'

Drake nodded. He had next of kin to trace as well as identifying where Murphy had been in the hours before he was killed. And there'd be house-to-house enquiries to initiate.

Kings left and Drake announced to Foulds, 'We're going to talk to the man who found the body and then we'll be back at headquarters. I need a report as soon as possible.'

'No problem – I won't hang around.' He cupped his hands and blew into them.

Drake walked purposefully through the garden, Sara in his slipstream and then towards the gardener's van. The man jumped out as soon as Drake had explained he wanted to speak to him. They stood in the layby.

'I want to know everything you can tell me.'

'I arrived as usual as I do on a Saturday in the winter. It's mostly boring stuff: clearing, tidying, cutting back and getting the place ready for spring. Ed wasn't around which isn't unusual. I brought tools from the van and it was only when I needed something from the shed that I went to the bottom of the garden. That's when I found him.'

'Was there anybody else around at the time? Did you see anybody leave the house, or nearby?'

'No, it was just an ordinary Saturday morning. I can't help you really. I'd worked for this man for a couple of years. It was good regular work and he paid on the button.'

Drake gave him his card. 'If you remember anything, contact me.'

Drake was pleased to be back in his car moments later and he turned the heating up to high. 'Let's go back to headquarters. We've got a killer to catch.'

Chapter 20

Drake returned to the Incident Room, having already messaged Gareth Winder and Luned Thomas to get started with adding the details of Edward Murphy to the board.

He'd spend the rest of the morning making certain all the priorities at the commencement of a new inquiry were dealt with. He cursed himself that he hadn't prioritised talking to Edward Murphy. Had he been too quick to accept the excuses about his absence?

'His death has got to be linked to the Peel Foundation,' Sara said.

'One thing I know for certain it's linked to the murder of Jack Holt. The croquet hoops used by the killer don't leave much room for doubt.'

'It might be a copycat, I suppose.'

Drake didn't respond, he had to gather evidence. He had to find a motive and he had to find the person with the opportunity.

He parked and they bustled over to the main entrance and up to the Incident Room. Luned was posting an image of Edward Murphy onto the board and Drake spotted a pin on the map showing the exact location of his property. Another pin identified the home of Teresa Ostler.

Drake marched over to the board just as Winder joined them. 'There's something I've got to tell you, boss,' Winder said. 'After you rang, I did some preliminary background work on Edward Murphy. I found his LinkedIn page. He went to school at Fremantle High.'

It took only a fraction of a second for the significance to sink in. 'That's the same school Jack Holt attended.' Drake paused. 'We need to do some serious digging into that boarding school. Were they in the same year? In the same class even?'

Winder looked pleased with himself when he replied, 'I've already checked that out, boss. Jack Holt was three years ahead of Edward Murphy.'

'So they might have known each other. They were almost contemporaries.' Drake turned to look at Holt's image on the board and then at Murphy's below him.

'Have you been able to find out if Edward Murphy has any family?' Sara said.

'He was a bachelor. We are trying to establish if he had siblings and whether his parents are still alive,' Luned said.

If there were members of his immediate family, they needed to be informed and while Drake wanted to interrogate everyone at the Peel Foundation it was more important to get details of Murphy's family first. 'Call the Foundation. They're bound to have some details about Murphy's life.'

'Yes, boss,' Luned replied.

Drake took a few moments to make certain house-to-house inquiries were being established in the area surrounding Murphy's home. His mobile would need to be traced and its records interrogated. 'Find out if he's got a car. I know it's Saturday but tell the DVLA to pull their finger out – we need all the details, now.'

'And we'll need details of his financials,' Sara said.

Drake nodded.

'I'm going to do some digging into Fremantle High. In the meantime, call the Foundation. If he has family, I want properly trained officers from the relevant force with them without delay.'

Drake marched over to his office and draped his coat over one of the visitor chairs. He sat down and noticed that the open page of the sudoku puzzle in the broadsheet had been placed neatly on an empty corner of his desk. He checked the arrangements for his Post-it notes and adjusted the placing of the photographs of his daughters and that of Annie by a few millimetres.

The initial buzz of an investigation never ceased to excite him. There was an urgency to what they were doing.

A life had been lost. A family would be grieving, and he needed to find the culprit. He took a moment to think through the consequences of Jack Holt's murder scene. It had meant two people, probably. Unless the crime scene investigators were able to find evidence of Murphy having been struck before being moved it could well be that Murphy had been killed by one assailant.

Once his computer had booted up, he clicked into the screen and began a Google search for Fremantle High. This time he paid the website far more attention than he had done on the first occasion. The institution boasted an alumni of leaders of industry, judges and journalists of renown as well as several politicians who had succeeded in the United Kingdom and overseas.

The school emphasised the small classes and a low turnover of staff. With the state school system in crisis because of a lack of funding, and graduates choosing a career that didn't involve facing a class of over thirty pupils, Drake could see the attraction of working in the private sector with classes of a dozen or so.

Once Drake had navigated away from the website, he found blog sites and Facebook groups with Fremantle High in their titles. These intrigued him, so he opened the first and read about reunions over the years. He guessed the attendees would probably be embarrassed if all the details about the celebrations were made public.

The contents of the second blog site were darker, making reference to abusive and aggressive teachers. Drake wrote the name of one who the authors had stated was long since dead and another who had emigrated to live in the deserts of southern Chile.

A Facebook group had regular contributors from several hundred members. Drake scrolled down through the posts, his mind focused on what information they would need from the school. He paused and jotted the details needed on a Post-it note. He resumed scrolling until he saw the heading "punishment rites", which caught his attention.

He clicked on the post; a tightness developed in his chest, giving him that brief excitement that he might have found something crucial. He began reading. There were forty-eight comments. The first one sharply focused his mind.

Do you remember all those stakeouts? I remember being shit scared when they pinned me to the quad. And then when the prefects ran at me with a dustbin full of water I could have died of fear.

Another post continued the thread.

You're right and Murphs was the worst.

Drake stared at the last sentence. Murphs had to be a nickname for Murphy.

Drake read all the comments. Several mentioned the stakeouts. They were described in clear terms, but it was when reference was made to croquet hoops being used to pin pupils to the quad where croquet was played in summer that Drake knew things had changed.

He marched through to the Incident Room board. The rest of his team looked up, waiting for him to say something. 'I've been digging into Fremantle High and I found a Facebook group where some of the former pupils talk about their time at the school. It doesn't seem to have been particularly happy.'

Drake turned to the board and pointed at the image of Jack Holt and Edward Murphy. 'There are comments about a punishment where pupils are pinned to the lawn using croquet hoops and then other pupils run at them with dustbins full of water.'

'So there's a link between Edward Murphy and Jack Holt,' Sara said.

'Or so the killer wants us to believe.'

'I want to make contact with the school. They must have lists of the pupils there at the same time as Edward Murphy and Jack Holt.'

147

'But it's Saturday, boss,' Winder said.

'I don't bloody care. Find a number for the headmaster or the bursar. It's a private school after all, so there's bound to be somebody there at the weekend. And, Gareth, tell them it's a murder inquiry. I don't want any excuses.'

'Yes, boss.'

Drake looked at his watch. He needed to update Superintendent Hobbs but first he'd visit the Peel Foundation.

Chapter 21

Visiting the Peel Foundation seemed to be a regular occurrence. Everything about both murders had a link to the organisation, but its secretive nature only added to the aura of suspicion surrounding it. Unless Mervyn Peel and his cronies were doing anything illegal then there was nothing Drake could do.

Drake was back in his office, where he hurriedly drafted a report to Superintendent Hobbs using the standard template. He was halfway through when his mobile rang.

He didn't recognise the number.

'Detective Inspector Drake, this is Brian Powell.' The voice sounded friendly, as though he were one of Drake's oldest friends. 'I'm covering Jack Holt's murder for an independent news agency.' Powell mentioned the name of one of the leading providers of reports to news organisations all over the world. 'I understand there has been a second death. Now I am sure you have your hands full. But I was wondering if you believe there is a connection between the two.'

'What did you say your name was again?' Drake reached for a ballpoint and a Post-it note.

'Brian Powell. You've probably heard my name before as I have covered a lot of important murder inquiries. I'm staying at the DeVere Royal Hotel. I understand your enquiry has an interest in the place. It is a bit rundown if you ask me, but quite comfortable nevertheless.'

Drake had had quite enough of Powell's let's-be-best-mates approach. 'I don't think I can help you Mr Powell.'

'It does seem to be a shocking series of events, having two murders so close together. And both men having been to the same school.'

And Drake was definitely not going to react to Powell's remarks, which suggested he thought the information about both men's schooling would surprise Drake.

'I suggest you call public relations.'

'Of course. And if you want to contact me or my team then you know where I am.'

'And how did you get my number?'

'It was good talking to you, Detective Inspector.' Powell rang off.

He left Drake mulling over his comments. He even had the audacity to refer to a team working with him. The last thing Drake needed was interference from some journalist poking his nose into the inquiry. But by the sound of things, he had already done that.

Drake tried and failed to curb his annoyance as he completed the report to Superintendent Hobbs. Once he had finished, he pressed send and turned his attention to his meeting with Mervyn Peel. First he'd call the inspector dealing with the fallout from the demonstration outside the Foundation. He found his number without delay.

'What's the latest on your inquiry?' Drake said.

'The CPS are still chewing it over. There was no damage to speak of. The demonstrators managed to prise open a window without causing any damage whatsoever. And nothing was stolen or removed.'

In order to prove a burglary charge any court would need to be satisfied the person involved was intent on stealing from the property. And if no damage had actually been caused, Drake could see the Crown prosecution lawyers deciding that public interest wouldn't justify charging the demonstrators.

'It doesn't sound as though the case is going anywhere.'

'I'll leave that to the lawyers to decide. But Mervyn Peel has been badgering me every day for an update.'

Drake rang off and pondered for a moment. It struck him that he had an unfinished conversation with Zoe Lloyd, the demonstrator he had spoken to at the area custody suite. Did she know more than she had shared with him or was it simply a gut feeling? He resolved that another chat with Zoe was overdue.

He dragged on his jacket and left his office. 'Let's go,' he said to Sara.

A dusting of snow covered the vehicles in the car park. Underfoot the slushy surface would soon harden if the cold temperatures persisted. The car didn't take long to warm up and by the time they had reached the Peel Foundation Drake had turned down the fan.

The gate opened smoothly once Sara had introduced herself at the intercom. Drake drove the short distance up to the front door. Light flooded out of all the upstairs windows.

Drake fiddled with his phone, switching it to silent: he didn't want any interfering telephone calls while speaking to Mervyn Peel. Martin Swan met them at the front door. His jacket was buttoned and he stood with his feet slightly apart.

'He asked me to show you to a conference room.' Swan pointed at a door to Drake's left.

Drake didn't move. 'Is Mr Peel waiting for us?'

'He won't be long.'

'If he's not in the conference room then please take me to his office immediately.' Drake looked over his shoulder down the corridor into the bowels of the building.

'Mr Peel won't be long.' Swan gestured with his hand: an invitation for Drake to enter the room.

Drake turned to Sara. 'Let's find Mr Peel's office.'

Swan barred his way. 'Mr Peel has asked me to show you to the conference room.'

'And if you continue to obstruct me exercising my lawful duty it could be a serious matter.'

Swan didn't move.

Drake stepped to one side of Swan who moved too, but thought the better of stopping Drake who swept past him and headed down the corridor. He had no idea where Mervyn Peel's office was, but he certainly wasn't going to be sitting in a conference room waiting for him.

Drake entered all the rooms down the corridor and his

interruption was met with startled faces from the occupants. But there was no sign of Mervyn Peel or his wife Martha, so Drake retreated and began the same exercise along another corridor. Drake retraced his steps to the main hallway and took the stairs to the first floor.

From a room at the far end he heard Mervyn Peel's voice so he marched over. As he reached the door Martin Swan exited, almost bumping into Drake as he did so. Mervyn Peel stood behind him. Drake entered Peel's office.

There was a sumptuous feel to the place. Four table lamps of matching onyx design and expensive-looking shades had been strategically placed on cupboards and tables. Modern abstract paintings hung in perfectly curated order.

'Martin told you I was busy and that I would see you in the conference room,' Peel said.

'I don't believe he did,' Drake replied, walking over to a bookcase filled with self-help books, three of which had been authored by Peel. 'Say that you were busy, I mean.'

Drake had deliberately invaded Peel's personal space. He was in charge and things would be done as he wanted. Drake sat down in one of the visitor chairs and motioned for Sara to do likewise. Peel stood and then stared angrily at Drake. But in the end he had no alternative so he stepped over to his desk and sat down on the leather executive chair.

'I'm investigating the murder of your accountant Edward Murphy. And you keep me waiting as though I'm trying to sell you a photocopier. Do you realise how bad that makes you look?' Drake said.

'I don't know what you mean.'

'I mean that anybody in your circumstances would have seen me immediately. What do you have to hide?'

'I don't like your tone.'

'I don't care what you like or dislike. I want to know where you were last evening.'

'I was here, home, of course.'

'Can anyone vouch for you?'

Peel looked away, avoided eye contact. 'I had a meal with my wife and had a couple of Zoom meetings early in the evening with some associates in the United States. Then I watched television, went to bed and read. Am I a suspect in Ed's murder?'

'We will need details of the Zoom meetings.'

Peel continued to stare at Drake.

'Now, Mr Peel. We need the details now.' Drake nodded at the computer. 'I want the names of the people who you spoke to and the times at which the meetings started.'

'I'm not certain I have that information.'

'Don't take me for a fool, Mr Peel. I can easily get a warrant to seize everything in this office, but I'd much prefer your cooperation.'

Peel wasn't going to win a staring competition, so he logged into his computer and shared the data Drake wanted.

'Do you know anyone who would want to kill Edward Murphy?'

Drake wasn't going to waste any time dancing around Mervyn Peel, asking some oblique questions about Murphy.

'He was well liked and he was an important part of the Foundation. I was shocked and surprised at his death.'

So why the hell would he keep us waiting, Drake thought.

'Did he have any family?'

'He never mentioned any. I think his parents died years ago and he was an only child. But I didn't know a lot about his private life.'

'So you wouldn't describe him as a friend?'

'Yes, but we never discussed things like family and...'

'So, what did you talk about? Football? Or cricket or were you rugby fans?'

'No, nothing like that.'

'So, you didn't know him that well at all.'

'You're twisting everything I say.'

'What did Edward Murphy do here?'

'He was in charge of our finances. He was indispensable. Who would want to kill him?'

'That's what we're going to find out, Mr Peel. Do you have personnel records? So that if there are any family members you don't know about, we can inform them.'

'We don't need a human resources department. Everyone knows how we run things. We haven't got disgruntled employees. Everyone's position is valued here and everyone who is part of the organisation knows their place.'

'Does that mean everyone does as you say?'

'Your attitude is unnecessarily belligerent, Detective Inspector.'

'I want to see Edward Murphy's office.' Drake stood up.

Peel did likewise but he paused, clearly nonplussed, trying to contemplate objecting to Drake's request.

Drake walked over to the door. 'Please show me Mr Murphy's office now.'

Peel hesitated. Then he relented and led them to the opposite end of the building and pushed open the door into Murphy's room. Drake scanned its contents, urgently looking for any sign of recent activity. The place wasn't a crime scene but Drake could insist nobody enter until he and his team were satisfied they had recovered everything of interest. And he was certain that wouldn't please Mervyn Peel.

Drake turned to Peel. 'We'll need all of Edward Murphy's passwords.'

'It can't possibly be of any relevance. It has all the Peel Foundation financial information. It's completely irrelevant to your work.'

Drake walked over to the computer. 'I'll decide what's relevant.' Drake nodded at Sara. 'Organise for the CSIs to work on accessing any of the data on the computer.' Sara nodded. Drake turned back to look at Peel. 'We'll do as little damage as possible, of course.'

Peel gave him another one of his angry looks.

'I'll get Martin. Give me a minute.'

Peel returned directly with Martin Swan who glowered at Drake.

'Martin is… I mean was Edward's assistant.'

'We need to access Edward Murphy's computer. Do you have the passwords?'

Swan looked at Peel who nodded his agreement.

'There's a small notebook in the drawer of his desk,' Swan said.

Drake looked at Peel. 'Can you please organise for all members of staff to gather in one of the conference rooms downstairs. Within, say, half an hour?'

Peel nodded.

'We'll work through some of Murphy's papers before that. There's no need for you to stay. And we'll need the keys to this room until the computer and the papers can be removed.'

Peel looked affronted but left with Swan moments later when he realised he had no choice.

As he turned to leave, Drake announced, 'And I need to see Mrs Peel before we see the rest of the staff. Can you tell me where her office is?'

Peel explained where they could find his wife and left them.

Sara began rummaging through the desk. 'What did you make of that boss?'

'There was no word of surprise or expression of sadness at the death of a colleague. Peel is completely devoid of emotion. He must have an utterly empty heart.'

Drake started work on various filing cabinets which contained folders and files with tabs identifying their names and the barest summary of information inside. It all seemed to be administrative and mundane.

'I think we'll need to find out exactly what Edward

Murphy did here. Somebody had a motive to kill him.'

Drake stopped and looked over at Sara. 'And his death must be connected to Jack Holt's. Let's hope the CSIs find his mobile so that we can trace his calls.'

Sara found the notebook with the passwords and other personal folders and documents in the drawer of the desk which she removed and placed in her bag. She called the administrative support unit and made certain somebody would attend whilst they were present to remove the computer.

'He was an accountant after all,' Drake said. He walked over to the artwork on the wall of the office which complemented the abstract canvases in Peel's room.

'Let's talk to Mrs Peel.'

Sara pulled the door closed behind them and used the key Mervyn Peel had given them to make certain it was securely locked. It was a short walk to Mrs Peel's room and Drake didn't bother to knock, he simply barged in. He saw the flash of anger in her eyes, that same cold calculating darkness he had seen before.

'I'm sure you've heard by now that Edward Murphy was killed last night.'

'Tragic. It is so desperately sad.'

'Did you know him well?'

'I can't say I did particularly. I think my husband knew him better. He was quite an insular character. He enjoyed his own company and lived alone in that house he'd turned into a museum.'

'Do you know if he had any family?'

'I can't tell you. He never mentioned his parents, so I'd assumed they weren't around any longer. And before he joined the Foundation... I can't remember what his background was.'

'How long has he been with you?'

Martha Peel frowned as though in deep thought. 'It must be well over twelve years.'

'And do you know if he had any enemies, someone who would want him dead?'

'I can't think… certainly not amongst the Foundation. Perhaps you should be looking at his previous life and his background. Maybe he had enemies from the dim and distant past.'

Drake sat for a moment. Making certain they investigated Edward Murphy's schooling and career as an accountant would be the top priority. But he couldn't shake off that nagging sense the motive for his death was in the present and not the past.

'I don't think he had a particularly happy childhood and he was sent away to school somewhere. If you're able to trace some of his family members, then they might be able to shed more light on his upbringing. I'll get one of the admin team to dig out any details we can find.'

Martha Peel's reaction was certainly more constructive than it had been in their first meeting, but Drake still wanted to ask the question. 'In order for us to eliminate you from our inquiry it would be helpful if you could confirm where you were last evening.'

'I was tired and went to bed early. I think my husband had some Zoom meetings. I took the opportunity of catching up with some reading I need to do.'

'Thank you, Mrs Peel,' Drake said; the difference in reaction between herself and her husband certainly needed some careful thought.

Chapter 22

Peel Foundation staff who were present in the conference room that afternoon wore suitably glum faces and expressed their shock and horror at Edward Murphy's death. Their emotions all seemed authentic enough. Two rooms were made available, and Drake and Sara got to work, wasting no time. The questions would be simple and straightforward – did they know Edward Murphy? If so, did they know of anyone who might want to cause him harm? Did they know anything about his personal circumstances and whether there was anyone on the staff who had been to his home?

Drake stared at Phoebe Parkinson, willing himself not to mention Gareth Winder, her cousin, being part of his team. There was no hint of acknowledgement on her face that she knew he knew Gareth. She had an attractive face with clear, confident eyes. She kept to the party line when she answered the questions, but Drake sensed she was holding back as though she wanted to share something but couldn't face doing so.

Drake handed her one of his cards and she studied it a fraction too long. 'If there's anything you want to share with us then please do not hesitate to contact me.' She pocketed the card, nodded briskly, saying nothing.

Drake could see how Winder felt the loss of his cousin. Perhaps it was worse than a bereavement. At least she was still alive, but out of touch and unwilling to contemplate the barest family contact.

The next member of staff was Martin Swan.

'I worked with Edward and his death is profoundly sad.' Swan expressed all the right words but without any emotion, as though he had memorised the words from a script.

'Yes, it is. Did you know him well?'

'I can't say I did.'

Like everyone else here, Drake thought, distancing themselves from Murphy.

The rest of Drake's conversation with Swan was equally unhelpful. All the staff were closing ranks. Protecting their precious Foundation.

Sara was waiting in the room she had used to interview the members of staff allocated to her when Drake joined her. She was sipping on a glass of water.

'None of the members of staff I spoke to had anything constructive to tell me,' Drake said.

'Likewise. A couple of the admin support personnel arrived to remove Edward Murphy's computer whilst we were interviewing.'

Drake nodded. 'I spoke to Pheobe – Gareth's cousin. She stonewalled me although I did feel she wanted to tell me more.'

'Peel has an iron grip on everyone.' Sara got up and finished her drink. 'Murphy didn't seem to have any friends on the staff. Nobody described him as a mate. And their sadness at his death seemed to be an emotion they thought they should express.'

'As though they were reading it from a book?'

'That's right, boss.'

'Everything about this place is odd and cold and sterile. Let's get back to headquarters.'

More snow had accumulated on the roof and bonnet of Drake's BMW. It felt as if the temperature had fallen too. They drove back to headquarters, Drake mulling over how the investigation into Edward Murphy's murder was going to be run at the same time as that of Jack Holt's. Did he need more officers? If so, he'd need to make a formal request to Superintendent Hobbs. It was another addition to his to-do list.

He arrived back at headquarters and after walking to the entrance he stamped his feet on the matting by the door, depositing bits of snow and ice. He detoured to the kitchen on the way to the Incident Room. He was overdue a decent coffee and after flicking on the electric kettle he measured the exact amount of coffee grounds into the cafetière. He set the timer on his watch to ping, once the kettle had boiled, for the requisite time and then he poured the hot liquid over the grounds. Once the second essential time period had been set on his mobile, he took the cafetière and his mug through into the Incident Room. Sara had already made cups of coffee and tea for herself and Winder and Luned in the time it had taken Drake to organise his.

'How are we doing with the background work on Edward Murphy?' Drake said, sitting down at one of the chairs by an empty desk.

'I've been able to talk to the bursar of the Fremantle High. I've emailed him a formal request for the information we need. He promised to send me details of the other pupils in the same classes and years as Jack Holt and Edward Murphy.'

'Did you ask him about the punishment rituals?'

'He sounded a bit vague. He'd only been with the school for a year. He suggested we speak to the headmaster,' Winder said.

'And what did he have to say?'

'He is skiing in the French Alps, apparently – back tomorrow.'

'I've had details of the vehicle Murphy owns,' Luned said. 'A couple of the officers doing house-to-house inquiries have reported that Murphy's immediate neighbour had seen him leave the house yesterday.'

'Anybody arriving?' Drake said.

'No, sir. And they knew very little about Edward Murphy.'

'It matches what we knew from our discussions at the Foundation.'

'One interesting thing, sir,' Luned continued. 'The house is owned by the Peel Foundation.'

'So they reclaim the property after his death.'

'Something connects Jack Holt and Edward Murphy.'

'It could be a copycat killer,' Winder said.

'It would mean the killer knowing exactly the circumstances of Jack Holt's crime scene. Those details weren't made public.' Drake recalled the brief conversation he'd had with the journalist earlier. 'And I've been contacted by a reporter called Powell. He was asking some questions. He made himself out to be my new best friend. So if he calls tell him to contact public relations and then put the phone down.'

Three heads nodded their understanding.

Before he could continue, the door to the Incident Room opened and Mike Foulds entered. He walked over to the board and peered at the developing connections between the victims and the possible suspects.

'How are you getting on at the crime scene?' Drake said.

'It's bloody cold. I've told my team to work in short bursts. Cold enough to get frostbite otherwise.'

'Anything helpful?'

Foulds sat by a desk. 'A coffee would be nice, two sugars and a splash of milk.'

Winder got to his feet and returned moments later. It had given them barely time for some inane discussion about the crime scene and how some busybody neighbours have been asking awkward questions.

'You and the CSIs need to be aware there is some hotshot journalist from London camped out at the DeVere Royal Hotel. He thinks there's a massive story here. Just be careful.'

'Noted.' He cupped the mug with his hands. 'Jesus, it's cold outside.' He took his first sip of the drink. 'Our preliminary search has uncovered a lump hammer. There was a lot of blood residue and from the look of the wound to his head it was likely inflicted with that sort of tool.'

'Where was it found?'

'It had been thrown into the hedge along the edge of the garden. And there aren't any fingerprints on the handle but we did recover some hair follicles. There'll be DNA in due course.'

'And that only helps us if the suspect is on the DNA database,' Sara said.

Foulds took another sip of his drink. 'There's nothing to suggest Edward Murphy was moved after he was killed. My assessment is he was attacked where he was found – there are some blood splatters on the lawn near the body.'

'And the croquet hoops?' Luned said. 'Are they the same vintage as the ones used to pin Jack Holt to the bowling green?'

Foulds nodded. 'We'll test them of course, but they look similar.' He continued. 'We did some preliminary work in the house. There was nothing to indicate any foul play had taken place inside. No blood spots, and nothing to suggest a struggle had taken place. We've dusted for fingerprints, just in case he entertained the killer before being lured outside where he was battered to death. I must say I think it's a bit improbable.'

'There are lots of things in a murder enquiry that can be improbable,' said Drake, sounding a serious note.

'We recovered his mobile telephone. It was in a jacket inside the house. I'll get my team to go over it as quickly as we can.'

Foulds finished his coffee and stood up. 'I hope you don't get any more victims pinned to some lawn with croquet hoops. Or at least not until the weather has improved. I'll send you a full report by Monday.'

Drake left the Incident Room after Foulds and sat at his desk. He stared at the Post-it note on the edge of the monitor – *Annie, tonight*. He had forgotten all about the dinner that evening. If he left now he'd be late. He found his mobile in his jacket pocket and realised the handset was still on silent. He cursed when he read several messages from Annie. The last was the most belligerent. *Can you please answer my text.* No "Annie" or "X".

He hadn't even texted to tell her there was a new murder inquiry ongoing. He should have done that first thing and a guilty sense his obsessions ruled his life reared itself like a dark ghost in his mind.

He'd already warned Superintendent Hobbs that he wanted a preliminary meeting about the Edward Murphy murder. Would the superintendent wait for an update? Drake decided he would have to. Annie meant more to him than keeping Superintendent Hobbs happy. So he emailed Superintendent Hobbs, postponing their meeting, citing delays with progress with the post-mortem and the final report from the crime scene investigators.

Then he called Annie.

'Ian, I've been trying to get hold of you all day. Are you all right?'

'I'm sorry my phone is on silent. There's been another murder.'

'Oh my God, it is the same as before?'

'Yes, it all looks like the same killer. The victim was the Peel Foundation's accountant.'

'That sounds terrible.'

'I'm on my way back. You'll have to entertain Colin and his new girlfriend until I arrive.'

'Take care on the journey home. The roads are quite treacherous. Love you.'

'Of course. And I love you too.'

Chapter 23

Drake listened to the early morning news as he drove from his home to the mortuary but there was no mention of the death of a man in Colwyn Bay. No details would be released until they were entirely satisfied Edward Murphy did not have a next of kin. It avoided embarrassing situations where the names of victims were published before their families were informed.

A steady shower of light snow fell as he travelled along the A55. It wasn't sticking to the roads but formed a delicate white dusting over the fields. The wipers of the car made swift work of any deposit on the windscreen.

The car park was empty first thing, so he was able to find a slot not far from the main entrance. As he left the vehicle, he noticed a man emerging from an Audi estate car a couple of slots down from his own. The man paced up to him and gave Drake a welcome greeting.

'Good morning, Detective Inspector. It's Brian Powell, the reporter. We spoke yesterday over the telephone.'

Drake frowned. What was this man doing here?

'I appreciate you're on your way to Edward Murphy's post-mortem but I was hoping you might be able to confirm a couple of points. I understand he was pinned by croquet hoops to a lawn at the bottom of his garden.'

Drake didn't respond. He was more than accustomed to journalists trying to catch him out. And he wasn't going to be goaded into demanding to know how Powell knew this information.

'Mr Murphy also worked for the Peel Foundation, didn't he? He was an accountant so he must have had access to all their financial details. Is that going to form part of your inquiry?'

Drake wasn't going to be sucked into a reply that suggested Powell's information was correct.

'How much do you know about Edward Murphy's

background?' Powell continued.

Both men had almost reached the entrance to the mortuary.

'Will there be a press conference?'

Drake was about to repeat his standard refrain about contacting the public relations department, but Powell persisted.

'I understand Superintendent Hobbs is your superior officer. He certainly does have quite a reputation.'

Drake paused. 'Please contact our PR department. The professionals there will be able to help you. How well did you know Jack Holt? If there is any scrap of information you feel might be of relevance I'm sure you'll share it with us immediately as part of your public duty.'

Powell gave Drake a disdainful look. Then Drake yanked open the door of the mortuary and entered. Still furious at the journalist, Drake scribbled his name on the health and safety form Denver, the assistant, pushed towards him. Then he marched down the corridor to the mortuary. He wasn't going to tolerate any more interference.

'Good morning, Detective Inspector,' Lee Kings said.

'It's bloody cold,' Drake said. 'And I've just been doorstepped by a reporter sticking his oar into our investigation.'

'Don't trust the press. Those big smart firms in London are unscrupulous enough to try and hack your phone.'

Drake nodded, recalling the publicity about journalists being implicated in phone hacking scandals.

Once the trolley was wheeled into place Kings got to work.

'I suppose you're interested in the enormous head wound and the time of death.'

Drake nodded.

'I need to do the usual procedures of undertaking a full examination of the body and all the usual slicing and dicing, if you pardon the sudoku analogy.'

Somehow Drake doubted he would ever slice and dice a sudoku puzzle again without thinking of Kings carving up a cadaver.

The pathologist started with Edward Murphy's hands, arms and legs before turning to the main part of the torso. Once the "Y" incision had been completed, he pulled back the flesh, cracked the ribs apart and began the macabre task of removing various body parts. Once he was finished, he turned to Drake. 'He seems to be a reasonably fit and healthy individual. No sign of underlying issues. All the vital organs seem to be healthy.'

Kings moved Murphy onto his side and carefully examined the wound to the back of the skull. 'I understand the crime scene investigators have recovered a lump hammer from the scene which has blood residue.'

'It was discarded in a hedge.'

Kings stared at the wound. 'Well, the wound would be consistent with a blow from a hammer. I've already taken the precaution of having full X-rays undertaken and I'll include them with my report. The skull has been badly damaged and the brain inside would have suffered catastrophic injuries resulting in death. Whilst the skull protects the brain nothing could protect it against this sort of injury.'

'Was it a frantic attack?'

'I'll examine the X-rays in more detail and summarise my conclusions in my final report. But there were probably two or three blows to the skull.'

'Was a lot of force needed to cause death?'

'When you're wielding a lump hammer you don't need to use a lot of force. If you bring it down from a decent height with a lot of energy you're going to cause catastrophic injuries.'

Kings turned to the saw on the table by his side and began the exercise of slicing off the top of the skull. Once the grinding sound stopped Kings flipped off the top section.

He made regular voice recordings of his conclusions, as well as taking photographs of each stage.

'And what about time of death?' Drake said.

'Based on body temperature readings together with the ambient temperature and the extent of rigor mortis when I saw the body last night and today, time of death was between nine pm and twelve pm'

Once Kings had finished, Drake left the mortuary and retraced the steps to the entrance. He paused and stared out of the window, hoping he could see if Powell was still around. But the Audi had gone.

Drake buttoned up his coat and headed out towards his car.

Since the investigation had begun Winder had woken early, his mind churning over everything that had happened in the family after Phoebe had become embroiled with the Peel Foundation. He felt guilty he hadn't given the events more time and attention years ago. Comments made by his mum and Auntie Gwen troubled him. He wanted to be valued within the family and despite feeling he had been treated as second best whenever the subject of Phoebe was discussed, now he felt he did have something to contribute.

That Sunday morning, he had woken wondering whether he should call to see Auntie Gwen, see how she was. His girlfriend had already rolled her eyes when he had told her he had to work. Not even the prospect of watching Liverpool play Arsenal at home in Anfield on the television interested him. When he told a friend of his he wouldn't be joining him in the pub to watch the game he had received a dozen question marks and old man emojis to his mobile.

Football could wait.

It was time for him to focus on family.

He left his girlfriend sleeping, and over breakfast scrolled through Facebook, looking for Phoebe's page. All the posts described the work she did at the Peel Foundation and how it had changed her life. He was surprised at how generic all the posts sounded, as though she had cut and pasted from a bank of posts prepared by the Foundation. Why did she have to repeat that the Foundation had taught her everything about being a strong woman?

Winder concluded it was more for the consumption of other members of the Peel Foundation and its prospective members. It made him sad to read through some of the comments about Phoebe's life. She should have been enjoying a career in the law. Maybe she could have become a criminal solicitor and their paths might have crossed in the police station or she might have been a high-flying commercial lawyer. She had given up a bright future for one regurgitating and repeating the benefits of joining the Peel Foundation.

He spent an hour scrolling through other posts from Phoebe's friends who were equally involved with the Foundation. It wasn't the sort of Facebook activity he was used to. There were no pictures of groups of friends at restaurants or walking on the beach or recovering from hangovers or smiling at parties.

He was tempted to message her. But what would he say? How are you? Long time no see?

And if she was in a controlling environment, she wouldn't see her messages anyway. Perhaps the Peel Foundation regulated everyone's social activity. He scrolled through to the Facebook pages for Mervyn Peel and then to Edward Murphy's. All the posts repeated the same mantra – joining the Peel Foundation was good for everyone's well-being.

It made Winder thoroughly depressed to think his own cousin had been taken in by these people. Auntie Gwen and her husband had never recovered. He wanted to call at the Peel Foundation and knock on their door, demand to speak to Phoebe and talk some sense into her. Then she'd gather her belongings together and leave, to be reunited with her family. But Winder knew there were no happy endings in these sorts of situations.

He didn't even know if this was the sort of thing he could raise at the team meeting later. But it made him feel helpless he couldn't do anything directly to help Phoebe. He finished his breakfast feeling as useless and depressed as he did when he had woken up.

Chapter 24

It pleased Drake that Sara and Gareth and Luned were at their desks when he arrived at the Incident Room. After hanging his coat on the stand in his room he joined them and walked over to the board.

'I've just been to the mortuary for Edward Murphy's post-mortem. The pathologist reckons he was killed with a lump hammer. The CSIs recovered one in the hedge in Murphy's garden.'

'Why would the killer throw away the murder weapon like that?' Winder said.

It must have been difficult for Winder and his family to come to terms with Phoebe's involvement in the Peel Foundation. Drake hoped Winder would retain a reasonable objectivity, but he looked tired and drawn and Drake wondered if the combination of the inquiry and his family connection was taking its toll.

'Killers do stupid things; we all know that,' Drake said. 'I want both of you,' Drake nodded at Luned and Gareth, 'supervising the house-to-house enquiries near Edward Murphy's property. We'll have a further catch-up later this afternoon. And be careful of anybody asking questions. I was doorstepped by a Brian Powell this morning on my way to the post-mortem. He is the hotshot journalist looking into Jack Holt's murder, and now Edward Murphy's. He's got a good source of information. So don't share anything with anybody about the inquiry.'

'Will there be a press conference?' Luned said.

'I've got a meeting with Superintendent Hobbs later. A decision will be made then. Has there been any sign of the CCTV from the café?'

'Nothing yet, boss.'

'Chase it.'

Luned and Gareth nodded.

Drake walked back to his office, gesturing for Gareth to

join him as he did so.

'Close the door and sit down,' Drake said, once he was at his desk.

Winder did as he was told and Drake looked into the officer's face. It was closed and grey, not at all like the usual Gareth Winder.

'I appreciate the inquiry must be raising difficult painful associations for you and your family.'

Winder gave a brief confirmatory nod.

'How are Phoebe's parents?'

'Auntie Gwen was over at mum's place yesterday. She just talked for hours, reliving everything that had happened and blaming herself. She's lost weight and mum is very worried about her.'

'You don't seem to be yourself.'

'I'm okay, boss.'

'You look tired, Gareth – are you getting enough sleep?'

Winder shrugged. It was always difficult looking in at yourself and recognising when things were not okay. Drake knew that from his own experience with his OCD. He wanted to reach out and reassure Winder that he valued his input, but if there was any question of his objectivity being compromised then it might be best to redeploy him to another team.

'I don't want you making mistakes, Gareth. A personal connection to a case can be very difficult.'

'I'll be fine, honest, boss.'

'I suppose your mum and Auntie Gwen are pestering you about progress reports and maybe even asking if anyone has interviewed Phoebe?'

Grudgingly Winder nodded his confirmation.

'I don't want Phoebe's connection to the Peel Foundation having an impact on your work.'

'It won't, boss. Seriously, everything is okay.'

'Keep a proper perspective. Superintendent Hobbs is bound to ask me about the position later today. One option is for you to be temporarily moved to another team.'

'Everything is under control; I want to be part of the team.'

'I'll talk to you again, but I want you to be honest with me and with yourself.'

Winder stood up, clearly desperate to avoid further interrogation about his private life and his mental health. They weren't the sort of things police officers discussed.

Drake pondered for a moment about exactly how much he should share with Superintendent Hobbs. He had already flagged up to his superior officer that a member of Winder's family was involved with the Peel Foundation. Nothing more had been said but he knew Hobbs would probably raise it at some point. He was good on detail, but Drake suspected that his superior officer's reaction would simply be to move Gareth Winder to another team and appoint a replacement. It was the simple answer but not the right one and Drake assembled in his mind the counterarguments in case Hobbs raised the matter.

Drake spent the rest of the morning working his way through the class lists and material from the bursar of Fremantle High. He started with the pupils in the same year as Jack Holt. None of the names featured in the investigation. None were members of staff at the Peel Foundation, although Drake reckoned there'd be other members of staff in different foundation locations. There were several lists for each of the years Jack Holt had attended the school. The names all needed to be double-checked – Luned could prepare a detailed spreadsheet in due course.

Drake recognised the name of one of the pupils as a member of parliament and another who had exactly the same name as a prominent journalist on the BBC news. It justified the boasts on the school's website about the achievements of its former pupils.

He opened the second folder, relating to pupils in the

same year as Edward Murphy. It had pages of details with names of the pupils as well as the names of members of staff. Drake added this information to the exercise Luned would have to undertake. It was the sort of task that could take hours of time but might unearth another nugget of information to connect both men.

A doubt surfaced in his mind that he had been too focused on the Peel Foundation but now they had the link to the school that Holt and Murphy had attended. He couldn't ignore the similarity between the staging of Holt's and Murphy's deaths and the punishment rituals at the Freemantle High. The discovery might have changed the focus of the inquiry but whoever was responsible for their deaths needed to be caught.

He scanned through the names on the lists for the year Edward Murphy began at Fremantle High. His name was included in four of the years and he wondered what had caused Murphy's parents to move him halfway through his education. He hadn't completed reading all the documentation when the telephone on his desk rang.

'Detective Inspector Drake.'

'Good morning, this is Harry Yeo, the headmaster of Fremantle High. I understand you want to speak to me.' The accent was exactly what Drake expected – clear, confident and very posh. 'I've only just got back from a skiing trip. The bursar suggested it was most urgent I call.'

'I'm the senior investigating officer in relation to the murders of Jack Holt and Edward Murphy. Both men had been pupils at your school.'

'Yes, the bursar told me about their deaths. It's most shocking. But I'm not certain how I can help.'

'As part of our inquiries we've uncovered various blog posts and Facebook groups relating to a punishment ritual where pupils were pinned to the lawn of the school quad with croquet hoops. And then dustbins full of cold water are emptied over them.'

'It was something that happened many years ago before my time as headmaster.'

It sounded like Yeo was opting out of responsibility.

'From what I've read it seemed quite brutal.'

'And also dangerous.'

'Edward Murphy's name features quite often as one of the main protagonists.'

'I can't really comment because I wasn't here at that time. I wasn't even on the staff.'

'Are you aware of any members of your current staff who might have been teaching at that time?'

'I very much doubt it. After all, we are talking over thirty years ago.'

'The school does pride itself on a low turnover of staff.'

'Even so, Detective Inspector, very few members of staff stay in the same post thirty years. But come to think of it there are two members of the humanities department, one has taught Latin here for many years and another history. I shall contact them and tell them you need to speak to them.'

'Thank you. Are you aware of the Facebook groups organised by former pupils?'

'I am, but that has nothing to do with the school, of course.'

'It doesn't portray your institution in a very good light.'

'The events you're talking about are shrouded in the mists of time, I'm afraid. They don't have any bearing on us now. Things were very different back then.'

'Do you know if there are any other members of staff from that time still alive?'

'I haven't the faintest idea. The headmaster before me had been here for about ten years and he retired. And before him… The head had been in place for several years so it's possible he was around at the time of the events you're alluding to. But he died recently.'

'Get back to me with confirmation about the two members of staff who might recall Holt and Murphy, please.'

'Of course, Detective Inspector I'll get around to it immediately.'

Drake finished the call and got back to the information the bursar had provided.

The work on the documentation was interrupted by an email reaching his inbox with the preliminary report from Dr Lee Kings. The pathologist had been as good as his word in expediting the report. Drake read the standard wording he had seen so many times before and skipped forward to the conclusion. The cause of death had been catastrophic brain damage.

Then he read the report from the forensic department. Mike Foulds had done his usual thorough report. Drake imagined it had been difficult work completing the search of the garden in the cold, icy conditions. There was nothing to suggest Edward Murphy had been moved post-death. Spots of blood had been found on the lawn near the body, but they were consistent with a blow to the rear of the head. It confirmed Edward Murphy had been struck where he was standing and then pinned to the lawn.

Drake paused for a moment, thinking. Murphy had walked to the rear of the garden for some reason. What had taken him there or who had taken him there? Drake decided he needed to see the garden once again, he needed to get a feel for exactly what had taken place.

He got back to the documentation provided by Fremantle High. He focused on the data for Jack Holt, deciding to start from the final year in which his name had appeared as a pupil. Then he worked back methodically until one name caught his attention. He stopped, surprised when he read the name David Ackland. Surely it was the same David Ackland that was in a relationship with Jack Holt.

Why on earth hadn't anyone mentioned their connection to Fremantle High?

Ackland had made no reference, nor had Holt's parents.

Drake didn't like coincidences. And this one made him feel uncomfortable. They were overdue another discussion with David Ackland.

When Drake asked to see Gareth Winder, Sara realised there was every possibility the detective constable would be moved and another officer allocated. But it wasn't as though there was a direct conflict – Phoebe wasn't a suspect. It must have been difficult for Winder, and Sara could guess the nature of Drake's conversation with him. He probably even warned him that Superintendent Hobbs might decide he didn't have the objectivity to be on the team.

It had been a good idea getting Winder out of the Incident Room, Sara realised. She'd seen him mulling over things far too often over the past few days, and getting him out doing the ordinary day-to-day work of policing for an inquiry like this would help.

It gave her time to focus on chasing the CCTV from the café Winder and Luned had requested. She called the café owner who gave her a bland excuse for the delay in responding. Sara had demanded that she send the footage immediately.

'But it's Sunday and—'

'And this is a murder enquiry so unless I have the footage within the next hour I shall be calling on your property with a couple of uniformed officers to make certain it's made available.'

'All right. Just keep your shirt on.'

The woman finished the call abruptly and Sara made a mental note to call her back within half an hour. It gave her the opportunity of doing some digging into the two men who had assaulted Jack Holt in London. They already had the name of one – Martin Swan. They needed a better image than the one on the board so she requisitioned a search at the DVLA. The government body that kept records of every citizen's driving licence would have an image of Martin

Swan, assuming he had a driving licence.

She googled the Peel Foundation and found dozens of videos with hundreds of hours of footage. In addition, there was a specific channel created by the Peel Foundation and Sara clicked into it. She watched a few moments of one video which all seemed to be directed at persuading people to join the Foundation so that they could maximise their personal potential and live their lives to the full. It was no better than selling snake oil, Sara concluded. It disgusted her that people like Mervyn Peel could operate unchecked.

There would be hours of work scanning through all the videos. Normally she would have expected Gareth Winder to have revelled in that task but now she assessed that he probably needed support to do so. She and Luned could help him. It would be part of their teamwork.

If it had taken two people to assault and then drag Jack Holt to the lawn of the bowling green, Martin Swan and the other of Mervyn Peel's henchmen were ideal candidates. She resolved to mention it to Inspector Drake at their catch-up session later.

She checked back into her emails and found the footage from the café owner. Pleased that the woman had seen sense and cooperated, Sara clicked it open.

She reminded herself of the time she needed to check. She scrolled back to a couple of minutes before they knew the red car had been stationary at the junction. She watched in real time. A taxi went down the road outside the café. A man and a woman in their twenties, hand-in-hand, walked past before she spotted the red car driving up the road and slowing at the junction.

Sara paused the footage and scrolled back until she could freeze-frame an image of the vehicle. Then she read its number plate. She felt pleased she had something to go on. She punched in the details into a search request for the DVLA and waited for the owner's details to be sent to her.

Chapter 25

Drake dragged on his overcoat, having already checked the weather outside from his office window. It wasn't snowing but it looked cold. He left his room and found Sara focused on the monitor on her desk.

'I've got a meeting with Superintendent Hobbs later but first I want to see Edward Murphy's property again,'

'Yes, boss.' Sara got up and found her coat and joined Drake as they headed downstairs.

Salt had been distributed all over the steps leading down onto the path and the car park. Carefully they made their way down to the car and Drake slowly headed out towards the junction with the main road.

'I've done some work on the Freemantle High pupil classes this morning. I also spoke to the present headmaster. He knew all about the staking out punishments, but it was long before his time. He promised to check with another two members of staff he thought might have been there at the time Holt and Murphy were pupils.'

Drake pulled up at the junction, indicating left but he had to wait until a string of slow-moving traffic passed.

'That doesn't really help us,' Sara said. 'We might need to talk to some of the pupils who were there at the same time. But it's such a long time ago it's difficult to believe anyone would bear a grudge for that long.'

Drake pulled into the traffic. 'People do bear grudges for a long, long time. And something recent may have been a trigger. I discovered David Ackland had been at the school at the same time as Murphy.'

'Really? So why the hell didn't he mention that?'

'And why didn't Jack Holt's parents refer to it?'

Sara didn't reply. Drake wasn't expecting her to.

'We received the video from that café and it does record a red car approaching the junction. It turned at the junction, as spotted by the dashcam footage on the police vehicle.'

'And it confirms Danny's version of events.'

'I've requisitioned details of the owner from the DVLA.'

'Good, hopefully whoever was driving that car might have seen something.'

'And the CCTV footage records a taxi driving from the junction a couple of minutes before the red car approached. And I spotted a couple walking down the road.'

'It was hardly the weather for an evening stroll.'

'I've asked the taxi company for details of the driver.'

'Good, some progress at least.'

Drake didn't need the satnav. He knew his way to Edward Murphy's property. He pulled up when he could see the mobile incident room. It would give anyone with information the opportunity of speaking to an officer. They left the car and walked over to the property. Crime scene tape still fluttering across the gate. Drake ducked under it and held it aloft for Sara. They walked down the side of the property to where they could see the rear door and patio.

'There's never enough time when we visit a crime scene to get a real sense of what happened.' Drake said, looking down at the garden. The patio area was made of random stones – some flat, others with raised surfaces – but they had all been pointed precisely. There wasn't a weed in sight and a dwarf wall that edged the patio had a wide section with steps leading down onto a lawn and lots of carefully manicured borders.

Drake walked over and stood with his back to the house. 'Murphy must have loved the garden.'

'It must have cost him a fortune.'

Drake peered over at the right-hand side. 'Is there any way inside the garden other than from the front entrance?' He didn't wait for Sara to reply as he marched down onto the lawn and then followed the paths through the garden and the apple trees and shrubs and gazebos, all the while checking to see if there was any entrance from the garden onto the adjacent fields.

When he reached a summer house at the bottom he was satisfied that on the right-hand side of the garden the hedge was thick enough and well maintained, with no possibility of anyone gaining access.

'It looks like something out of one of those glossy magazines.' Sara gazed at the summer house and the tables and chairs inside.

Beyond it Drake found another section of garden with a fish pond and then a polytunnel. Benches inside were filled with the accessories for potting plants and shrubs. Drake retreated to the area where Edward Murphy's body had been found. Again the area was lined with thick hedges trimmed and cut carefully. He judged they had probably been in place for years, long before Murphy had lived at the property.

Behind the hedge was a stone wall and from its condition Drake guessed it had been built when the house was constructed. But it certainly didn't have gaps or gates into the adjacent field.

Drake stood for a moment near the spot where Murphy's body had been pinned to the grass. Sara stood by his side.

'He came down here for a reason,' Drake said.

'There's nothing here apart from the shed and composting bins.'

'It's away from the house and private.'

'I think it's clear he knew his killer. He was lured here. Maybe the killer wanted to borrow a piece of garden equipment. The killer could hardly persuade Murphy to show off the planting in the garden at this time of year.'

'And it's freezing.'

'What was Murphy wearing?'

'It was a thick winter coat.'

'So the killer knocks on his front door, offers some explanation for why he or she is there which means Murphy accompanies them to the bottom of the garden.'

'Which means he probably knew the killer.'

Drake turned to look over at the shed and composting

bins nearby. A padlock kept the door safely closed. He stepped over towards it and peered inside at rakes and other garden tools hanging in neat rows.

Sara joined Drake as they retraced their steps to the rear entrance. The hedging on his right had no gaps or holes. They stopped and Drake looked back at the garden. 'There's no way the killer could have accessed the garden other than through the main entrance.'

'It certainly looks that way. Have the forensics been able to find any other evidence?'

Drake shook his head. Visiting the property had given him greater clarity which vindicated his decision to tramp around the garden. The use of the croquet hoops was clear evidence the murder wasn't random. When he had his suspect in the interview room across the table he wanted to be able to tell that person he knew what they had done.

Drake turned to Sara. 'Let's go and talk to the officers in the mobile incident room.'

'Yes, boss.'

Sara followed Drake as he walked back to their car. He spotted two uniformed officers, suitably muffled up, standing on the pavement.

'Good to see you sir,' the older of both officers said.

Drake didn't recognise him but the younger one exchanged small talk with Sara.

'Who's in charge here?'

'Sergeant Turner was here a while ago but he and DC Winder and DC Thomas left. They had a witness to speak to.'

'Have there been any developments?'

'Nothing much, sir. There have been the usual time-wasters but nobody knew Edward Murphy. He kept himself to himself.'

Frustration clawed at his thoughts. Somebody knew something about Murphy's death, surely? Drake read the time on his watch and turned to Sara. 'Let's get back to headquarters I've got a meeting with Superintendent Hobbs.'

Hobbs read the briefing memoranda Detective Inspector Drake had prepared twice in anticipation of their meeting. Then he read an email from the public relations department warning him that Brian Powell was making a distinct nuisance of himself. Members of his team had even been talking to civilians working at Northern Division headquarters.

The death of Edward Murphy was still fresh in his mind, as it was only the previous morning the body had been discovered. This had meant Hobbs having to change his domestic plans to be present that afternoon for an update with Detective Inspector Drake. He tried to keep Sundays sacrosanct for family. His wife had long given up any attempt to criticise his decisions about the long hours he worked.

He kept the door to his office open and when he heard movement outside shouted a greeting for Drake to join him.

Hobbs immediately felt wrongfooted. Drake was dressed formally: a decent suit, a powder blue shirt and matching tie. Normally Hobbs would have been in uniform, but he had decided to dress casually. His trousers were dark grey, the shirt underneath the thick green sweater a neutral cream colour.

'Bring me up to date,' Hobbs said, once Drake had sat down.

'The body of Edward Murphy was found yesterday morning pinned to the lawn at the back of his property by croquet hoops. We are treating both his murder and that of Jack Holt as connected.'

Hobbs nodded.

'We've discovered Holt and Murphy were pupils at the same school.'

'But that's years ago.'

'It's still a connection.'

'And a very tenuous one at that. What did Murphy do with the Peel Foundation?'

'He was an accountant, a pen pusher.'

'Then you should be focusing on something in his work or his background that's more recent than his schooldays.'

'It could have had a significant bearing on him. We've researched the school on social media and pinning pupils to a lawn and then pouring dustbins of water over them was a common punishment.'

'It's all sounds very public school to me. And have you thought that whoever was responsible might be aware of that ritual to throw sand in your face.'

'Of course, sir, but we can't just ignore the link to the school. Especially as David Ackland, Jack Holt's partner, was a pupil there too.'

'And I would suggest he should be your main suspect. Arrest him, get him in for questioning and see if he cracks.'

'Yes, sir.'

Hobbs knew the detective inspector wouldn't follow his suggestion until he had far more evidence to implicate David Ackland.

'And another thing, Sir. A Brian Powell a journalist from London has spoken to me on the telephone and he doorstepped me outside the mortuary before Edward Murphy's post-mortem.'

'Damn. The PR department told me he is making a nuisance of himself. I don't think we have any choice other than to organise a press conference.'

'Press conference,' Drake replied, his reservation about its efficacy clear in his voice.

'I'll coordinate and I'll send you the details. Does Edward Murphy have any family? Any next of kin?'

'We spoke to the Peel Foundation who were extremely awkward with us. They have no information about his family.'

'What sort of people are we dealing with here?'

'I've spoken to an investor who gave Mervyn Peel an alibi for part of the night of Jack Holt's murder. But apart from some Zoom meetings early in the evening he alleges he was at home when Murphy was killed.'

Hobbs nodded. 'I still think you should be focusing on David Ackland. And I was concerned about your reference to a member of Detective Constable Winder's family being involved. Do you think his performance is affected?'

Hobbs searched for prevarication in Drake's response, and he did suspect a degree of obfuscation. 'I've discussed the position with Detective Constable Winder, and he assures me his judgement isn't impaired.'

Hobbs sat back in his chair. 'Keep me posted.'

Drake made his way back to the Incident Room. Superintendent Hobbs hadn't directly ordered him to remove Gareth Winder from the inquiry, but he was clearly signalling that if there was any possibility the detective constable was hampering the inquiry he would be moved. But Drake didn't want a replacement detective – he wanted Gareth Winder to continue. He knew the young officer. Introducing somebody new at this stage could compromise their work.

He detoured into the kitchen and fussed around making coffee which he took on a tray back to the Incident Room. The other officers sat at their desks. Drake found an empty chair and deposited his mug and cafetière on a desk.

'How did you get on with the house-to-house enquiries near Edward Murphy's property?' Drake said.

'It didn't prove to be very helpful, sir,' Luned said. 'It's too cold to be walking your dog far at this time of year, especially in the evening.'

Winder nodded.

Luned continued, 'Uniformed officers doing the house-to-house referred us to Murphy's immediate neighbours. But they barely knew him. It wasn't as though they had fallen out. They simply had nothing to do with him.'

'Depressing, isn't it?' Sara said.

'And what about other people living near to him?'

Winder added. 'Some of them knew him as the man who lived in the posh house. An older man living in one of the terraces nearby had seen Murphy in the local newsagent and had ventured a few words with him. Murphy had barely acknowledged him.'

'So the house-to-house enquiries aren't going to help us.'

'I've been working on Murphy's mobile,' Luned said. 'It doesn't take us any further because there were no calls to it or made by Murphy on the day he was killed.'

'What about the day before?'

Luned nodded. 'Calls to the Peel Foundation and to Martha Peel's mobile.'

'He had barely joined the twenty-first century,' Winder said. 'I've also had the results from the land registry. I had to double-check the details but it confirms the Peel Foundation actually owns Murphy's property.'

Drake frowned. If, like Winder's cousin, Murphy had given a chunk of his capital to the Peel Foundation for its greater collective good and his own personal advancement it was a surprise he had been allowed to live in the property.

Winder continued, 'And I found details of the Peel Foundation's property interests. They've just acquired a row of shops in Flint.'

'How the hell did that happen?'

'I don't know, boss. I did a search against Martha and Mervyn Peel's names too and they have a tract of land in their own name. It was recently transferred from the Peel Foundation into their joint names.'

'That's the land Leonard Ferrier mentioned. Do some more digging into that.'

Drake got up, checked the time and realised the team needed to rest for that afternoon and evening. 'There's likely to be a press conference tomorrow. So everyone in first thing. For now, let's get home.'

Chapter 26

Winder returned home but his mind was still at the Incident Room, his thoughts consumed by how he could protect Phoebe. His girlfriend sat in the sitting room sharing a bottle of wine with a girlfriend, making steady progress through two enormous packets of potato crisps and watching a romcom. Being sociable was the last thing on Winder's mind so he headed upstairs to the shower.

He allowed the hot water to wash over him, and he turned his face to the showerhead, closing his eyes, hoping it would refresh him for the evening ahead and the following day's activities. Once he'd towelled himself dry, he dragged on a pair of jeans and a clean shirt. The clothes he'd worn earlier were discarded into the linen basket. He sat on the edge of the bed as he picked up his mobile from the bedside cabinet.

He noted there was a call from his mum as well as a text asking him to call her. He frowned. It must have been important, so he called her.

It took four rings for his mother to answer and when she did so her voice sounded breathless as though she'd been crying.

'It's Steve,' his mother managed between breaths.

'What do you mean?' Winder didn't need to ask who she was referring to – Steve Parkinson was Phoebe's father.

'He's… in hospital.… They think it's an overdose.'

A tightness gripped his chest. Anger pierced his mind.

'Where are you?'

'We're at home.'

'I'm leaving now.'

He finished the call, threaded his arms through a sweater and took the stairs to the ground floor two at a time. He put his head round the sitting room door simultaneously as he shrugged on his coat. 'I'm going to see mum. Something's wrong with Uncle Steve.'

He didn't wait for his girlfriend to reply. He pulled the door tightly closed behind him and trotted down towards his car. It was a short journey to his mum's home. He drew up in the drive and ran over to the front door.

His father opened the door and from the sombre look on his face Winder knew something was seriously amiss. He followed his father into the kitchen at the rear of the property where his mum was sitting at a table.

She gave him a look that said she was pleased he was there as support.

'What happened?'

'Uncle Steve has been taken to the hospital. He took an overdose earlier,' Winder's mum said. Her face was puffy and it was clear tears had been spilled, but Winder could only imagine what his Auntie Gwen was going through.

'When did this happen?'

'Gwen rang me just before I called you. She is on the way to the hospital with him.'

'Why did it happen? Is it about Phoebe and this business with the Peel Foundation?'

Winder sensed his pulse increasing as he thought about the impact Mervyn Peel and his evil organisation had on ordinary people like Auntie Gwen and Uncle Steve and Phoebe.

'He's not been well. He finds it very difficult to come to terms with things.'

'Are you going to go to the hospital?'

'He's unconscious. Gwen is going to call me.'

When his father suggested he sit, Winder refused, pacing around the kitchen. He was barely able to stand still. It was time somebody did something about the Peel Foundation and its hold over Phoebe. Sitting around doing nothing wasn't going to be an option. Every muscle in his body seemed to be tensing.

'I'm going to sort this out.'

'What do you mean?' his father said.

'It's time somebody did something about Phoebe.'

Winder stormed out of the house, and once he was in his car he accelerated out of the housing estate where his parents lived. If he had blue flashing lights available on his vehicle he'd have switched them on. And the siren too. But he broke every speed limit through Colwyn Bay, flashing his car headlights and sounding the horn whenever a slowing vehicle irritated him. He had only one thing in mind – getting to the Peel Foundation, finding Phoebe and talking sense into her, and dragging her back to her family that loved her.

It didn't take Winder long until he arrived at the Peel Foundation's premises and was pleased the main gate was open. He drove up towards the main entrance, parked and dashed over to the door. He wasn't going to follow the usual courtesies of knocking on the door and expecting a polite welcome. The handle opened when he tugged at it, which surprised him. He found himself inside the main entrance hall. Being uncertain exactly where he might find Phoebe, he headed off down one of the corridors familiar to him from when he had visited before. He heard voices in a couple of the rooms and when he opened the doors and peered in, startled faces looked over at him. 'What the hell do you want?' The voice sounded alarmed.

Winder pulled the door closed and headed down the corridor. By now there was a pounding in his ears and he was going to find it difficult keeping his anger in check. In a second room one of those present raised his voice. 'You can't be here.' Winder scanned those present and, much like in the first room, there was no sign of Phoebe.

Winder barged his way into a dining room where several people were congregated around the table eating a meal, drinking wine and chatting amiably. He was doing nothing wrong. In fact he was making things right. For Auntie Gwen and Uncle Steve and also for Phoebe. He didn't care about the consequences any longer: he just wanted to get his cousin out of this hell hole and back to her family, back to the people who cared for her.

'Who the hell are you?'

'Where is Phoebe?'

The man got to his feet and stepped over towards Winder. 'You've got no right to be here.'

He moved closer to Winder, who pointed at him. 'Don't come any closer to me. You will regret it. Now tell me where Phoebe is.'

'I'm calling the police.'

'Just tell me where she is.'

The man retreated and picked up a mobile handset from near his place setting at the table. Winder left the room and immediately bumped into Phoebe who was returning to the dining room with a tray of desserts.

'Phoebe,' Winder almost shouted. 'You've got to come with me. Now. I'll get you out of this place. Your dad is in hospital, for Christ's sake. The family need you.'

'What are you doing, Gareth?'

Winder grabbed Phoebe by the shoulder as the tray of desserts in their glass dishes crashed to the ground. He tugged and pulled her by her shoulder down the corridor back towards reception. But Martin Swan and Mervyn Peel were waiting for him. They blocked his exit.

'How dare you break in here and cause such a commotion.'

'I'm taking Phoebe home.'

Peel looked over at Phoebe. 'Do you want to go home with this man?'

She shook her head.

Winder couldn't believe she had done that. He released his hold on her arm and turned to her. 'Your dad is in hospital. Surely that means something.'

'We are taking this very seriously,' Peel announced as he nodded at Swan, who marched over to Winder. Swan reached out to grab Winder's arm but he waved Swan away.

'I don't believe you're doing this, Phoebe. I really don't believe it.'

'Please leave my premises immediately. I shall of course be reporting you to your superiors first thing in the morning.'

Swan pushed Winder out of the front door and for a few seconds he stood looking down at his vehicle. He had done all he could. What more could he have done to protect Phoebe? What more could he have done to look after Uncle Steve and Auntie Gwen?

Chapter 27

Drake recognised his mum's Toyota when he arrived home. He had already texted Annie before leaving headquarters, telling her when to expect him. A smiley emoji had reached his mobile moments later.

He had been late the previous evening for a dinner with one of Annie's colleagues and a new girlfriend. He had been distracted by the events at Edward Murphy's property and all he had been able to share with Annie and her friends had been the barest details that he was in charge of another murder inquiry.

So today he had made a determined effort to be home at a reasonable hour. He let himself into the house and made his way upstairs where he heard conversation between Annie and his mum. It pleased him immensely that his mum got on so well with Annie. Her relationship with his ex-wife Sian had been so different and he now realised it was Sian's aloofness that contributed significantly to the lack of warmth between both women.

'How are you, Ian?' Mair Drake said, after Drake had kissed her on the cheek.

'It's been a busy week or so.'

'Annie was telling me all about this latest case. I do hope you're not working too hard.'

'I'm looking after him, don't worry.' Annie smiled.

'We've been talking about the arrangements. It must be a record for our family to have two weddings so close to each other.'

It had only been a few months since his mum had married Emlyn. And the immense happiness she enjoyed from sharing her life with her new husband was clearly evident.

'We've arranged to visit the wedding venue at the Town Hall in Portmeirion,' Annie said. It had been the venue where Mair and Emlyn had married. And where Drake had proposed. 'We're going this Saturday. Helen and Megan will be with us so it'll be a good opportunity for the four of us to spend time together.'

Drake nodded and gave a mumbled half-hearted agreement. All he could think about was the possibility the investigation would still be live on Saturday. In fact that was a racing certainty. The enquiry into Edward Murphy's murder had only just started.

His mum stayed to share an evening meal with them, explaining that Emlyn was visiting an elderly relative and wouldn't return until much later.

It wasn't until after his mum had left that Drake began to relax. And by the time of the evening news he could barely keep his eyes open. Sleep beckoned and after setting the alarm for the usual early start Drake fell soundly asleep.

He chose his best suit the following morning, explaining to Annie there was every possibility he'd be asked to attend a press conference later. He picked a new white shirt from his wardrobe and neatly knotted a tie with a paisley design to the collar.

He stood by the mirror by the front door and then looked at Annie.

'Very presentable.' Annie smiled. He pulled her close and kissed her on the lips. He grabbed his winter coat and left for the car.

He found BBC Wales on the radio and listened to the news which carried a brief mention of Edward Murphy's death. He wondered which of the journalists from the TV stations covering Wales would be present at a press conference. If one was organised, Brian Powell was certain to be there.

He took the Colwyn Bay exit from the A55 and made for the regular newsagent he visited over many years. He jumped out and headed inside finding his regular broadsheet and exchanging a few brief words with the shop owner about the weather. As he left the store Brian Powell entered.

'Good morning, Detective Inspector Drake. How is the investigation going?'

Drake glared at Powell, biting his tongue before walking over to his car, Powell following behind.

'I understand you've had a full team of officers doing house-to-house enquiries near Mr Murphy's property. Any positive results?'

Drake turned to Powell. He was wearing a full-length camel jacket and matching leather gloves.

'I suggest you talk to public relations.'

Powell grinned. 'Regularly, of course. And they mention every time that you're the senior investigating officer. Is it true Edward Murphy knew his killer?'

Drake narrowed his eyes. Nothing would give him greater pleasure than taking Powell by the scruff of his neck and making it quite clear he was interfering with a criminal investigation. Common sense got the better of Drake as he realised there were probably several members of Powell's team filming him. The last thing he'd wanted was a confrontation between him and the reporter splashed all over social media.

'I'll text you the number for our public relations department. They're very helpful.' Drake managed an utterly insincere smile and got into his car and drove away.

His anger at Brian Powell hadn't subsided by the time he reached reception, when one of the civilians on duty called his name.

'DI Drake, Superintendent Hobbs wants to see you immediately.'

Drake acknowledged the message and headed for the senior management suite.

The senior officer's secretary ushered Drake into his office without delay.

'Morning, sir. What's this about?'

'Have you spoken to DC Winder this morning?'

'No, I came straight here.'

Hobbs waved a hand at the chairs in front of his desk for Drake to sit down.

'He went to the Peel Foundation last night. Walked right in and tried to haul Phoebe Parkinson from the premises against her will. He created quite a disturbance.'

Drake wanted to defend Winder, knowing there had to be an explanation. 'Having his cousin involved with the Foundation has been difficult.'

'He's lucky Mervyn Peel and Martin Swan don't want to press charges. Apparently he threatened to assault Swan.'

Drake couldn't believe Winder had done such a thing. 'I'll talk to him.'

'And make certain he stays well away from the Peel Foundation. I've a good mind to transfer him but this time I'll depend on you to make certain he doesn't go anywhere near the Peel Foundation again. I don't like that Mervyn Peel one bit so I'm not going to give him the satisfaction of knowing DC Winder has been transferred.'

Drake stood up, his mind focusing on the dressing down he'd give Winder.

'Thank you, sir.'

Drake marched through to the Incident Room and shouted at Winder, 'My office now.'

The DC joined Drake and after closing the door Drake sat down.

'I've just spoken to the super. What the hell were you thinking?'

'I wasn't, sir. I'm sorry. I've let you down.'

'Damn right you have. What possessed you?'

'Phoebe's dad tried to commit suicide yesterday. I couldn't think straight.'

'What! How is he?'

'In hospital, but he'll pull through, thankfully.'

'Good. You're lucky Mervyn Peel and Swan don't want to complain or else you'd be in deep trouble.'

'Yes, sir.'

'That's all and don't go anywhere near the Peel Foundation again.'

Drake checked his emails and adjusted the photographs of his daughters as his anger at Winder and annoyance with Powell subsided. Then he walked through to the Incident Room.

'That bloody journalist has tried to speak to me again,' Drake said to the team sitting at their desks as he paced over to the board.

'There's been a development,' Luned said. 'The result on the registration number of that red car came in this morning. It belongs to David Ackland.'

'We should bring him in for questioning,' Sara said.

'He's certainly got some explaining to do.' Drake paused gathering his thoughts together.

Sara continued, 'I've been trying to find the name of the second of Mervyn Peel's henchmen we saw on that video. There are hours and hours of footage on YouTube.'

Drake nodded at Winder. 'That's a job for you and Luned.'

'How does that help us with the enquiry into Edward Murphy's death,' Luned said.

'There's a connection between both. We haven't found it yet. Luned, we've still got to work through the rest of the papers Jack Holt's editor gave us and we need to go through Edward Murphy's computer. We're going to find that link, and we need to find it soon. And before that bloody Brian Powell puts his fat nose into more of our business.'

Drake turned to look at Sara. 'We need to prepare for a press conference.'

Drake's attention to detail always impressed Sara, even if he could be obsessive about making copies in triplicate of case summaries and to-do lists. He had reservations about press conferences but she had sensed a growing anger in him that morning about the repeated attempts by Brian Powell to bounce him into sharing information. Winder's behaviour would have unsettled Drake and she had warned the DC that if he did anything that stupid again he could expect to be disciplined.

They sat in his office, Drake occasionally reading the time on either his watch or the computer monitor. She had always found the superintendent to be a difficult officer to get to know. His predecessor, Wyndham Price, had been straightforward and uncomplicated. Luckily she had little to do with Hobbs on a practical day-to-day basis but it pleased her Drake included her in his meeting with the superintendent.

'We need to include a statement asking for the couple seen walking down the street on the evening Jack Holt was killed to come forward. We can even post a photograph on the force website and issue copies to the press,' Sara said.

'I'm not certain Superintendent Hobbs will favour the second of your suggestions. At least not at the moment.'

'I suppose it would be an open invitation for someone like Brian Powell and his team of investigators to track these people down and hassle them.'

'It's the last thing we want. Have you had any response from the taxi company?'

'They're going to get back to me later.'

Sara could see from the troubled expression on Drake's face he wanted feedback from the taxi company there and then. It was often the case in an inquiry that information came in piecemeal. It could feel like one step forward and two steps backwards.

'Will we be mentioning the croquet hoops?' Sara said.

Another pained expression flashed across Drake's eyes. 'Brian Powell knows about them. He mentioned them to me. I don't see how we can avoid it. And he and his team must have been able to find the information from someone – maybe the CSIs or a civilian.'

Usually the nuts and bolts of the actual crime scene as it

related to the dead body wouldn't be shared in the public domain. But could they take the risk Brian Powell wouldn't ask about the croquet hoops in the press conference?

Drake got to his feet. 'Let's see what the superintendent says.'

Drake gathered his papers together and led Sara through to the senior management suite. John Westcott from the public relations department was waiting when they arrived.

'Hello, Ian.'

'John, you know Detective Sergeant Sara Morgan.'

Westcott nodded, smiled at Sara.

'Brian Powell is making himself a bloody nuisance. He even tried to tackle me this morning outside a newsagent in Colwyn Bay. I was sorely tempted to give him a piece of my mind.'

'Not a good idea. He was probably filming it all.'

Drake nodded. 'Can't you tell them to back off or something.'

Westcott shrugged. 'It's a free country. And he's very determined and he's very good.'

Hobbs' secretary announced they could go through into his office where he was waiting at the conference table.

'Let's discuss this proposed press conference for later,' Hobbs began.

'Nothing proposed about it. I've got everyone lined up,' Westcott said. 'I've drafted a statement to be read by Detective Inspector Drake as the senior investigating officer. We don't have any immediate family members we can invite other than David Ackland. It would be clearly inappropriate for him to feature.'

Westcott pushed over an A4 sheet for everyone present.

Sara read her copy and realised it said nothing of substance. Which was exactly what the public relations department wanted, she guessed.

'We'll need a reference to the two people seen on the CCTV footage from the café. They could be crucial eyewitnesses,' Drake said.

Westcott nodded. 'I'll need their full details. We could always issue a still photograph of both individuals.'

'It's not going to be an invitation for people like Brian Powell to find them and pester them,' Hobbs said.

'An image would reach a much wider audience,' Westcott said.

'I agree with John, sir,' Drake said. 'We need to speak to these people as a matter of urgency.'

'Agreed. Let's just hope someone knows who they are. And make sure it's made clear they are witnesses only.'

'And what about the croquet hoops?' Drake said. 'Brian Powell knows the detail.'

'If he asks you about them you then simply reply that you don't make any comment on the specifics of the crime scene. We move onto the next question.'

'Will he be happy with that?'

'He'll have to be.'

Chapter 28

Drake returned to the Incident Room wanting to believe the press conference had been a success. He wasn't at all certain it was likely Brian Powell would be satisfied when his expected question had been squashed unceremoniously. He didn't seem to be angry or annoyed and Drake guessed he'd simply be redoubling his efforts to get information double-checked before publication.

The reporters from the television news channels had been less aggressive and Drake had provided an interview to the Welsh language channel S4C which added nothing of substance other than calling for the eyewitnesses on the CCTV footage to come forward. He needed coffee and he detoured to the kitchen with Sara. His routine was well practised.

'What did you make of the press conference, boss?' Sara said.

'I just hope the witnesses come forward. The images are pretty grainy.'

'Somebody must know who they are.'

They took their coffee through into the Incident Room and sat by the desks. Drake wanted to hear from Luned and Winder about progress.

Winder was the first to respond. 'I think I've tracked down the second of Mervyn Peel's henchmen. He was on a video showing various aspects of the background work the Peel Foundation did to support community groups in South Africa.'

'South Africa?' Drake said.

'But he is English, and he's called Simon. I managed to drag his first name from various interviews and conversations they had for promotional videos. I've added his name and screenshot of his face to the board.'

Drake glanced over at the board and noticed a photograph of Martin Swan and the image of Simon alongside each other under the smiling face of Mervyn Peel.

'Good work, Gareth. Next step is to establish if this Simon is at the premises locally.'

Drake looked over at Luned. 'How did you get on with Edward Murphy's computer?'

'There's a lot of material. There are dozens of folders relating to the various properties in the Peel Foundation's portfolio. And I haven't had an opportunity of going through all of them as yet. He had a folder relating to a property owned by Martha and Mervyn Peel in a personal folder. I was quite surprised to find it there.'

'We know that property was transferred from the Peel Foundation to their personal ownership quite recently. There must have been a reason for that,' Drake said.

'But he also had an estate agent's brochure relating to a new acquisition in Cape Town.'

'Circulate a list with all the details.'

He was well overdue a mind map exercise and rather than scribble it out on his desk he decided to undertake the exercise at the board. He finished his drink, stood up and walked over to it.

'Jack Holt was murdered at the park in town. His head was caved in and his body pinned to the bowling green.' Drake drew an arrow to the picture of Edward Murphy below Jack Holt. 'And the circumstances of Murphy's death are very similar although he was killed with a lump hammer recovered from the scene.'

'I'll chase the CSIs about the forensic results on that hair follicle they recovered,' Sara said.

Drake turned away from the board for a moment and nodded at her. He stepped back and paused and then he turned and pointed at David Ackland. 'Ackland went to the same school as Jack Holt and Edward Murphy. He would have known all about the punishment ritual. And we know Ackland lied about where he was the night Holt was killed.'

'What would be Ackland's motive to kill Edward

Murphy?' Sara said.

'Revenge?' Winder said.

'After thirty odd years, that's stretching it,' Luned said.

'Let's look at the evidence. We might be able to track David Ackland's mobile to Edward Murphy's property, but we need it first. I don't think we delay.'

'But what about Mervyn Peel?' Sara said. 'He must have had a perfect motive for killing Jack Holt. After all, the journalist was on a one-man mission to expose the Peel Foundation.'

'But why would he want to kill Edward Murphy who worked for him?' Winder said.

Drake looked over at Luned. 'There's something in those folders and files on Edward Murphy's computer. Perhaps he found something he shouldn't have done. Perhaps he was going to expose Mervyn Peel. Peel gets wind of what's going to happen and decides the only way to protect the Peel Foundation is to get Edward Murphy out of the way.'

Three heads nodded over at Drake in unison.

'Is there any point in looking at Edward Murphy's career before he joined the Peel Foundation?' Luned said.

'Of course there is. We need to know everything about Murphy.' Drake looked over at Sara. 'Let's get organised for an interview with David Ackland in the morning.'

Chapter 29

Drake arrived early at headquarters after a journey where his mind had been dominated by the punishment rituals meted out to pupils at Fremantle High. The person responsible for Jack Holt and Edward Murphy's deaths knew all about the staking outs. And David Ackland had to be a prime suspect. Drake had already warned the custody sergeant to expect them with Ackland for interview that morning.

Before leaving the previous evening, he had outlined an interview plan with Sara. But things never went according to plan, and he often had to adapt and improvise. He indicated off the A55 and made for the newsagent where he'd buy his broadsheet for the sudoku puzzle. He parked and scanned adjacent vehicles for any sign of Brian Powell. Satisfied there was no sign of the London hack he left his vehicle and returned moments later with the newspaper which he opened to the right page. Completing a few squares always settled his mind. It gave him order for the day.

He laid the carefully folded newspaper on the passenger seat and drove over to headquarters. Sara was already in the Incident Room, a coffee mug on her desk.

'Morning, sir.'

'Morning, I wonder what David Ackland has planned this morning?'

Drake sauntered over to the board.

'Whatever it is we're going to disrupt it big time.'

Drake looked over at Ackland's image.

'I've organised for two uniformed officers to assist us,' Sara said.

'And we'll need a search team once we've arrested him.'

Drake pointed a finger at Ackland's image.

'Do you want a coffee before we leave?' Sara said.

Drake turned towards her. He shook his head. 'Let's get Ackland into the custody suite as soon as possible so he can be interviewed.'

Sara finished her drink and called the two uniformed officers waiting to assist with the arrest. Then she followed Drake down to the main reception. There was still a scattering of snow on the parkland outside Northern Division headquarters. Temperatures had increased since the very cold snap at the weekend when there had been a dumping of snow.

Drake's BMW formed the second vehicle in the short convoy that took the journey to David Ackland's home. He pulled in at the kerb behind the marked police car. Drake and Sara walked up to the front door. They rang the bell and waited. Moments later Ackland stood at the threshold, coffee mug in hand. The quizzical look he gave them soon evaporated into a hard defiant stare when he saw the marked police vehicle.

'David Ackland, I'm arresting you on suspicion of the murder of Jack Holt.' Drake completed the standard police caution.

'I don't believe this. You must be absolutely mad.'

'We'll need you to come with us.'

Ackland paused for a moment as though he expected Drake and Sara to leave and that all of this was a nasty dream. But he turned on his heel and Drake and Sara followed him into the house. He deposited his coffee mug on the breakfast table, dragged on a coat and left with the two uniformed police officers.

The kitchen had an ordered atmosphere. Drake admired the complicated coffee machine standing in one corner. There was no sign of any breakfast materials – no boxes of cereal or plates with crumbs of toast or jars of marmalade.

Sara was already working her way through the other rooms on the ground floor when Drake joined her in a room where a piano had pride of place.

'This is a music room, I'd say,' Sara said.

Drake nodded.

They paused for a few moments in the sitting room

where they had first spoken to David Ackland at the beginning of the inquiry. Drake didn't recall the heavy and substantial furniture. They all looked uncomfortable as though they had been designed to inflict pain on any user.

'Let's have a look upstairs.' Drake looked at his watch. 'The search team should be here any minute.'

They took the stairs to the first floor. There were three bedrooms and a bathroom. The master bedroom was as neat and tidy as the kitchen. Drake would have expected an unmade bed, perhaps clothes draped over a bedroom chair, socks on the floor. It looked as though nobody had slept in it the night before. The beds in the other two rooms had bare mattresses.

'I don't like this place, it's soulless,' Sara said.

'It's completely different to the home of Teresa Ostler.'

'I can't imagine how Jack Holt could have lived here if he was going to make a life with her.'

Drake heard a vehicle in the drive outside and he retreated down to the hallway. A sergeant entered, two uniformed officers behind him.

'It's all yours. Let me know when you have finished.' The sergeant nodded at his officers who entered the kitchen.

Drake turned to Sara, realising one thing that had struck him. 'Did you notice any condolence cards?'

Sara shook her head.

'There wasn't one.'

'Maybe he's kept them all out of sight or shredded them.'

'It's all very sad. Something really wrong here.'

It was a short drive to the area custody suite, where Drake parked before marching over to the entrance where he punched in his security number. The door buzzed open and he entered.

The temperature inside never varied. A dull hum reverberated around the place and the smell of bleach hung in the air. Drake walked over to the custody sergeant's desk.

'Ackland's solicitor has just arrived,' the custody sergeant turned to Drake.

'That was quick.'

'He knew exactly who he wanted to instruct.'

Drake organised the tapes he needed for the interview. He found the room allocated. Sara left to arrange for Ackland and his representative to join them.

Drake didn't have to wait long for Ackland to enter and sit at the table opposite Drake. His solicitor was someone Drake knew well. Frances Owen had short, cropped hair and a stern jaw. She had an aggressive style which clients seemed to love.

'Morning, Frances,' Drake said.

She nodded back in acknowledgement.

'You know Detective Sergeant Sara Morgan.'

'Yes, of course.'

Drake looked over at Ackland. He sat perfectly still looking over at Drake – his defiant stare replaced by a hard gaze.

Drake dropped the cassettes into the tape machine and once it was ready Drake asked his first question.

'How long have you been in a relationship with Jack Holt?'

'Eight years.'

'And how would you describe your relationship?'

'It was loving and permanent.' Ackland emphasised the last word.

'Did he get on with your family?'

'I don't have anything to do with them.'

'Why not?'

'They refuse to acknowledge who I am... my sexuality.' He looked over at Frances for support. She nodded.

'And how did you get on with Jack's parents?'

'We rarely saw them.'

'And why was that?'

'I can't tell you.'

'We've spoken with Jack's parents and they painted a picture of you as a manipulative, difficult individual who didn't want anything to do with them. Would that be an accurate description?'

'Jack and I were making a life together and they didn't want anything to do with us.'

'What you mean is they didn't want anything to do with you. Did you realise they saw Jack regularly?' Drake looked straight into David Ackland's eyes searching for any reaction, any sign of weakness.

He blinked and struggled to maintain eye contact. Then he swallowed awkwardly.

'Whenever Jack was away with his work he would always make a point of visiting his parents, without you. Were you aware of that?'

Ackland stiffened and raised his head, pinching his lips together as though he couldn't demean himself by replying.

'It must have made you angry he was maintaining a loving relationship with his parents against your wishes.'

'You don't understand.'

'Then please explain.'

'It's difficult.'

Drake waved a hand over at the tape machine. 'We have enough tapes to record hours of interview if that's your preference.'

Ackland pouted.

Drake consulted the interview plan and Sara nodded at the next bullet point of his proposed questioning.

'You had quite a fiery relationship with Jack. We have evidence of regular and vociferous arguments between you. Can you tell me what those arguments were about?'

'You cannot possibly rely on the evidence of Mr and Mrs Wakeling.'

'Why not?'

'They're homophobic bigots.'

'What makes you believe that?'

Ackland shot a desperate look at his solicitor. She gave him a neutral nod.

'Let me come back to the subject of your arguments with Jack. Is it true Jack settled a number of your gambling debts at the beginning of your relationship?'

Sara reached into the file of papers and extracted a copy of the record provided by the credit card company clearly listing the various gambling firms where Ackland had spent money. She slipped it across to Drake who pushed it over the table at Ackland. 'This is a detailed list of the debts at the time your relationship with Jack Holt began. Can you confirm he settled all these?'

Ackland nodded.

Drake had to interject. 'For the purposes of the tape Mr Ackland is nodding his head.'

Sara gave him another sheet of paper with the latest debts owed by Ackland.

'And this is a summary of your existing credit card debts. They are quite substantial and have been outstanding for some time.'

Ackland gazed at the piece of paper as though it was the first time he had seen it.

'Did Jack refuse to pay these debts?'

Ackland didn't reply.

'We believe he wasn't prepared to bail you out a second time. That must have made you really angry.'

Ackland fidgeted with his fingers.

'You must have been desperate. Who was going to pay your debts if Jack didn't do so?'

'You're twisting everything.' Ackland spat out the reply.

'How am I twisting things, Mr Ackland? You've got massive financial problems. We know about arguments between you and Jack. It must've all been too much for you. He had made a will leaving you everything. The red mist must have descended and you thought the only way was to kill him.'

'All this is a bit thin,' Frances said. 'Are we going to move on?'

Drake paused. It had been agreed Sara would take the next stage of the questioning.

'Where did you go to school, Mr Ackland?'

He frowned at her but Drake could see the worry in his face.

'I went to Freemantle High in Dorset. It's one of the best regarded public schools of England.'

'And you must be aware Jack had also been a pupil.'

'Of course, that's a stupid question.'

'One of the other inquiries we have in hand is the murder of Edward Murphy.'

Frances Owen interjected. 'What the hell is this about? Are you treating my client as a suspect in that murder?'

'It would help if your client would simply answer our questions,' Sara retorted. 'And Mr Murphy was a pupil at Freemantle High too.'

'What the hell has that got to do with anything?' Ackland sounded desperate.

'You must be aware one of the punishment rituals common place at Freemantle High during the time you were a pupil was "staking out". It basically used croquet hoops to pin a pupil to the lawn of the quad and other pupils would run at the prone body with a dustbin full of water. It must have been a frightening experience. Were you ever subject to a stakeout?'

Ackland didn't respond. He looked visibly shrunken and colour had drained from his face.

'Both Jack and Edward had been pinned to the ground with croquet hoops. It suggests their killer knew about the punishment ritual, at Freemantle High. Were you ever subjected to that punishment?'

When Ackland replied his voice was small, pinched. 'Very often it wasn't just punishment. If you said something wrong to one of the prefects or did something they didn't like you could be staked out. It was a vicious place and the masters at the time just allowed it to take place.'

Ackland looked down at the table, his lawyer adding. 'Anyone familiar with Freemantle High could have found out about this 'staking out' as you call it.'

Drake turned his attention back to the outline plan for the interview. He asked the next question.

'I'd like you to examine this photograph.' Drake pushed over a screenshot of the CCTV coverage from the café with an image of the red car. 'We've been able to identify from the registration number of this vehicle that it belongs to you.' Drake shared the registration number.

Ackland nodded.

'It was seen travelling in Colwyn Bay late in the evening Jack Holt was killed. When we asked you to account for your movements on the evening he died you said you had been at home. That's not true, is it, David. Why did you lie to us?'

Ackland opened his mouth as though he were beginning to say something but the words didn't form.

'And were you aware that Jack was having a relationship with another person?'

A flash of recognition crossed Ackland's eyes. Drake knew then that Ackland knew about Teresa Ostler.

'It must have driven you insane with jealousy when you knew that Jack Holt was planning to leave you, for a woman.'

Ackland looked at Frances Owen for support. Then he glanced at Sara before looking at Drake.

'Your relationship was coming to an end. There was nothing you could do about it and you were going to be left homeless and with no money. You decided that Jack had to die didn't you?'

Unadulterated terror broke out on Ackland's face. It crumpled and twisted. He drew a hand through his hair and over his forehead. 'I don't believe this is happening.'

Chapter 30

Luned settled down to a morning's work, pleased Winder wasn't in the Incident Room. He had been called to the house-to-house team near Edward Murphy's property. It was the sort of trip out of headquarters he would enjoy. It gave her an opportunity to focus on the paperwork provided by Alex Normanton, Jack Holt's editor. She expected Inspector Drake and Sara to be back by early afternoon after having concluded their interview with David Ackland. She wanted to have something concrete to report to them when they got back. And it would be interesting to hear exactly what David Ackland had had to say.

If he admitted immediately he was responsible for Jack Holt's death then at least that would be progress. But it would leave Edward Murphy's murder unresolved. She started on the papers Alex Normanton had left. The folders contained working papers and notebooks Jack Holt had assembled for investigations he had conducted. One of the more interesting that grabbed her attention was a people-trafficking ring bringing young girls in from Eastern Europe. It disgusted Luned that anybody would seek to take advantage of women in this way. They were no more than teenagers, promised good salaries and comfortable homes only to find they were expected to work in the sex industry.

Another related to a financial scam perpetrated on individuals who wanted to maximise returns on capital. Luned's initial reaction of little sympathy was soon changed when she saw the figures bandied about by the conmen as possible returns. They were taking advantage of vulnerable people although one part of her mind reminded her they really should have known better.

Jack Holt travelled a lot if he found a story that interested him. He had travelled to the Channel Islands when he thought he had a story about smugglers moving cheap liquor into the United Kingdom. Another story about animal cruelty had taken him to the Highlands of Scotland. Luned marvelled at his attention to a good cause and wondered how he kept an objective mind. He had investigated all sorts of people who were the dregs of society.

She turned to papers relating to the Peel Foundation. It was a substantial collection of notebooks, papers and photographs. Jack Holt had clearly been obsessed with his work on the Foundation. The drafts of the articles he had written made it quite clear what he felt about Mervyn Peel and his impact on vulnerable people. Jack Holt had spoken to a number of families who had lost loved ones to the Foundation. Many had described it as a cult, like those fanatical religious sects she heard about on the television occasionally.

It amazed her how a man like Peel could have such control over individuals. People could be naïve and trusting and if they were in the right frame of mind they might be taken in by anything. She found photographs of Mervyn Peel taken outside various properties. She recognised one as the Foundation's offices in London. Another had him hailing a yellow taxi in New York. There were others taken in various cities around the globe. She was certain she recognised Sydney Harbour Bridge in one photograph and the harbour in Stockholm in another.

Jack Holt had managed to get hold of photographs of Mervyn Peel with celebrity TV presenters. There were other smiling faces with Peel that Luned didn't recognise. It took a few moments to scan the images into the Incident Room system and she shared them with the rest of the team.

It struck Luned as odd there was a collection of photographs of Martha Peel, independent of her husband. Jack Holt must have decided to follow her, hoping perhaps she might have helped him with questions about the Foundation.

There were photographs of her in cafés and restaurants. She was frequently photographed with Martin Swan, who

Inspector Drake had met and who had assaulted Holt in London. Martha Peel clearly enjoyed the man's company. He looked to be younger than her but it was difficult to be precise from the photographs.

Although she was intrigued Luned knew she had to move on to the computer removed from Edward Murphy's office.

Inspector Drake had been focused on making the connection between Jack Holt and Edward Murphy and the Peel Foundation. Luned suspected there was more going on. After making herself a coffee she began the work of examining the contents of Murphy's computer.

There was a lot of information about the finances of the Peel Foundation. She found dozens of Excel spreadsheets and taking a cursory look at each she knew she needed more technical help. She rang a colleague in the economic crime unit.

'I need some help,' Luned said.

'And I thought everyone in Detective Inspector Drake's team was invincible.' Hywel Lloyd had joined the force at the same time as Luned and she knew him from various training courses.

'We're investigating the murders of Jack Holt and Edward Murphy, who was an accountant with the Peel Foundation.'

'I've heard about the case. From what I've heard it's a bit macabre, didn't the killer use croquet hoops to pin them to the ground?'

Luned could see now how easy it would be for information to have reached the ears of Brian Powell.

'I need to have some spreadsheets prepared by Edward Murphy examined. And I need it done quickly.'

'And here I was sitting at my desk thinking that I might take the day off and play golf.'

'Don't be silly, Hywel.'

'Okay, just send them over to me. I can probably spare

an hour this morning.'

Luned sent the various spreadsheets over to her colleague and hoped by the time Drake and Sara had returned she'd have something positive to tell them.

She turned back to the rest of the documentation in Edward Murphy's computer. After half an hour of scrolling through various folders she had an idea of how he organised everything. At least that gave her a place to start. There were annual accounts and formal Companies House records as well as tax returns. The accountants for the Foundation prepared annual reports and from cursory examination the capital assets were substantial.

Every course organised by the Foundation had its own folder with details of the activity and who the new recruits had been. It led her to examine another folder with the names of new supporters of the Foundation. The numbers surprised her. How could people part with such capital without any guarantee of return? They were being sold nothing better than empty promises their personal well-being would be enhanced by joining the Foundation.

She found a folder with photographs that included a separate folder titled "Martha P and M". The image of Martin Swan appeared in the folder with Martha.

She turned to social media recalling that Winder had already mentioned his cousin having a Facebook page. She had barely begun when the telephone rang.

'Thanks for sending me the spreadsheets,' Hywel said.

'Did you make any sense of them?'

'The Peel Foundation certainly has a lot of assets but they're struggling for income. There are different items of expenditure which could very well be the cost of maintaining Mr Peel in the lifestyle to which he has become accustomed.'

'Anything illegal?'

Lloyd snorted. 'It's taken me an hour to look at them. And that is literally a snapshot. If you want us to have a look at the Foundation in more detail you need to get your inspector to make a formal request to allocate time and resources.'

'Do you think it's worthwhile doing that?'

'Are the finances of the Peel Foundation an issue in the murder investigation?'

Luned wasn't at all certain that was the case. She thanked Hywel for his help and returned to the work in hand. She took a screen shot of one of the images of Martha Peel and Martin Swan. Then she pinned it to the board. Why did Jack Holt and Edward Murphy have photographs of Martha Peel and this man together? She didn't know the answer but guessed Inspector Drake would want one soon enough.

Chapter 31

'So what did you make of that?' Sara said.

'We'll keep him overnight. Hopefully the search team will turn up evidence we can put to him in the morning.'

'He knew all about Jack Holt and Teresa Ostler, right enough.'

Drake nodded. 'He's a nasty piece of work. He's more than capable of murdering Jack Holt.'

'I'm not certain about his reaction to Edward Murphy.'

'The atmosphere in that school must have been vicious.

'Aren't all public schools the same?'

Sara sat with Drake in the canteen at the area custody suite. She'd chosen a flaccid tuna sandwich which she washed down with an odd-coloured soft drink. She knew better than to offer to buy Drake coffee so she'd included a bottle of water when she ordered his lunch.

A proper debriefing after an interview with the suspect always took time and they needed to assess exactly how they proceeded. If David Ackland wasn't charged with Jack Holt's murder he'd be released pending further investigation. There had been enough to justify his arrest and interview. His angry comments about the Peel Foundation and the impact they had on Jack Holt's life had stuck in her mind. Was there something he hadn't said?

Once they had finished their lunch Drake announced he wanted to visit David Ackland's property on the way back to headquarters. Sara had hoped she'd be able to finish early that afternoon. The freezing cold weather had meant it was impossible for her to run on the road. She didn't feel safe doing so, and now looked forward to a session in the local gym.

On the journey from the custody suite Sara took the opportunity to re-evaluate everything they knew about David Ackland. 'We can place him near the scene. We know they had vicious arguments. And we know Jack Holt was intending to leave him for a woman which must have made him incandescent with rage.'

Drake slowed at a roundabout. 'He certainly ticks all the boxes.'

'We can't place him in the park, delivering the fatal blow.'

'Let's see what the search team have to tell us.'

The search team vehicle, a van big enough to carry several officers, was tucked discreetly into the rear of the driveway at Ackland's property. Drake reversed up the drive and parked.

The door into the house was ajar and Drake pushed it open. The sergeant in charge must have heard him as he emerged from the sitting room.

'We've just finished the first interview with Ackland.'

'Did he confess?'

'No, we're going to be holding him overnight. I want to know if you found anything and once we've had a full report by the morning I'll interview him again.'

'We haven't found anything to help your inquiry. No clothes with any blood residue in the house or the garage or garden shed.'

'Anything at all to spark your interest?'

The search team supervisor shook his head. 'We should have finished later today. Then I'll get a report done. Don't hold your breath.'

Drake nodded at Sara who followed him back to the car.

They sat in the vehicle for a few moments. Unless they had some physical evidence to link Ackland to Jack Holt's murder he wasn't going to be charged immediately. The case would have to go for review by a Crown prosecution lawyer. And that meant delays. Drake wouldn't like that, Sara knew.

'Let's get back to headquarters. Hopefully Luned will have made some progress.'

Drake drove the short distance back to headquarters. After parking they made their way up to the Incident Room.

Sara was surprised Gareth Winder wasn't present and Luned offered an explanation immediately.

'He went down to assist the house-to-house enquiry team near the home of Edward Murphy.'

Drake emerged from his office after shrugging off his winter coat. He walked over to the board and immediately noticed that Luned had added a photograph next to the image of Martha Peel.

'That's an image of Martin Swan.'

'You'd better explain,' Drake said.

'I've been working on the papers Alex Normanton left you, boss. I discovered a lot of photographs Jack Holt had taken. There were dozens and dozens of images of Mervyn Peel and other members of his organisation. However, what took my attention was the fact he photographed Martha Peel with Martin Swan on several occasions.'

'Swan was most uncooperative when we visited the Foundation.'

Luned nodded. 'It's going to take me a couple of days to work through everything. I sent some of the spreadsheets in the folder to DC Hywel Lloyd in the economic crime department. He suggested the Peel Foundation has a lot of assets but issues with their cash flow.'

'And presumably he suggested I contact his inspector if I want their time allocated.'

'Yes, boss.'

'Good work, Luned.'

'How did you get on with David Ackland?'

'He didn't confess, unfortunately,' Sara said. 'And we called at the property on the way back but the search team haven't unearthed anything to help us.'

'At least not yet.' Drake was staring at the images on the board. 'Let's go back over the CCTV footage from the dashcam of the police car as well as from that café. And I want to go over all the house-to-house enquiries around the park. Before I submit a file to the Crown Prosecution Service about deciding on whether to charge David Ackland, we need to have exhausted every line of inquiry.'

Winder entered the Incident Room. 'Have I missed something?'

'We've completed the interview with David Ackland. We believe he knew about Teresa Ostler but he didn't admit to it. And he knew Edward Murphy from school but denied he was responsible for his death.'

Sara said to Winder, 'Why did you go down to the mobile incident room near Murphy's place?'

'It was a waste of time. There was a time-waster who insisted on speaking to a senior detective from the team in charge of the inquiry. God knows how he was satisfied with me.'

The other officers didn't have an opportunity to reply before Mike Foulds the crime scene manager barged in.

'All the team gathered together in one place – excellent,' Foulds said. 'We've had the results of the DNA test on the hair follicle we recovered from the lump hammer.'

Foulds walked over to the board and scanned the faces on it.

Sara hadn't seen him draw out sharing information with quite such theatricality before.

'Get on with it, Mike. If you got something to share, spill the beans,' Drake said.

'The results have come back and it's quite clear the hair belongs to a woman.'

Nobody said anything for a moment.

'That is not very helpful,' Winder responded.

'And her DNA isn't on the national database,' Foulds added.

'At least we have a DNA sample,' Drake said.

Sara thought about the implications. It didn't rule out David Ackland as the murderer. It didn't rule Mervyn Peel out as the killer; it just meant a woman had left a hair follicle on the lump hammer.

Drake thanked Foulds, who left, and he walked over to the board and pointed at Martha Peel. 'She and Teresa Ostler are the only women who feature in the inquiry.'

'I don't think anything points to Ostler as the killer,' Luned said.

Sara nodded. 'We haven't found anything to suggest she might be involved.'

'Which leaves Martha Peel and Mervyn Peel, possibly working together,' Drake said before turning to the team. 'Let's make progress.'

Chapter 32

Drake sat at his desk peering at the monitor. The answer to Jack Holt and Edward Murphy's murders was on the board in the Incident Room. He just couldn't see it now and frustration was the dominant emotion in his mind. He hated the prospect the killer or killers would go unpunished. There was something missing: some essential piece of the jigsaw they hadn't found.

Sara put her head around his office door and offered to make coffee. And when she returned he waved a hand for her to sit.

'I can't help feeling we've missed something. We'll wait until the morning before deciding about his release. Hopefully the search team will have something we can use for a second interview.'

The mobile on Drake's desk rang as he was halfway through his coffee. He wanted to compliment Sara as she had got the drink tasting just as he liked.

He didn't recognise the number. 'Detective Inspector Drake.'

'It's Zoe Lloyd.'

Drake wasn't expecting her to call, and he looked over at Sara who gave him a quizzical look. 'How can I help you, Zoe?'

'I need to speak to you.'

'You know I can't discuss anything about the complaints made by the Peel Foundation against you and the others.'

'It's not about that.'

'I'll be at headquarters all afternoon if you want to call in.'

'You must be joking. I wouldn't be seen dead there. There's a café in Deganwy called The Hungry Ferret. I'll be there in an hour.' She finished the call.

Drake looked over at Sara. 'That was Zoe Lloyd.'

Sara frowned.

'She was one of the demonstrators outside the Peel Foundation I suspected knew more about Jack Holt. She wants to meet.'

It had been two days since Drake had seen Superintendent Hobbs for his formal review. Drake reckoned it would take fifteen minutes or so to reach Deganwy so he had at least half an hour to prepare an updated progress report for Hobbs. He completed the standard template in good time and after he pressed send, he left his office, Sara joining him as they headed downstairs.

'Have you ever been to The Hungry Ferret?' Drake said, starting the engine of his BMW.

'I can't say I've had the pleasure,' Sara said. 'And where is this café exactly?'

'Deganwy and there's no need to bother with the satnav.'

Drake pulled out of the junction by headquarters into the stream of traffic and then indicated left towards the A55. He left the dual carriageway at the exit for Llandudno and Deganwy. It wasn't long until he saw a parade of shops and a colourfully designed sign with the café's name.

He found a slot to park and they walked the short distance down to the café.

The place had an old-fashioned bell that was triggered when the door opened. The owner gave Drake and Sara a surprised look as though he wasn't expecting to see a man in a suit and a woman dressed smartly to frequent his premises.

Drake scanned the customers and spotted Zoe in the far corner. He ordered drinks for himself and Sara. He couldn't resist the opportunity of a millionaire shortbread so he ordered two.

Drake sat down at the table with Zoe. He hadn't noticed when he first met her that she had lively, attractive eyes but he had been distracted by her nose and ear piercings.

'You sounded as though it was urgent,' Drake said.

Zoe gave Sara a challenging glare.

'You remember Detective Sergeant Sara Morgan, don't you?' Drake added making clear he wasn't going to have her challenge Sara's presence.

Zoe nodded briskly.

'Word on the street is you've arrested Jack Holt's partner.' Zoe sounded remarkably well informed.

'And who gave you that information?'

'I've got my sources.'

A waitress came over with Drake's coffee and Sara's tea as well as the biscuits he'd ordered. He took a mouthful, enjoying the chocolate and shortbread.

'You said you wanted to talk to me.'

'It's about the Peel Foundation.'

'What can you tell me about them?' Drake recalled Zoe's voice when she had shared with him her family's experience of Mervyn Peel.

'You don't need me to tell you Mervyn Peel and his operation are basically a scam.'

Drake paused to take a mouthful of coffee. 'You didn't invite me here to tell me something I already know.'

Zoe sipped on the tea she was drinking. She looked at him intensely.

'I've been talking to somebody inside the Peel Foundation.'

She made the statement sound like an important announcement.

'Who is it?'

'I can't tell you; I won't tell you until you promise me that everything will be kept confidential.'

Drake took another chunk of the biscuit, realising he was enjoying the sugar hit. A sandwich from the canteen at area custody suite at lunchtime was hardly going to be enough sustenance.

'And how does this help us? I've got a murder enquiry.'

'And Mervyn Peel is one of your suspects isn't he?'

Drake didn't respond. He took another sip of coffee.

Sooner or later Zoe would tell him exactly why she wanted to meet.

'We have several lines of inquiry.'

'Jack Holt was a thorn in Mervyn Peel's side. He was working on a major story that would have meant Mervyn Peel being investigated for fraud.'

'So is time running out for Mervyn Peel?'

Zoe nodded. 'There's somebody I want you to meet.'

'Who is it?'

'I can't tell you unless you agree not to involve that person in your inquiry. The person is very concerned about their safety. Mervyn Peel has tentacles everywhere and my friend will only agree to see you on those terms.'

'How do I know this person has anything constructive to share with us?'

'You have to trust me.'

Drake wasn't at all certain he was prepared to do anything of the sort. He wasn't going to indulge Zoe and her friends. But why she had made contact intrigued him. The detective in him wanted to hear what this person had to say, wanted to decide if it was valuable evidence.

'The only basis upon which I'm prepared to see your friend is the basis I'd see any witness in any murder inquiry. If this person has anything of value, I want to hear it. And I want to hear it without delay. This isn't some sort of game, Zoe. Two people have been killed. If your friend has any information, he or she has a public duty to come forward.' Drake was tempted to get up there and then and leave but he looked over at Sara who was staring over at Zoe.

'Does this friend of yours fear for their personal safety?'

Zoe nodded.

'If the evidence is helpful then we can always provide witness protection. But we need to see your friend first.'

Drake got to his feet. They had accommodated Zoe as much as they could. He wasn't going to be held to ransom by an unknown person with unknown evidence.

'You know where I am. Contact me at any time.'

Chapter 33

Drake arrived early the following morning. It was dark when he left his home and night would have fallen before he arrived back. It meant the working days seemed long.

He arrived at the Incident Room and the first thing needing his attention was a decision on David Ackland. It surprised him Zoe Lloyd knew he'd been arrested. How on earth did she know that had happened? Leaks to reporters happened routinely but it surprised him she was so well informed. He checked his inbox for a report from the search team supervisor and noted it had been sent a little after seven am.

He clicked it open and began reading its contents. He knew after the first summary paragraph there was nothing to help him make a final decision about David Ackland. He needed to have the case reviewed by a lawyer and the Crown Prosecution Service before charging. And that meant putting the papers together, but more than anything it meant releasing Ackland on bail to come back to the police station at some future point.

They still had Ackland's mobile and personal computer to examine. By tracking his mobile they might be able to establish his movements for the evenings Jack Holt and Edward Murphy had been killed.

He heard Sara arrive in the Incident Room and he called her into his office.

'We've had the report from the search team.'

'Not good news I take it.'

Drake nodded reluctantly. 'We'll need to release him pending further enquiries.'

'I'll get Gareth and Luned to work on his mobile and personal computer.'

'Thanks.' Drake reached for his mobile and called the area custody suite. He didn't need to be present when Ackland walked free. He didn't want to watch his gloating face.

After simple instructions to the custody sergeant Drake got back to work.

Zoe Lloyd's comments the previous afternoon were bubbling in the back of his mind. Peel had an alibi for most of the evening of Jack Holt's murder – Leonard Ferrier's confirmation saw to that – but he could still have killed Holt. And what Luned had learned about the finances of the Peel Foundation clearly helped. They needed cash. Getting Holt out of the way was solving a problem.

A regret played in his mind that perhaps he should have agreed to see Zoe Lloyd and her friend on her terms. But he couldn't agree to treat her any differently to any other witness. Mervyn Peel's motive for disposing of Jack Holt was clear enough but why would he want to kill Edward Murphy? Unless the accountant had learned something he shouldn't.

Drake clicked into the files and folders from Murphy's computer; despite the work Luned had completed already, he wanted to undertake the exercise himself. Get a feel for the man. Identify what exactly was going on. After all, a fresh mind might well pick up something Luned had missed.

He glanced over at the Post-it notes on his desk, realising that since yesterday he hadn't double-checked for progress. Scribbled on one at the back was the word "taxi" and he realised he didn't know about progress with the taxi company.

He went through into the Incident Room. 'Has anybody tracked down the taxi driver spotted on the CCTV footage?'

'We're still waiting to hear from them,' Winder said.

'Dammit. I'll get down there now.' He nodded at Sara for her to join him. 'And double-check that we haven't overlooked anything else.'

'Yes, boss,' Winder and Luned replied in unison.

Drake accelerated a little too quickly out of headquarters and had to brake hard at the junction. He knew it was a simple thing to overlook but the taxi driver might have seen something or somebody they could connect to the murder of Jack Holt.

'Everyone's working as best they can,' Sara said.

'I realise that, Sara. But we can't afford to allow something like this to slip through the cracks.'

Improving temperatures had meant fewer cars appeared in traffic with snow topped roofs. But it was still slushy underfoot, so Drake was especially careful as he pulled up and parked outside the offices of the taxi company.

Colwyn Taxis was an old, established company he had used personally when he lived in the town. A tall, thin woman with a long face sat at a reception desk behind a screen. 'Can I help you?'

Drake pushed over his warrant card. Sara did likewise.

'I'll call the boss.' She disappeared before Drake had an opportunity to explain the nature of their visit.

A man in his fifties with greased, slicked-back hair entered the office vacated by the receptionist.

'What's this about?'

'I'm in charge of the investigation into the death of Jack Holt. His body was found in the park a week last Monday. We've recovered some CCTV footage that shows one of your vehicles,' Drake nodded for Sara who repeated the registration number, 'driving down a street near the park.'

'And you want to talk to the driver? Give me a minute.'

He sat by the desk and clicked through into a computer.

'If it was last Sunday, it might be easier.' He bobbed his head at the board which had a table displaying which driver was using which vehicle. 'After a week the board is cleaned.'

Drake began tapping the fingers of his right hand on the shelf of the opening looking into the office. Waiting patiently in the middle of a murder inquiry wasn't one of his talents.

The owner continued to stare at the monitor. Seconds

felt like minutes and Drake was about to encourage the man when he announced, 'You need to speak to Derek. He was driving that night.'

'And where will I find him?'

The owner glanced up at the board. 'Let me check.' He reached over and picked up a radio handset and after a few seconds was connected to the driver. 'Where are you, Derek?'

'I'm at the railway station. Front of the queue and there's a train in real soon.'

'Stay where you are.'

'I heard,' Drake said. 'Thanks for your help.'

The car was still warm when Drake and Sara got in. He wound his way through the town centre towards the railway station and parked on a double yellow line near the taxi rank.

Drake left the car, Sara following in his slipstream as he headed purposefully over towards the first taxi. He leaned down towards the driver's side window, pushing his warrant card against it.

A startled face looked at him before the window buzzed down.

'Are you Derek?'

'I haven't seen him this morning.'

'His boss spoke to him a few minutes ago. Where the bloody hell is he?'

'How would I know?'

Sara was already talking to the next car owned by Colwyn Taxis. She gestured to Drake for him to join her.

'I've got an address for Derek.'

'What the hell is wrong with these people? Let's go and find him.'

Drake almost jogged back to the car and Sara punched the details of the address into the satnav. Soon they had the disembodied voice telling them how to reach Derek's home. Drake wasted no time and less than five minutes later he was parked outside the taxi driver's home. His vehicle was parked a little distance along the street.

The front door badly needed more than just a lick of paint. It was falling apart and Drake was almost reluctant to thump on it. As he hammered it made a noise inside. There was a shout of protest and a man in his seventies with silver stubble appeared at the door ready to tackle the people disturbing his morning.

'Who the fuck are you?'

'Police.' Drake got as much aggression into his voice as he could. They flashed their warrant cards. 'Detective Inspector Ian Drake.' He didn't bother introducing Sara. Then he pushed his way into the house.

'What the fuck?'

'We have your vehicle on CCTV from a café in the middle of town driving down from the park Sunday before last when a Jack Holt was murdered there.'

Drake had found his way into the kitchen at the rear of the building. The place smelled and every surface was cluttered with pots and pans and empty bottles and cans of beer.

'It wasn't me, mate.'

'Your boss told me it was you.'

'That's what he thinks. I swapped with Tony. Know what I mean?' He tapped his nose with his forefinger as though he were sharing a state secret.

'No, I don't bloody know what you mean. And you better tell me double quick where Tony lives.'

'Keep calm, pal.' Derek dragged a mobile from his back pocket and made a call.

'Tony, it's Derek. I've got the cops here they want to talk to you.'

There was a pause. Drake said. 'Tell him he's not in any trouble.'

'You're not in any trouble, mate.'

Derek finished the call then turned to Drake dictating the address and postcode. Sara made a record of the details and extracted Tony's mobile number for good measure.

They left Derek and minutes later they were outside the block of flats where Tony lived.

'I hope this isn't another wild goose chase,' Drake said.

They reached the entrance door and found the bell for Tony's property. The door buzzed open seconds later. The front door of the flat on the second floor was ajar when they arrived. 'Tony,' Drake called out.

'In here.'

Drake followed the voice into the kitchen where a man in his twenties was coaxing a young baby to eat from a bottle of readymade food. A woman the same age fussed around.

'Are you the cops?' Tony said.

Drake flashed his warrant card but the man didn't pay it any attention.

'Go through and sit down,' the young woman said.

The sitting room had a comfortable sofa and strategically positioned scatter cushions. The sweet smell of perfumed candles lingered.

'How can I help?'

'Is it correct you were driving Derek's taxi the Sunday before last. We've got CCTV footage showing the vehicle near the park. You were turning at a junction near a café. I'm in charge of the investigation into the death of Jack Holt whose body was found on the Monday morning.'

'Yeah, I heard about it. And I was driving, but I don't know that I can help you much.'

'Did you see anything or anybody that took your attention?'

'There wasn't much traffic that night and I was on my way home. I'd just dropped off my last fare. I noticed a young couple walking. I remember that because it was freezing.'

'Do you remember any other vehicles?'

Tony looked away as though he were deep in thought. 'There wasn't much traffic. Come to think of it I saw a

Mercedes C-Class coupé. Those are really dead smart.'

'Anybody else walking?'

Tony shook his head.

'Do you remember anything about the C-Class coupé? How old was it? It's colour?'

Tony looked blank. 'It was late and I wanted to get home. I was doing Derek a favour. I don't think he told the boss.'

Drake got up. Sara followed.

'If you think of anything else, please contact me.' Drake was already thinking about the report he should be preparing for Hobbs and the work he needed to get done on all the paperwork on Murphy's computer.

'Sure thing. But do you want to see the dashcam footage?'

Chapter 34

Winder got straight to work on Edward Murphy's mobile. Top priority would be building a list of the numbers Murphy had called and the numbers that had called him. He had to be able to cross-reference everybody who had contacted the accountant. Since the demonstrations outside the Peel Foundation and the murder of Edward Murphy, Winder's mum had called him every evening. She always got straight to the point and asked if there were any developments.

He had told his mum and Auntie Gwen all about seeing Phoebe the previous Sunday, but he hadn't shared with them her refusal to return home. Instead he had invented a tale of how Martin Swan and Mervyn Peel had manhandled Phoebe to avoid him talking to her.

His Auntie Gwen couldn't possibly have known David Ackland had been arrested and interviewed but when he called her that morning before he left for work she sounded distant, detached, and he had the impression she had been awake for hours. He asked after Uncle Steve as he had every day since Sunday. 'He's out of danger,' Auntie Gwen had said. It pleased Winder and he promised to visit once he could.

Winder didn't have children, and he didn't anticipate being a father if his present girlfriend's steadfast opposition to parenthood continued. So he could only imagine what it must feel like for Auntie Gwen to be unable to contact her daughter, and to feel the hostile estrangement her involvement with the Peel Foundation created. He had told her clearly there was no information he could share with her.

Luned was focused on continuing to interrogate Edward Murphy's computer from the Peel Foundation. She had barely exchanged a word with him since Inspector Drake had left earlier with Sara. Somehow chasing the taxi company had been overlooked and Winder was annoyed with himself. He knew Inspector Drake would be irritable and brusque when he got back.

Edward Murphy had made no telephone calls immediately before he was killed. There were WhatsApp messages to and from other members of the Foundation, and it amazed Winder that Murphy had no social life or any life at all outside the Foundation.

Winder found it difficult to concentrate, knowing Phoebe was in the middle of that place. Did she know Edward Murphy? Had she worked with him?

When his mobile rang he snatched it off the desk, pleased at the interruption.

He didn't recognise the number. 'Detective Constable Winder,' he announced.

'Gareth, somebody you need to see.' Winder recognised the voice of Sergeant Turner who was coordinating the house-to-house inquiries near Edward Murphy's home.

'I'll be there as soon as I can.'

Winder announced to Luned he had a follow-up interview near Edward Murphy's home. She nodded but it didn't interrupt her flow or concentration.

He knew the journey well and within a few minutes he had reached the mobile incident room not far from Edward Murphy's home. He parked, dragged on a winter coat and found Turner sitting inside, shivering.

'It's bloody cold,' Turner said.

'What have you got for me?'

Once they were in Winder's car Turner gave him directions.

'One of the uniformed officers followed up the house-to-house enquiries at a property that was empty when we first called. The homeowner has information of assistance.'

The journey took them into the countryside and eventually Turner indicated for Winder to take a gravelled driveway up to a converted barn.

'It's a Mr Morrison.' Turner looked out of the windscreen. 'He's a bit eccentric.'

Winder nodded.

They left the vehicle and used the knocker on the door. It was a substantial cast-iron version that made a racket outside as well as inside.

There was no one on the threshold when the door opened. Winder noticed a figure disappearing down the hallway. 'Come in, and close the door,' the man shouted.

Turner and Winder entered the property. Turner closed the door firmly. They walked to the end of the hallway and through into a corridor that eventually led into a kitchen where logs crackled and hissed in a fireplace. Even so, the place felt cold. Morrison was wearing a thick cardigan, red corduroy trousers and a butcher's apron.

'This is Detective Constable Gareth Winder, Mr Morrison,' Turner said.

Morrison stopped chopping meat with an enormous cleaver and looked over at Winder. 'Are you in charge?'

'The senior investigating officer is Detective Inspector Drake. I'm part of his team. How can I help you? I understand you have information you want to share with us.'

'I spoke to one of the uniformed officers.' Morrison waved the cleaver in the direction of both officers. 'Apparently they'd called when I was away.'

'Did you know Mr Edward Murphy?'

'Of course not. Whatever gave you that idea? Never seen the man.'

Winder started to believe this could be a waste of his time. But he had seen and interviewed odd people before.

'I returned home,' Morrison continued, 'on the evening Edward Murphy was killed. It was late and it had been snowing badly. There were hardly any other vehicles on the road but I was taking the last few miles at a snail's pace. I wasn't going to take any risks.'

Winder glanced at Turner, who gave him a look that encouraged him to be patient.

'After I passed Edward Murphy's home, I noticed a car

in the layby on the left-hand side. It didn't have any snow on the roof or the bonnet which suggested it had recently been parked there.'

Winder sighed to himself – another armchair detective.

'It was a Mercedes C-Class coupé. I was going to buy one myself a couple of months ago but I opted for an SUV. It's a bit more practical living out here in the country.'

'Were you certain it was a Mercedes C-Class?'

'Yes, of course. I've seen it before.'

'Where was that?'

'Pulling out of Edward Murphy's drive a couple of months ago.'

Drake's tone of voice became more and more belligerent as he demanded the owner of Colwyn Taxis provide him with the dashcam footage.

'You wait till Derek comes in. He had no right to switch with Tony. I've got to know who's driving my cabs.'

'I just need the dashcam footage. And I need it now. Not tomorrow or next week.'

The owner looked at his watch and then at the time on a clock on the wall as though he needed to double-check.

'It might take me a while to find it.'

'Get onto it.'

'I don't know where she keeps all the recordings.'

'Well bloody well call her then and find out,' Drake snapped.

It had the desired effect of galvanising the owner into action and within half an hour Drake left with a hard drive. He made straight for the Incident Room and barely noticed Winder wasn't present. He didn't bother going to his office, getting Sara to plug the device into her computer. Moments later she had access to its content and the recordings appeared on screen.

'Fast-forward it to the right time and the Mercedes C-Class. Then you can watch the whole thing in real time.'

Sara nodded. Drake gave Luned a potted version of events, and she told him that Winder had been called to interview a potential witness from the house-to-house enquiries near Edward Murphy's home. Drake mumbled his understanding.

His frustration grew as Sara played the footage. There was no sign of a Mercedes C-Class. Why the hell had Tony said he had seen such a car? And he had been vague about where he had seen it. Speeding up the footage any more might well mean they'd miss a vital clue so Drake resolved to be more patient.

After twenty minutes he spotted a Mercedes C-Class.

'Where is that?' Drake said, frustrated that he hadn't been able to identify the location.

'It's that road leading to the park.'

'Why the hell was Tony there?"

'Maybe it was a short cut?'

'Is there any way we can identify who the driver was?'

Sara shook her head. 'It's not the best quality recording.'

Drake jotted down the registration number and headed for his office. Sara and Luned followed. Then he called the DVLA and demanded to be put through to the department dealing with police enquiries.

'Have you completed the usual form?' the voice said when Drake explained he needed a result immediately.

'This is a murder enquiry, for Christ's sake. I want to know who owns this vehicle immediately.'

'I don't know about that. I'll have to talk to my superior.'

'No, don't bother. Put me through to that person.'

Seconds later there was another voice. 'Is this really urgent?'

'Every murder is urgent. Now I want the owner's details immediately.'

After a brief period of silence Drake heard fingers on a keyboard and then a muffled conversation. The first person he spoke to came back on the line. 'The vehicle is registered to a Mervyn Peel and his address is—'

'I don't need the address.'

'I'll send you the details in the usual way.'

Drake slammed the phone down. Now he had more evidence that pointed at Mervyn Peel. His pulse quickened with the buzz of excitement that they were making progress. He turned to the two officers standing in his room. 'Mervyn Peel owns the Mercedes C-Class.'

Chapter 35

'I think it's time I did a full review with the superintendent and Andy Thorsen.' Drake referenced the senior Crown prosecution lawyer as he spoke to Sara standing by his side looking at the board. He stared at the image of Mervyn Peel and then at Martha Peel. Was it her DNA on the hammer? Had they both been present when Holt and Murphy had been killed.

'It might be Martha Peel's DNA on the murder weapon,' Sara said.

Drake nodded, pleased she was thinking the same as him.

Mervyn Peel had a perfect motive for Jack Holt's death. And now, with this record of his vehicle being spotted near the park on the evening of his death, they needed to ask him again whether he stuck to his alibi.

Leonard Ferrier had confirmed Peel's alibi for only part of the evening when Jack Holt had been killed. Now it was clear Peel had lied to them. Drake hated it when people lied to him.

He retreated to his office. He checked that the photographs of his family on the desk were just so before he tapped out a brief email to Superintendent Hobbs, copying in Andy Thorsen. It notified both he needed a meeting later that afternoon.

Drake heard Winder's voice when he returned to the Incident Room and immediately got to his feet and joined him.

'I've spoken to a witness this morning who gave me details about a vehicle he'd seen parked near Edward Murphy's home on the night he was killed. The car was out of place as there wasn't any snow on the roof or the bonnet and he'd seen the same model leaving Edward Murphy's home previously.' Winder said, discarding his coat over the back of a chair.

'And we've made progress with the footage from the taxi driver's dashcam,' Drake said, walking over to the board.

'This witness saw a Mercedes C-Class coupé. It's a pretty smart car and he recalled the make and model because he'd been thinking about buying one himself.'

'Mercedes C-Class. Excellent.' Drake raised his voice. 'That's exactly the make the taxi driver recorded on his footage and the car he spotted was owned by Mervyn Peel.'

Drake turned to face the board. 'I want a picture of a Mercedes C-Class on the board. We're overdue another conversation with Mervyn Peel.'

As Drake made his way back to his office the sergeant in charge of the search of David Ackland's home entered, carrying a holdall. Drake motioned for the officer to follow him into his room where Drake pointed at one of the visitor chairs.

'We found a box Ackland had secreted at the bottom of a drawer. It was full of press cuttings and articles about Freemantle High and stuff about Edward Murphy. It goes back over ten years. It looks like Ackland was obsessed with Murphy.'

The officer leaned down and pulled out a lever arch file from the holdall.

Something else for them to consider at the review with Andy Thorson and Superintendent Hobbs.

Drake yelled for Gareth, who appeared at his door moments later.

'I want you to go through this box of cuttings the search team recovered from David Ackland's home. Apparently they're all about the Freemantle High and Edward Murphy. I want a summary by late this afternoon when I've got a review with the Superintendent and the CPS.'

'Yes, boss.' Winder picked up the box.

Drake turned to the sergeant. 'Anything else of interest in David Ackland's home?'

'No, nothing. I've been to some odd houses in the past but that was one of the strangest.' The sergeant got up and left.

Drake turned his attention to preparing a memorandum for his meeting later that afternoon, when his mobile rang.

'It's Zoe Lloyd.'

'How can I help you?' Drake stared at his monitor, his mind thinking about his meeting with Hobbs and Thorsen.

'My friend will agree to see you. But it's got to be you, nobody else from your team.'

A mix of emotions crossed Drake's mind. Was this person going to have valuable evidence? He couldn't dismiss the possibility that somebody inside the Peel Foundation might offer a valuable insight. Demanding only to see him sounded odd and it just meant that he had to be more careful.'

'Otherwise, no preconditions?'

'Be at the Tesco supermarket in Llandudno Junction in an hour. Don't be late; we won't hang around.'

Drake went through into the Incident Room and found Sara finishing a telephone call.

'I've just spoken with the two people who were on that footage from the café. They're coming in for an interview later.'

'Good. You speak to them. I'll go and talk to Zoe Lloyd and her friend.'

Sara raised a quizzical eyebrow. It shared with Drake exactly how he was feeling too – suspicious.

Sara realised by early afternoon that she hadn't eaten anything all day. She visited the canteen and bought herself a salad bowl. Luckily she'd been able to visit the gym that morning where she'd run eight kilometres on the treadmill. It wasn't quite the same as running outdoors, but it was certainly safer than pounding the streets covered with ice and snow.

She returned to the Incident Room and revisited the footage from the café on the evening Jack Holt had been killed. She copied it to her laptop so that she could share it with the witnesses attending that afternoon.

She had finished her salad and was halfway through a Braeburn apple when reception called to tell her that two individuals were waiting to see her. Sara dropped the remains of the apple into the plastic salad bowl, then gathered up her papers and laptop and headed downstairs.

'I'm Detective Sergeant Sara Morgan,' Sara said.

'I'm Connie,' the girl said.

'Brandon,' the man alongside her said.

Sara showed them to a conference room. She opened the laptop on the table and once the footage had appeared on the screen she turned to Connie and Brandon.

'We are investigating the murder of Jack Holt who was killed a week last Sunday.'

They both nodded their understanding.

'We recovered CCTV footage from a café at the junction of a road near the park where he was killed. The recording identifies two people walking down the street quite late in the evening.'

'I'm sure it was us,' Brandon said. 'Walking home.'

'We didn't have any cash or our card to pay for a taxi,' Connie said.

'And although it was cold it was quite nice walking, hearing the snow crunching under our feet.'

Sara turned the screen of the laptop to face Connie and Brandon and played the footage. 'Can you please check that this is you?'

Connie and Brandon looked at the monitor intently. Once it finished, they turned to Sara. 'Yeah, that was us,' Brandon confirmed.

'Do you remember anything else from your walk home that evening?'

'What do you mean?'

'Was there anybody else walking?'

Brandon and Connie shared a puzzled look.

'I don't remember,' Brandon said. 'It was late and we'd had a bit to drink.'

'I remember seeing a taxi go past and thinking I was annoyed that I couldn't pay for one.'

Brandon nodded. 'And there was a couple in the distance, near the park. They were walking away from us. I'm almost certain it was a man and a woman.'

'Did you notice a Mercedes C-Class coupé?'

Brandon shook his head. Connie followed suit.

Sara spent a few more minutes challenging both Brandon and Connie about their recollection and hoping they'd be able to add more detail, but once Sara realised she had exhausted all the information they could provide she thanked them. 'And do please contact me if you remember anything else.'

Sara saw them to the main reception entrance. They had another small piece of the jigsaw; Brandon recalling a man and a woman contradicted Danny's evidence of two women but it would need to be checked. Had there been two couples out that evening?

Chapter 36

Drake arrived a few minutes before the time allotted by Zoe Lloyd for their meeting. He parked and surveyed some of the customers streaming from the car park into the supermarket. Drake left his vehicle and headed for the entrance and then over to a café where he sat at a table giving him a view of the other customers.

He checked the time on his watch. He had another five minutes to wait if Zoe and this mysterious third party were going to be prompt. So he surreptitiously scanned the other customers in the café. He didn't recognise any of the faces.

He tried to spot Zoe. Perhaps she had adopted a disguise of some sort, but all he could see were retired couples in their seventies enjoying a coffee and a piece of cake as part of their shopping routine.

The coffee was so bad he decided he needed sugar so he paced over to the condiments shelf and found two sachets and a stirrer. It gave him the opportunity of observing as unselfconsciously as he could the faces of the customers whose backs were turned to him where he sat.

Still there was no sign of Zoe.

He stirred the sugar into his coffee and took a mouthful. It tasted like sugary water, almost as bad as days-old lemonade. His attention was taken by two women who came into the café area. One looked exactly like Zoe but the other was much older and he craned to see if he recognised both. When he saw the face of the woman he thought was Zoe he realised she didn't have the same eyes or cheekbones.

He finished his drink and read the time – Zoe was ten minutes late by now.

He pulled the mobile from his jacket and texted her – *in the café*.

He stared at the handset willing her to reply, but no response came.

Annoyance and irritation built in his mind that Zoe

Lloyd was taking him for a fool. After all, she was one of the demonstrators outside the Peel Foundation and she'd been responsible for illegally entering their property.

He picked up the handset and called Zoe's number. He half expected to hear the number ringing out somewhere nearby. But the call just rang and rang. No voicemail and no personal invitation to leave a message.

After twenty minutes Drake got up and left.

He got back to the Incident Room annoyed and frustrated.

'I've spoken to the two people recorded by the CCTV footage passing the café.' Sara joined Drake as he walked to his room.

'I hope you had better luck than me. That Zoe Lloyd didn't show up.'

Sara sat in one of the visitor chairs. 'They also saw two people walking near the park. They thought it was a man and a woman.'

'But Danny thought he had seen two women?'

'I know, boss, perhaps there were two couples out that evening?'

'It was a freezing cold night. Who would want to be out in that weather?'

'Jack Holt and his killer.'

'I've got a meeting with Superintendent Hobbs and Andy Thorsen.'

Drake glanced at the time on his monitor. 'I'm not going to keep them waiting.'

Sara left and Drake began to review everything. When he revisited the notes of his call with the headmaster of Fremantle High it reminded him that the teacher the headmaster had mentioned still hadn't called him. So he called the school and after a brief conversation with the headmaster, who apologised profusely that the teacher hadn't made contact, he was put through to another extension. After waiting several minutes he heard a tentative voice.

'This is William Vickers.' The voice was straight out of a period drama. 'Headmaster tells me you want to speak to me.' Even from his voice, Drake could tell Vickers was well into his sixties.

'I understand you've been teaching at Fremantle High for many years.'

Vickers chortled. 'Man and boy, don't you know.'

'Do you remember a pupil called David Ackland?'

'Headmaster told me about Jack Holt and Edward Murphy. Terribly, terribly sad.'

'But do you remember David Ackland?'

'Yes, of course. I was his tutor. I remember all of my boys and he was one of the brightest, I have to say.'

'Jack Holt and Edward Murphy were pinned to the ground using croquet hoops. I understand it was a punishment ritual at the school many years ago.'

'Yes... I know. It wouldn't be allowed these days, of course.'

'Can you recall if David Ackland was subjected to that ritual?'

'I always felt helpless at the time. I was, and still am, a simple educator.' Vickers offered this as an explanation for doing nothing, Drake guessed, only to regret it later. 'It deeply affected David Ackland at the time and I remember it very well indeed.'

Drake had worked with Andy Thorsen on many cases in the past. Thorsen had taken lawyerly indifference to an art form. The absence of any personality made it difficult to get to know the prosecutor. Frequently his judgement on cases had been proved unerringly correct. He was sitting opposite Drake at the conference table in Superintendent Hobbs' office flicking through copies of the various updates Drake had sent his superior officer.

'So you've released David Ackland?' Thorsen made it

sound like a criticism.

'I took the view that the evidence needed to be reviewed before a decision to charge could be made.'

'Very wise.'

'Has the position changed?' Hobbs said.

'The search team have recovered a box from Ackland's home full of cuttings about Edward Murphy and articles written about Fremantle High.'

'That's the school Ackland attended at the same time as Jack Holt.'

Thorsen pitched in. 'And Edward Murphy was a pupil.'

'I spoke to a teacher at the school who had been there when Ackland was a pupil.'

'He must be ancient,' Hobbs said.

'He's been at the school most of his career. So he must love it there.'

'And did he have anything helpful to add?' Thorsen said.

'The punishment rituals were common at the school all those years ago. He remembers Ackland as a bright pupil who took the staking out punishment badly. I know it seems difficult to believe a man would carry a grudge for all these years but the fact he has kept a box full of articles referring to the school and Edward Murphy makes me believe the treatment he received is still raw in his mind.'

'We can only go on the evidence,' Thorsen added. 'It would certainly seem to be the case that Ackland had a strong motive to kill Jack Holt and this recent development from the search team certainly puts his relationship with Edward Murphy under the microscope. Have you finished examining his mobile telephone and personal computer?'

'Not yet. It should be completed very soon.'

'Good. Let's turn to Mervyn Peel. He also had a motive for killing Jack Holt. And we know he and the two thugs with him in London assaulted Holt.'

'And there's been a development this morning,' Drake said. 'We've recovered footage from a dashcam on a taxi that we've established was in the vicinity of the park on the evening Jack Holt was killed. It has recorded a Mercedes C-Class coupé belonging to Mervyn Peel in the area that evening.'

'I thought he had an alibi supported by a business associate?'

'The Mercedes was spotted after he had left Leonard Ferrier.'

'Are there any other witnesses?'

'We made a public appeal for two individuals recorded on the same CCTV footage as the Mercedes to come forward. Detective Sergeant Sara Morgan spoke to them this morning. They weren't able to confirm seeing a Mercedes but they did see two people in the area.'

'What do you make of the hair follicle that was recovered from the lump hammer at the scene of Edward Murphy's death?' Hobbs said.

'The DNA results makes clear it belonged to a woman,' Drake said. 'The only woman who has featured in the investigation is Martha Peel. She could well be his accomplice.'

'Any evidence against her to justify her arrest which in turn would enable you to get a DNA sample,' Thorsen said.

Drake shook his head.

Thorsen nodded. Hobbs looked down at his papers.

'This Mervyn Peel is a nasty piece of work,' Thorsen said. 'Colleagues of mine in the CPS in London have investigated the organisation but the inquiry fizzled out.' He paused and then looked over at Drake. 'This is different. This is murder. I suggest you bring him in for questioning.'

Drake nodded. 'I'll organise it first thing in the morning.'

'I'll be here all day so I shall expect a progress report once you've concluded the interviews.'

Drake pulled into the drive at his home, pleased that his working day was at an end. He needed to unwind and the journey from headquarters usually enabled his mind to switch off, but that evening his thoughts had been dominated by his plan for an interview with Mervyn Peel.

Was he a man capable of murder? Drake didn't harbour any doubt. He was single-minded in the way he had built and developed the Peel Foundation. He would do anything to protect it. The violence he had had his two henchmen inflict on Jack Holt had been more than enough evidence that he was a dangerous individual.

He left the car and once inside the house heard the television upstairs. He was looking forward to spending time with Annie, telling her about his day and what he faced in the morning. He sat at the kitchen table while she organised an evening meal. He often regretted that he wasn't more domesticated. He didn't thank her often enough for her support.

'Thank you for putting up with me. I don't tell you often enough that I couldn't do my job without you.'

Annie came over and kissed him on the forehead. 'What's your day been like?' She finalised their meal moments later and a cast-iron pot full of chicken stew was placed on the table. Drake tucked into the meal with the mashed potatoes and broccoli Annie had prepared. He couldn't remember what he had eaten that day but he had drunk at least one bottle of water.

'Sometimes it feels like I've been running around like a headless chicken. I've got an interview with Mervyn Peel in the morning. He is our main suspect in the Jack Holt case.'

'So you've got a busy day tomorrow.'

Drake parked the finer details of the enquiry and the plan for the interview with Mervyn Peel into a recess in the corner of his thoughts. He was focusing now on Mervyn Peel even though he reserved a small place in his mind for David Ackland. He spent the rest of the evening enjoying Annie's company and looking forward to their visit to the wedding venue at the weekend.

Chapter 37

'What the hell do you mean Mervyn Peel is dead?' Drake said, conscious his voice sounded borderline hysterical. 'I was going to interview him this morning.'

'He won't be doing much talking,' the officer on the other end of the telephone said. 'It looks like suicide, sir. One of the members of staff found him in his office this morning.'

Drake stood up from his desk kicking his chair to one side. It clattered against the radiator under the window. He bellowed for Sara. She appeared in a doorway seconds later and he gesticulated for her to come in as he continued talking into his handset.

'I want all the details. No, don't bother. I'll be there in a few minutes.' He turned to Sara. 'You can forget all that work about interviewing Mervyn Peel. He's dead.'

'What do you mean? What happened?'

'Get your coat let's get over there.'

All the snow had cleared from the roads near headquarters and temperatures had risen. Despite this, Drake was wearing his winter coat as he jogged over to his car. Luckily the traffic was light that morning and they reached the Foundation in good time. He sped through the open gate and up towards the main entrance where he spotted two marked police cars. A uniformed officer stood at the doorstep waiting.

'His office is upstairs, sir.'

'I know. What's the latest on the CSIs and the pathologist?'

Drake didn't wait for a reply as he heard the scientific support vehicle drawing up behind him. Mike Foulds, the crime scene manager, was the first to get out followed by a second investigator. Moments later a second CSI vehicle arrived.

Drake led Mike Foulds into the building, Sara following

behind. 'Is it true?' Foulds said.

'I've only just got here, Mike.'

Drake and Foulds walked through the building to Peel's office. Another uniformed officer stood by the door. Drake entered. He heard Foulds and the investigator depositing boxes of equipment in the corridor outside.

Sara followed Drake inside. He stood for a moment looking over at the figure of Mervyn Peel sprawled over his executive chair. Drake stared at the gaping wound under the man's chin. There was blood, lots of it, everywhere. Dark stains had drenched his suit jacket and white shirt.

Drake stepped over towards the desk. Papers on the desk had been stained too. He didn't want to get too close, conscious that Mike Foulds wanted to preserve the crime scene to gather every last scrap of evidence. Was it fanciful to think Mervyn Peel had realised his time was up and that he was going to be questioned and possibly charged with two murders? And that he had decided he couldn't face a life behind bars, a life deprived of the luxurious lifestyle his Foundation allowed him.

Drake neared the desk and craned over to see if there was any sign of a gun. He spotted a handgun on the floor and Peel's empty hand pointing towards it where his arm had fallen.

'Jesus Christ, what a sight,' Sara said.

'Who found the body?'

'I spoke to the uniformed officer who told me that it was Martha Peel. She heard the gunshot and came rushing down. She called 999 immediately.'

Drake hadn't taken his eyes off Mervyn Peel. Driving into work that morning his thoughts had been entirely dominated by the possibility of interrogating Peel about his involvement with the murders of Jack Holt and Edward Murphy. Peel gazed lifelessly at the ceiling. Drake stepped back into the rest of the office.

'Get Mike Foulds in here.'

Sara did as she was told and the crime scene manager entered.

'Is there a firearm?' Foulds said.

'It's at his feet.'

'That's the first thing we need to secure. We are going to be here all day. Is there any suggestion that any other room in the building may be a crime scene?'

'We'll check with the uniformed officers. And I want to know immediately if you find a suicide note.'

'Noted and until you tell me to the contrary, I will treat this room only as the crime scene. Now get the hell out of here whilst I do my work.'

Drake retreated with Sara to the corridor.

'It certainly looks like suicide,' Sara said.

'I know. But until we've had a full report from Mike Foulds and we have an opportunity to examine everything we'll treat his death as suspicious.'

'Okay, boss.'

'Let's go and talk to Mrs Peel. And get Gareth and Luned over here. I want all the members of the Peel Foundation spoken to.'

'Gareth too?' Sara said.

'Yes. Mervyn Peel is dead so he's not going to complain about Gareth, and if anybody else does they can go to hell.'

Sara smiled, clearly pleased that Drake wanted Winder's full participation.

She walked with Drake to Martha and Mervyn Peel's private accommodation. He heard her one-sided conversation. Once she had confirmation both officers would be en route Drake turned to her. 'Get one of the uniformed officers to warn us as soon as Gareth and Luned have arrived. You can brief them and, in the meantime, let's talk to Mrs Peel.'

The top floor of the building had been converted into a luxurious apartment for the Peels, befitting their status as the owners and inspiration behind the Foundation to which they had given their name.

Martha Peel was sitting in the kitchen at an island that was the size of three average dining tables. She drew a finger up and down a tall glass, its contents fizzing seductively. Drake and Sara stood to one side; there wasn't an invitation to sit down.

'I don't think Mrs Peel is up to talking to anyone,' Martin Swan said. His was an unwelcome presence for Drake and Sara but clearly one Martha Peel valued.

'It's all right, Martin.'

'I understand you discovered your husband this morning.'

'Yes, I heard a sound. It just sounded like a gunshot. I rushed down to his office.'

She was avoiding eye contact, avoiding sharing how she really felt at the death of her husband.

'Was there anything to suggest from your husband's behaviour that he was contemplating suicide?'

'He'd been under a lot of stress recently. The Foundation has been struggling with cash flow issues, and Jack Holt and your involvement in the murders haven't helped.'

'Has your husband suffered in the past with mental health issues?'

'Don't be absurd.'

'It's a serious question, Mrs Peel,' Sara said.

Drake could see Sara was suspicious, unhappy with Mrs Peel's reaction.

'Were you aware your husband owned a firearm?'

Martha Peel nodded.

'Where did he normally keep it?'

'In the firing range. I don't know what possessed him to bring it home.'

She looked over at Martin Swan who gave her the briefest of smiles. 'I think Mrs Peel has been through more than enough this morning. I think she should be resting.'

'We may need to speak to you again,' Drake said. 'And

we can organise for family liaison officers to be present as a support for you during this difficult time.'

Martha Peel shook her head. 'I don't think that will be necessary.'

Downstairs, away from the private quarters, Sara whispered to Drake. 'There was something odd about that. It was as though his death was perfectly normal. And remember all those photographs of her and Martin Swan. I reckon there's something going on between them.'

'I agree, and we need to check back with Mike Foulds about the scene in Peel's office. We treat everything as suspicious.'

Uniformed officers along the corridor called out for their attention. 'The detective constables on your team have arrived.'

Chapter 38

Drake found Luned and Winder in the hallway with uniformed officers who were standing by the door. 'We need to interview all the staff as soon as possible,' Drake said.

'Is it true he shot himself?' Winder said.

'It looks that way,' Drake said.

'Did he know you were going to interview him this morning?' Luned said.

'There's no way he could have known that. Unless he's left a suicide note there is no way we can determine what his motives may have been. So we keep an open mind as we do in every criminal investigation. The CSIs should have finished by later today. The post-mortem should be either today or tomorrow so for the rest of today you know what the priority is. Establish facts, gather evidence. Make certain you ask about any signs of suicidal behaviour or feelings – did he say anything about his mental state? Was he drinking more than normal? Did anything change in his personal routine or habits?'

'Yes, boss.'

Drake led them through to the conference room where they had interviewed members of staff before. He scanned the individuals present, noticing Martin Swan was a notable absence. Phoebe kept her gaze firmly on her feet.

'Mervyn Peel was found dead this morning in his office. We need to speak to all of you about your movements last night and first thing today. Please do not speak to each other about the events until you have spoken to one of my officers here. Detective Sergeant Sara Morgan will be in charge and both detective constables on my team will undertake interviews as well. You will all remain in this room and a uniformed officer will be present with you until all the interviews have been conducted. Do I make my position clear?'

Drake was pleased when everyone in the room nodded.

It was probably too late to prevent them talking to one another but his lecture had been a useful reminder he didn't want them talking out of turn until they had spoken to one of the team.

Drake left the room and headed back for Mervyn Peel's office. A text reached his mobile from Superintendent Hobbs – *Is it true that Peel is dead?* Drake replied – *Apparent suicide. Full team of detectives on site. I will report back later.*

Hobbs didn't reply. He didn't need to. Drake reached Peel's office just as Dr Lee Kings was emerging. 'I thought he was one of your suspects?'

'I was due to interview him this morning.'

'Death would have been instantaneous. A shot from a handgun directly into the brain has that effect.'

'Anything about the circumstances that strike you as odd.'

'Come off it, Ian, you don't think this was staged?'

'I'm keeping an open mind.'

'I'll be doing the post-mortem as soon as I get back to the mortuary. Don't be late.'

Drake nodded and made his way into Peel's office where Mike Foulds and two investigators were busy.

'You've just missed Lee Kings.'

'I saw him before he left. Any preliminary results?'

Foulds stood up. 'It looks exactly as you'd expect. He fired the gun under his chin into his head. He died and the gun fell onto the floor.'

'So it's suicide?'

'I didn't say that. All I can do is give you the facts of my forensic analysis. And no doubt it'll be up to the coroner in due course to make a finding of suicide or not.'

'What I want to know, Mike, is if there is any sign of third-party involvement?'

Foulds frowned. 'Ask me again once we've finished. And we did find a suicide note.' Foulds pointed to a sheet of

A4 paper in an evidence pouch. Drake used his mobile to take a photograph. He left Foulds and the rest of the team and rejoined Sara in the conference room after she had completed an interview.

Drake motioned for her to join him outside in the corridor.

'Anything from the staff members?'

'Nothing, some of them don't even recall hearing a shot. The first they'd heard was Martha Peel screaming.'

'And did you make sure you were interviewing Phoebe Parkinson?'

'She was the first one I spoke to. Didn't hear the shot, only Martha Peel's scream.'

'There's a suicide note, apparently.'

Sara nodded.

'Once you've finished get back to headquarters. I'm going to the mortuary as Lee Kings is doing the post-mortem immediately.'

All the procedures surrounding a possible suicide flooded into Drake's mind as he drove over to the mortuary. The coroner would need to be informed and the officer attached to his office might even have to be involved in the investigation. He pulled into the mortuary just as the undertakers arrived with Peel's body. Drake had already taken the precaution of notifying Superintendent Hobbs of progress.

It was certainly unusual that a suspect had committed suicide the day before a planned interview. Drake didn't like coincidences.

Once he had joined Lee Kings in the mortuary he had to wait until the body was prepared.

'I had a slot available this morning unexpectedly. I was supposed to do a post-mortem on an elderly man who died but his family have objected as they want their own pathologist.'

'So Mervyn Peel gets special treatment?'

'The dead always gets special treatment from me.'

The mortuary assistant wheeled the trolley in with Mervyn Peel's body.

Kings removed the sheet covering the body. Drake briefly recoiled at the site of the bloody wound. Kings completed the preliminary examination of the arms and legs and then he opened the torso with the usual "Y" incision. Dictating his notes, Kings made clear he was entirely satisfied the cause of death was the gunshot wound that he was equally convinced was self-inflicted.

'How easy would it be for a person or persons to stage this to look like a suicide?'

'It would need at least two people to keep the victim in one place – in this case sitting on his chair. But I guess if they could do that quickly enough then discharging the gun into his head would have been over quickly. Death would have been instantaneous as I said before.'

'If he had been held down or restrained would there be some bruising on his body?'

'You're getting ahead of yourself, Detective Inspector. This man's brains were blown to smithereens by a gun found at his feet. What more evidence do you need?'

Kings turned to dictate the details of his examination of Mervyn Peel's skull. Drake began to feel very queasy as the pathologist trimmed the top of his skull with the handheld saw and removed what remained of the brain. He removed the bullet which he dropped into a stainless-steel container.

Once everything was complete Kings stood back. 'Mervyn Peel had no underlying health conditions that I could see for a man of his age. He was killed when a bullet entered his skull fired from a handgun.'

Drake stared at the body for a moment. Was he losing a sense of perspective by focusing on the possibility Peel had been murdered simply because he had been denied the opportunity of interrogating him? He might have to face the simple truth that Peel had killed himself. And that the murders of Jack Holt and Edward Murphy might never be solved. That prospect filled him with the dread of failure.

'Thanks Lee. I need your report as soon as.'

Drake turned on his heel and left the pathologist to complete his work.

Chapter 39

Drake sat at one of the desks in the Incident Room. He looked over at Sara and then at Winder and Luned. He had already circulated a copy of the suicide note.

He looked down at the details:

> *I am sorry, Martha. I know you will find this difficult, but it will be for the best.*
> *I cannot see any way out of the predicament. Our enemies are circling. I have made mistakes but Holt and Edward left me no choice.*
> *I know that finding me in this way will be traumatic but I cannot see another option.*
> *The dark forces of our enemies think they have won.*
> *I know you will continue our work and triumph in the future.*
> *All my love*
> *Mervyn*

'Who the hell types out a suicide note?' Winder said.

The same question had been uppermost in Drake's mind.

'If I'm reading this right he is admitting to killing Jack Holt and Edward Murphy,' Luned said.

'If that's what he means when he says Holt and Edward had left me no choice.'

'And if that's correct we have our murderer.'

Drake stood up and walked over to the board. He pinned a copy of the suicide note alongside the image of Mervyn Peel which had been moved from its original position. The board badly needed to be reorganised, but it wasn't a priority.

'He apologises to his wife and tells her he loves her and that his death will be for the best,' Sara said.

Drake resumed his seat by a desk. 'Tell me about the interviews with the members of staff.'

Sara began. 'All the members I spoke to hadn't noticed any change in Mervyn Peel's behaviour. He was his usual self. I asked them all if there was any sign he'd been drinking but they all shook their heads.'

'I did the same,' Winder said. 'And most of them just dismissed out of hand any suggestion Peel's behaviour had changed.'

Luned nodded. 'It was the same for me. All the staff I spoke to said his behaviour in the last week had been entirely normal. He hadn't given anybody any sign he was suicidal.'

Drake peered again at the suicide note, determined he was going to exhaust every line of enquiry to establish Mervyn Peel's state of mind.

'Is there any chance David Ackland might have been responsible' Sara said.

'Let's at least eliminate him from our enquiries. I want one of you to go over to his house and establish his movements for last night and first thing this morning.'

Winder got to his feet. 'Yes, boss.'

'Sara, you're with me. We need to talk to Martha Peel again. I don't care if she's recently widowed. I want to see what she thinks about this suicide note.' Drake turned to Luned. 'We need to find exactly who was resident at the Peel Foundation last night and this morning. Get a timeline for everyone's movements. And do some research into Martha Peel. I want to know more about her.'

Luned nodded her understanding.

'Don't take long Gareth, you can help Luned when you're back.'

Martha Peel had moved from the island in the kitchen to the spacious sitting room in the apartment. She still looked grey and drawn but she had changed her clothes and looked more presentable. There was no sign of Martin Swan.

'I need to understand your husband's state of mind in the days before his death,' Drake said.

Martha gave him an anxious look. 'I don't know what you mean?'

'How was your husband sleeping?'

'Well, he never complained.'

Sara asked, 'Do you have separate bedrooms?'

Martha nodded.

'And had there been any changes in his eating habits?' Drake said, determined he was going to ask open questions.

'None that I'm aware of. He had a good appetite.'

'And what was his mood like?'

'He'd been complaining about the investigation into Jack Holt and Edward Murphy's murders. I can see why now.'

'What do you mean?'

'He's killed himself. All the pressure you've put him under was too much for him. It must be apparent Mervyn was terrified of Jack Holt and his type of gutter journalism.'

'Do you think Mervyn killed Holt and Murphy?'

'How could I possibly know that?' Her voice quivered. 'Holt's despicable work certainly took its toll on Mervyn.'

Drake wasn't convinced by Martha Peel's explanation. If her husband had killed Holt and Murphy there must have been more to it. 'And how do you explain the croquet hoops used to pin both men to the ground?'

'I've told you before there was something dark and foreboding in Edward's background and his schooling. And he told me that Holt's partner had been at the same school. Its name escapes me.'

'Did Mervyn ever mention David Ackland?'

Martha shook her head.

'I'm sure the coroner and his officer will want to question you in more detail so it is important, Martha, that you can provide us with as much information as possible about your husband's mood and anything he might have said in the past few days.'

'But he's left a note hasn't he. There can't be any

doubt?'

'I know this must be a most distressing time for you.'

'I don't know how he could have written that note. I shall live with it for the rest of my life of course.'

'Thank you for your time.' Drake stood up and nodded for Sara to join him as they left.

Martha Peel didn't react. She kept staring into a space only she could see.

Drake and Sara walked down through the building and out towards Drake's vehicle.

'What you make of that, boss?' Sara said.

'She was pretty emphatic about the effect of the note wasn't she?'

They sat in the car for a moment. Drake adjusted the heater, although it didn't need to be full on now that the snow and ice had disappeared.

'There was something odd about her.'

'She's just lost her husband.'

Drake nodded. 'But there was more to it than that. She mentioned Edward's schooling but how would she know about that?'

'Maybe he told her.'

'Maybe, but it points to Ackland too easily, too conveniently. Let's get back to headquarters. I need to think.'

Winder jumped to his feet when Drake and Sara entered the Incident Room. 'David Ackland wasn't at home last night or this morning.'

'Details, please,' Drake said.

'He went to stay with a friend in Leeds last night. Apparently he gave the details to Mr and Mrs Wakeling, who were shocked he made any sort of contact with them.'

'And that rules him out.' Drake turned to the board. 'Something else has been on my mind. Danny saw two women on the night of the murder. The witnesses from the

CCTV footage from the café were clear they had seen a man and a woman. Get Danny in here again I want to ask him exactly what he saw.'

Drake turned to face the officers on his team and saw the scepticism that a homeless man could provide them with any information that could be of assistance. 'And talk to Connie and Brandon again. We need any description they can remember.'

'They told us they couldn't remember anything – that it was just a fleeting moment when they had seen them in the distance.'

'I don't care, get them in again.' Drake marched over to his office. He turned his mobile to silent so that he wouldn't be disturbed and was tempted to put a "Do not disturb" sign on the door to his office. He had been mulling over various alternatives and he needed to focus on the evidence collected so far. But first he had to start on the suicide note. Everything about the note felt wrong. If Peel had been intent on providing some comfort to Martha, surely he would have written her a personal note rather than a typed letter?

Drake spent an hour researching. He wrote a preliminary email and the recipient responded almost immediately, which pleased Drake. Then he tapped out a memorandum which he checked and rechecked hoping it covered all the points he needed examining. Finally he added two attachments to the email, which he had marked as urgent, and pressed send.

Once he switched his mobile back on he realised Zoe had attempted to contact him again. He called her back. 'I was busy when you rang.'

'I've heard about Peel,' Zoe said without embellishment.

Drake would have expected her to have been pleased but she sounded neutral.

'My friend wants to see you.'

'Mervyn Peel is dead. How can this person help now?'

'This time it's different. Tomorrow morning eight am at

the same supermarket.'

Zoe abruptly finished the call.

Sara knocked on his door and he waved her inside.

'Gareth and Luned have found Danny. He is in a conference room downstairs. They've organised for him to have a full cooked breakfast from the canteen.'

'Good.'

Drake walked through the Incident Room with Sara and headed downstairs.

Chapter 40

Danny was shovelling baked beans into his mouth when Drake arrived in the conference room at reception. Bits of egg yolk had caught in the stubble of his beard. He still had three pieces of toast and rashers of bacon to finish. He looked up at Drake, who had a hungry, determined look on his face.

'Bloody good,' Danny said.

Winder and Luned were sitting at the other end of the table looking over at their voracious guest.

'How are you, Danny?'

'Okay. At least the snow stopped.' Danny continued eating the rest of his meal.

'I wanted to ask you again about the evening when Jack Holt was killed.'

Danny nodded, his mouth chewing energetically.

'Initially you confirmed seeing two people in the vicinity of the park. You were in a doorway not far from the entrance to the park.'

'Yeah, that's right. I couldn't find a better place to kip that night.'

'How far were they away from you?'

Danny shrugged. 'Dunno.'

Drake got to his feet and opened the door of the room pointing down the hallway towards another doorway. 'Were they as far away as that door?'

'Yeah, suppose.'

'Were they closer than that?'

Danny frowned. 'Maybe.'

'But they were no further away.'

'If you say so.'

Drake leaned over the table. 'Danny, could you be a little more specific?'

He looked out of the door and down the corridor, where Drake had suggested. 'Yeah, guess it was about to that door.'

'One of my officers is going to pace that out,' Drake looked over at Winder who got to his feet and duly obliged.

'It was twenty paces, boss.' Winder said.

Drake turned to Danny. 'That means you were quite close to them. Did you see their faces?'

He shook his head and folded a piece of toast over a rasher of bacon. 'I was trying to sleep.'

'When we spoke to you originally you said you had seen two women.'

'Yeah. One had her hair pulled tightly behind her head and the other one had hair down to here.' Danny tapped his shoulder.

'Was it like someone with a ponytail?'

'A woman, yeah.' Danny took another mouthful of the tea from the mug in front of him. 'She had a ponytail.'

Drake and Sara left Danny and returned to the Incident Room.

'Why do you think Danny might be helpful?' Sara sounded sceptical and the anxious look on her face suggested to Drake she was beginning to doubt his motives.

'I wanted to know whether he was still confident it was two women when Connie and Brandon had made clear it was a man and a woman.'

'How is this going to help us?'

'I don't want any threads unresolved in the Jack Holt case. I want to know who these two were. I want to know if they were working for Mervyn Peel, if he was actually the killer.'

Sara gave him a pensive look. 'Connie and Brandon have been in touch. They are going to call first thing in the morning.'

Drake got back to his office and checked his emails for updates from the pathologist and the forensic department. The pathologist was as good as his word and had provided a detailed report explaining clearly that the cause of death had been a gunshot to the head. Drake didn't expect anything else.

He dialled Mike Foulds' number on his mobile; the call was answered immediately. Drake heard Foulds' voice.

'What can I do for you, Ian?'

'Have you finished yet?'

'We'll be another couple of hours.'

'Is there anything important I need to know.'

'Everything suggests he committed suicide. There's nothing to suggest it was staged in any way, if that's what you're alluding to.'

Drake wanted to make sense of the conflicting issues in his mind. As he spoke to Foulds he glanced at the suicide note on his desk.

'Just let me have the report as soon as possible.' Drake knew he sounded impatient. It was the overarching emotion in his mind. He just had to make certain that bits of the jigsaw he could see could somehow slot together.

He spent the rest of the afternoon reviewing all the statements Winder and Luned had gathered from the staff at the Foundation. They had full details of the Foundation's finances and they had requisitioned any personal information on Mervyn and Martha Peel that afternoon. Drake looked forward to seeing it in more detail in the morning. He knew Sara doubted he was on the right tracks with the threads developing in his mind. He wasn't certain he knew exactly where he was going but he wanted to be certain.

He texted Annie telling her he was going to be leaving but that he had a call to make en route and that he wouldn't be too late.

'I'm going to be calling at the Tesco supermarket in Llandudno Junction first thing tomorrow morning. I've got a meeting with Zoe Lloyd.'

Three heads nodded at him.

'In the meantime, I'm going to talk to Leonard Ferrier on the way home.'

A Lexus saloon accompanied the Range Rover parked on Ferrier's drive when Drake pulled up outside his home. The business consultant stood waiting for him on the doorstep, a dark troubled look on his face. He reached out a hand. 'I wasn't expecting to see you again.'

'I expect you've heard about Mervyn Peel.'

'Indeed, I have.'

'He was found with a bullet in his head this morning in an apparent suicide.'

'Apparent?'

'It will be a matter for the coroner to determine formally if he committed suicide or not.'

'But I understand there was a suicide note so there can't be any room for doubt, can there?'

Ferrier turned on his heel and led Drake into the study he had visited on the first occasion they met.

'We will need to provide details to the coroner and his officer about Mervyn Peel's circumstances. It will help us enormously if you could provide us with some details of exactly where you are with the commercial development of the land owned by Mr and Mrs Peel.' Drake sounded as detached as he could afford.

'Not a lot has changed since I originally spoke to you. I have been working on the proposals and it's likely the land will significantly increase in value.'

'Do you see the proposal continuing now that Mr Peel is dead?'

'Of course, Martha Peel is the driving force behind the proposal and she spoke to me only this afternoon to make arrangements for our next meeting with the developers. We hope they will make a sensible offer for the land once preliminary planning permission is in place. And that is likely to be next week.'

It was hardly the act of a grieving widow, Drake thought.

'I thought the land was in their joint names.'

'She inherits the land automatically after her husband's death. I think there was some tax reasons why it was transferred out of the name of the Peel Foundation. I guess you'll need to talk to accountants about that. And she's given me full authority to deal with everything.'

Drake took a moment to gather his thoughts. Ferrier had made clear Martha Peel had a single-minded commitment to the development of this land. Mervyn Peel was dead. Was the Peel Foundation dead? It was one part of the inquiry that niggled Drake.

Chapter 41

Drake woke early the following morning. It was still dark and he looked forward to the spring when the clocks went forward and sunshine would seep round the edges of the curtains in the morning. He hoped by later that day he'd have a clearer picture of what was happening in the inquiry.

He didn't bother with coffee or breakfast. He reversed the car out of the parking slot and drove for the A55 and then east. He indicated left off the dual carriageway when the signs indicated the exit for Llandudno and Deganwy.

He didn't bother waiting in his car, even though he was a few minutes early. He marched into the store and then over to the café. This time he would give Zoe five minutes and then he'd leave. He spotted Zoe sitting opposite a person wearing a hoodie drawn tight over their head.

Zoe gave him a welcoming nod. He marched straight over and sat alongside her. He looked over at the person facing them. It was a face he had seen before. He hadn't expected to see Phoebe Parkinson.

'Is this the friend you are telling me about?' Drake said to Zoe.

Phoebe answered for her. 'I didn't want to get into any trouble. But things have changed now.'

'What do you have to tell me, Phoebe. I've got a murder inquiry to deal with so if you've got anything relevant you've got a public duty to share it with me.' Drake kept his voice low even though there were only two other customers at the opposite end of the café.

'I've been terrified,' Phoebe said.

'Terrified of what?' Drake said.

'You don't know what they're like. Once they have their claws into you then it is impossible...' Phoebe looked down at the cup and saucer on the table in front of her.

'Mervyn Peel and his wife are evil,' Zoe said.

'Martha Peel lied to you.' Phoebe said. 'In fact, they all

lie.'

'Tell me what you know. What do you mean by saying Martha Peel lied?'

'I guess she told you she was in the Foundation when Jack Holt and Edward Murphy were killed.'

'Go on,' Drake wasn't going to acknowledge details of the investigation until he knew far more about Phoebe.

'Martha Peel drove the Mercedes the night Holt was killed. I know because I was at the window looking out as she drove down the drive.'

'Can you be certain?'

'Of course I can. I've been terrified she'd find out I'd seen her.'

'Did Mervyn Peel know she had left the Foundation that night?'

'He was really surprised when Jack Holt had been killed and he was devastated when Edward Murphy was murdered. I've never seen him so upset.'

Drake paused for a moment. It sounded genuine. Mervyn Peel wouldn't need to have performed for his staff. Drake listening to Phoebe recounting the depth of Mervyn Peel's emotion gave him a new perspective.

'Do you know if there was anybody with Martha Peel when she left?' Drake said.

'I couldn't see clearly but Martin was with her, I'm sure.'

'Can you be certain?'

'Everyone in the Foundation knew about them. Except for Mervyn Peel, I suppose.'

Zoe read the time on her watch. 'You need to get back before she thinks something suspicious has happened.'

Phoebe turned to Drake. 'I made an excuse that I needed some shopping.'

Drake noticed the shopping bags on the chair by her side.

'I don't want to go back. I'm frightened,' Phoebe

continued.

'You don't have to go back,' Drake said.

Phoebe shook her head. 'You don't know what they're like. Where would I go?'

Drake softened his voice. 'You have a family that loves you. Go to them. You'll be safe.'

Drake could see the fear in Phoebe's face. She gathered up the bags and bustled out of the store with Zoe.

Driving into headquarters, Luned found it difficult to comprehend that Martha Peel might be responsible for two murders and the staged suicide of her husband. She arrived promptly and got to work immediately. Motive, there always has to be a motive, Luned reminded herself. And she persuaded herself Martha Peel must have been a strong, purposeful character to have been part of the Peel Foundation. Confidence and resilience must have been essential components of Martha Peel's make up to have allowed her and Mervyn Peel to succeed.

Preliminary work on the background of Martha and Mervyn Peel hadn't given them a great deal of information about Martha's background. Luned decided that if they were assuming she was responsible for Edward Murphy's death, there must have been something that gave her a motive.

She wanted him dead for a reason.

The Peel Foundation's assets were mostly in the capital value of its property, and the present cash flow difficulties the organisation found itself in had been created by Mervyn Peel's greed. She knew that from the money in his personal bank account. When she looked at the respective financial position of Mervyn and Martha Peel, it became apparent there was a disparity. Mervyn's personal bank accounts had substantial balances whereas Martha Peel's finances were more modest.

The previous afternoon she had started work on Martha's bank accounts and a decent night's sleep had given

Luned a renewed focus. Looking for patterns in bank statements that required further investigation always required concentration. And when she found a regular series of payments to an overseas account it piqued her interest. It didn't take very long to establish that a dozen payments have been made in the past eighteen months.

Who was the recipient of these sums? Luned had only one way to find out. She called the bank. It took her several conversations and much cajoling to extract information from the bank that the payments had been made to a bank account in Cape Town in the name of Terence Willis.

Luned sat back, thinking to herself, who the hell is Terence Willis?

They already knew the Peel Foundation had connections to South Africa. But if the payments were part of the financial activity of the Peel Foundation, surely they'd have been made from the Foundation's accounts?

Luned pulled from her memory a faint recollection from the folders and files removed from Edward Murphy's computer. She went back into the computer and found various folders relating to the Foundation's properties. If Edward Murphy had discovered something incriminating against Martha Peel he wouldn't have stored it in the usual Peel Foundation folders. So she clicked through into his personal folders and was rewarded when she opened a folder called "Holidays" with details of a property for sale in Cape Town.

She checked, but there were no details of the property in the Foundation's assets. It looked like a residential home in a gated community, not the sort of investment the Foundation would make.

Luned scooped up the handset of the telephone on her desk and called the agents. She had taken a few minutes to prepare a simple subterfuge of pretending to be Martha Peel's personal assistant. She soon had the crucial information she needed.

The next thing she did was to undertake a search of Facebook and Instagram. Everyone does social media these days, and she hoped Terence Willis would be no different. It didn't take long to find the information she needed, and she smiled to herself, pleased that she had made progress.

Drake was still pondering what he should say to Gareth Winder about his cousin when he entered reception at headquarters. He would have to share with the detective constable that she had spoken with him. He deserved to know, but a voice from reception interrupted his chain of thought.

'Detective Inspector Drake, there's someone to see you.'

Drake turned and looked over at the woman.

'There's a Dr Renton to see you. I've asked him to sit in the conference room. He asked me to tell you he doesn't have much time as he is on his way to a symposium at Bangor University.'

Drake hadn't expected Dr Renton to turn up at headquarters. He was going to telephone the academic later that morning. His email to him the day before had been simple and self-explanatory. He hoped the reason for Dr Renton's attendance at headquarters was equally straightforward.

Philip Renton was a man in his fifties with a shaved head that glistened in the artificial light. His suit was badly fitted and one of the ends of his shirt collar lifted over the lapel.

'Thank you for calling to see me, Dr Renton,' Drake said.

'No problem, no problem,' Renton said. 'I'm on my way to Bangor University.' He glanced at his watch. 'I left early so I could call in to see you on my way.'

'I assume it's about my email?'

'Yes, of course. Although it's not my main field of study, suicide notes are utterly fascinating.' Renton settled into his chair, relishing the opportunity of sharing his expertise. 'Have you heard of the truth bias, Inspector Drake? It suggests that we as human beings assume something is true unless it can be proved to the contrary.'

Drake nodded.

Renton had a printed version of Mervyn Peel's suicide note on the table in front of him.

'Let me start with what researchers have identified real note-writers are more likely to include in their suicide notes. It's well established that authentic notes have expressions of need that require some reaction from another person. By this I mean words like "don't feel bad" or "I hope you understand".'

'I don't think there was any of those sorts of expressions in Mervyn Peel's note.'

'Exactly. And descriptions of specific motives or positive emotional states are also more common in genuine suicide notes whereas non-suicidal individuals will use vague and abstract concepts, e.g., life, fate, et cetera.'

'I think I understand, Dr Renton. Please continue.'

'What is quite clear however is there is a preponderance of cognitive verbs here in this suicide note.' Renton tapped the document on the table. 'It uses the words "know", "think" and "see". And there is a clear emphasis on blaming others – for example it uses "our enemies are circling us" and "the dark forces of our enemies think they have won".'

'We were due to interview him yesterday morning as a suspect in relation to two murders.'

'I see. What you must understand is that the author of a fictitious note has to somehow get into the mind of the suicide individual's frame of mind. But it's so complicated because all our decisions are coloured by our individual experiences. It's a process called double hermeneutic.'

'I've never heard of it.'

'It's basically common sense. Try putting yourself into the mind of another person. It's impossible. What distinguishes a genuine from a fake suicide note can be distinguished by the themes around which the note has been constructed. I won't bore you with the technical formula for analysing suicide notes but... let me ask you this before I finish. Is there anything to suggest Mervyn Peel was suicidal from his behaviours?"

'None that we are aware of but our investigation is at a very early stage.'

'Then let me help you. In my professional view this is a simulated suicide note.' Renton stood up. 'I'll send you a formal report and my invoice for this consultation.'

'Is there any doubt in your mind Dr Renton.'

'None, but you must be aware that it's a professional opinion.'

'The coroner will need to be informed.'

'Of course.' Renton made for the door to reception. 'Coroners don't understand everything. But hey-ho, such is life.'

Drake watched Renton leave. Then he turned and raced upstairs.

Chapter 42

Drake pushed the Incident Room door open and it crashed against the wall before he paced up to the board. Then he turned, first to look at Gareth Winder. The detective constable needed to be informed, he needed to know about Phoebe.

'I saw Zoe Lloyd first thing with her friend from the Peel Foundation. It was Phoebe, Gareth.'

Winder's mouth opened but he said nothing, as though he was struggling to find the words. 'What did she say? How was she?'

'She confirmed it wasn't Mervyn Peel who left the Foundation on the evening Jack Holt and Edward Murphy were killed, but his wife Martha.'

'Makes sense,' Luned said. 'I've done some digging into Martha Peel. She's made regular payments over the past eighteen months to a bank account in Cape Town.'

'South Africa?'

'Yes, sir. There were payments to an account in the name of Terence Willis. I've been doing more digging into the various documents in Edward Murphy's computer relating to property transactions. I found details of a property for sale in Cape Town. I called the agency this morning and pretended to be Martha Peel's personal assistant.'

Winder and Sara each gave her an incredulous look. She continued, 'The agent confirmed he was expecting Mrs Peel tomorrow on a flight from the United Kingdom. And I did a search on social media for Willis. He's quite the Facebook and Instagram junkie. He posted a picture of the Cape Town property as the new home for Martha and himself.'

Drake turned to the board and stabbed a finger at the image of Mrs Peel. 'Of course, of course. She was planning a new life without Mervyn, and she needed the money from the sale of the land she had transferred into their joint names – now with him dead it belongs to her.'

'And the DNA on the hammer is probably hers too,' Sara said.

'She wanted us to believe her husband killed Holt and Murphy but she created enough confusion by using the croquet hoops to suggest a link to their shared schooling. And the fact that Holt and Murphy and Ackland went to the same school is a convenient bonus which muddied everything nicely.'

He turned back to the team. 'Apparently she was also in a relationship with Martin Swan.' Then Drake remembered what had been niggling in the back of his mind. 'Of course, Swan has a ponytail.'

'And that means Danny might mistake him for a woman,' Sara said.

'Exactly right.'

'And what he doesn't realise is that Mrs Peel isn't taking him to South Africa with her.'

'What about the suicide note?' Winder said.

'I've just spoken to Dr Renton. He is an academic with an interest in suicide notes. He is convinced it's a fake.'

'Makes sense,' Sara said. 'I can't see anybody typing out a suicide note.'

'We need to talk to her before she gets anywhere near a flight to South Africa. Let's go and arrest Martha Peel and Martin Swan. They've got a lot of explaining to do.'

Drake marched over to his office and called Superintendent Hobbs. It was a short, one-way conversation. Hobbs occasionally sought clarification but at the end simply agreed with Drake. 'Arrest them both.'

It took another half an hour for Drake to organise a full team to assist with the arrests. Four uniformed officers streamed into the Incident Room, together with two authorised firearms officers. The pistol Martha Peel had used to kill her husband meant she probably wouldn't hesitate to use a firearm again. And that threatened life.

Uniformed officers lined up behind the desks, Winder,

Luned and Sara sitting at their usual desks.

Drake took a few moments to explain exactly what they had to do. A map of the Peel Foundation property and the roads surrounding it and all means of access were highlighted.

'How many civilians are present inside?' one of the authorised firearms officers asked.

'There's no risk of a hostage situation,' Drake said. 'We're not talking about terrorists here.'

The uniformed officers nodded their acknowledgement of the position.

Half an hour later Drake's vehicle pulled up at the open gate of the Peel Foundation.

He was expecting it to be closed. Instead, he drove straight through the open gate and up to the main entrance, the three marked police vehicles following behind.

Drake left his vehicle joined by Sara. Luned and Winder emerged from their vehicle. They all wore stab jackets and with body cameras on their lapels.

Drake hammered on the front door. There was no reply. Winder had already stepped back and looked up at the windows. He shook his head. Drake nodded towards the rear of the property. But just as he planned to direct officers to the rear, the door eased open. Katie stood there, a terrified look on her face.

Drake barged in. The other officers streamed in behind him.

He turned to Katie. 'Is Mrs Peel here?'

She looked stunned, as though she were incapable of speech.

He didn't wait for an answer and ran off towards the stairs leading to the top floor apartment. He took the risers two at a time, listening to the sound of footsteps behind him as the detectives on his team followed him. He pushed the door open and they filed into what had been Mervyn and Martha Peel's home. The place was empty. Winder and

Luned checked each room and returned to the large kitchen shaking their heads.

'No one here, boss.'

Drake turned on his heel and headed out of the apartment and down to the first-floor corridor. He yelled instructions for the two firearms officers to join them and allocated one officer to accompany Luned and Winder as they searched another corridor. The other officer, who like his colleague drew his gun, joined Drake and Sara.

It didn't take them long to reassemble by the stairwell, satisfied there was nobody in the offices. No sign of Martha Peel or Martin Swan.

'Let's talk to Katie. Let's hope she hasn't completely lost the ability of rational speech,' Drake said.

Back in the hallway one of the uniformed officers told Drake that Katie was in an adjacent room, and when he entered she was sitting, staring at the floor. 'She's out of it, sir,' one of the officers said.

Drake went over to Katie. 'Where are the rest of the staff? Where is Phoebe?'

She looked up at Drake, a look of terror in her eyes. She seemed utterly lost. 'Home,' she said simply.

'What the hell do you mean?'

'There must be living accommodation at the back of the property,' Sara said.

Drake nodded at one of the uniformed officers to keep an eye on Katie. At the rear of the building he found a corridor that linked to other premises. In the kitchen area a dozen of the staff were huddled around a table, clearly startled when they saw Drake and the other officers barge in.

Winder rushed over to Phoebe and hugged her tightly.

'Where the hell is Martin Swan?' Drake said.

There were a dozen blank looks until Phoebe dislodged herself from Winder and announced, 'He's working in Flint.'

'And where the hell is Martha Peel?'

The faces staring at them were filled with terror now.

Chapter 43

'The foundation owns a property in Flint,' Drake said. 'What do we know about it?'

Winder gave Drake a noncommittal look and he could feel his anger developing until Luned announced. 'It is a small parade of shops. Somebody must know the details.'

Luned turned to the Foundation staff and raised her voice. 'It's imperative we know the address of the property in Flint.'

After a few seconds delay somebody stammered the address.

'We need to get over there fast.'

Drake led the officers back to the hallway at the front of the building where the uniformed officers, including both men authorised to use firearms, were standing. 'We need to get over to Flint. We believe both suspects are at a property there.'

'Do we have an address?' one of the officers said.

Drake gave them the details and the postcode. 'Let's go.'

They ran out of the building to their vehicles and moments later indicated right onto the main road. One of the marked police vehicles and another with the armed officers led the convoy. They switched on their lights as they accelerated hard towards the junction for the A55 that would take them the short distance to Flint. No sirens, yet. Sara punched the postcode into the satnav and the details of the journey came up onto the screen.

When they reached the A55 the two police vehicles ahead of them accelerated into the outside lane clearing any dawdling cars. 'It should take us about thirty-one minutes,' Sara said.

'Going to be there sooner than that.'

'I'll check the details about flights from Manchester.' Sara resumed staring at her handset.

Drake focused all his attention on driving and keeping

up with the vehicles ahead of him. He glanced in the rear-view mirror and noticed that Winder was keeping up a good pace.

'I've checked and there aren't any direct flights from Manchester to South Africa. She could be booked on a flight to one of the European capitals that have direct links to Cape Town.'

'Damn. Let's hope we're not too late.'

The marked police vehicles gave plenty of warning of their intention to turn off the A55 and Drake did likewise. It meant they could peel off into the inside lane safely as other traffic slowed to allow them to proceed. When they left the dual carriageway Drake released the iron grip he had on the steering wheel. He relaxed, a little, knowing he wasn't travelling at speeds of in excess of a hundred miles an hour.

The officer from the lead vehicle rang Sara, telling her they expected to arrive at their destination within five minutes. It had been significantly less than the thirty-one minutes Sara had anticipated. Entering the town they, slowed to a crawl as other traffic delayed their journey despite the lights on both lead vehicles flashing.

'It won't be long – it's just ahead,' Sara said.

The marked cars drew to a halt at the kerb and Drake did likewise, leaving the car immediately. On the opposite side of the street was a parade of three shops. One was a bookmakers, another a beauty salon and the third a butcher. Each shop had two bay windows above, with the larger having a dormer-style pitched roof. Drake couldn't see any means of entry into the flats from the front.

'Go into all the shops,' Drake said to Winder and Luned. 'I want to know if anybody has seen Peel and Martin Swan. We'll go round the back.' He jerked a head at the uniformed police officers to follow him towards the rear of the property.

They jogged to an open gate that led to a lane at the rear. It opened onto a narrow tarmac road. Ahead of them were several garages and, turning, Drake looked at the rear of the three shops. Each had a galvanised set of stairs to the first floor.

Drake turned to Sara and the uniformed officers with him. 'Did any of you see a Mercedes C-Class parked nearby?'

'No, sir.'

'She could have parked anywhere, boss,' Sara said.

Drake gave instructions for one of the armed officers to lead the way up the stairs and force an entry into the first flat. Once each had been secured, he and Sara would enter. He wasn't going to take any chances with Martha Peel.

They streamed up the first staircase, their footfall clattering against the metal. The officer shouted a warning. No response. The door buckled under the weight of the officer's repeated kicking. An officer had already drawn his firearm and he led the way into the flat. Moments later he appeared at the door. 'It's clear, nobody here.'

Drake entered and quickly scanned the empty flat. 'Next one.'

They repeated the exercise for the second staircase, the result inside the property was the same. Although the door had been locked, the place was empty apart from decorating equipment.

The door to the final flat above the third shop was ajar and the officer who led the way indicated for Drake and the others to stay well back as he entered shouting repeated warnings he was armed. Nobody replied. Moments later he shouted, 'You'd better get in here.'

Drake and Sara found him in one of the rooms overlooking the street outside. At his feet was the prone body of Martin Swan. Drake kneeled and felt for a pulse, Swan was alive, just. Once an ambulance had been called, Drake left Winder and Luned with the uniformed officers and descended the staircase with both armed officers and returned to their vehicles.

There was no question – they had to head for Manchester Airport. If needs be they'd drag Martha Peel off a plane. 'I'll get a warning to the Cheshire Road Policing unit. She can't have got far.'

Standard protocols meant Drake would have to warn the Cheshire Constabulary he was chasing a suspect. And he needed to notify the police on duty at Manchester Airport too.

The marked police vehicle switched its lights back on, and now its siren too. Drake followed as they accelerated out of the town and back to the A55.

'I'll call the road policing unit for Cheshire,' Sara said.

Drake nodded. 'There might be one of those specialist units that covers the motorways.' He remembered that sections of the motorway in the north-west of England had special units of highly trained officers who prided themselves on being the best in the world at high-speed chases.

Soon communication came in from the road policing units on the M56 that would eventually lead them towards Manchester Airport. He doubted Martha Peel would be taking any chances speeding and she was probably driving quietly in the inside lane, well under the speed limit. They reached the junction for Runcorn where the M56 swept to his right. He glanced at the satnav and noticed the next junction would be for Daresbury. It would be one more junction, which he guessed would be signposted for Warrington, before the M6 interchange.

'Where the hell is she?' Drake said.

'I warned the police at the airport to expect us,' Sara said.

The convoy raced on in the outside lane and after passing the junction for Daresbury powered on. Still no sign of any police vehicle having spotted Martha Peel's car. They reached the junction with the M6 and Drake began to realise they weren't too far from the airport itself. If she realised they were closing in on her, she might decide to change her plans. He slammed the palm of his hand against the steering wheel. 'Why the hell didn't we pick her up before?'

Moments later Sara took a call which played through the loudspeaker on the hands-free system of the car.

'I've just joined the 56. Suspect car four-hundred metres ahead. Request backup.'

Drake's pulse spiked. 'Where are you?'

'Approaching junction seven. Another car is joining the motorway ahead of her. We'll box her in.'

He finished the call and ahead of him the marked vehicle from Northern Division accelerated. Drake did likewise. Just as abruptly the vehicle slowed and a message reached Sara's mobile. 'About half a kilometre ahead.'

Drake peered into the distance and saw a marked police vehicle ahead of a Mercedes C-Class. Behind it a BMW 5 Series was going to box her in. The marked police vehicle in Drake's convoy joined the other cars as they forced Martha Peel to slow and eventually stop. At least she had the good sense not to try to outrun three police cars.

Drake pulled up on the hard shoulder of the motorway. He joined the three police vehicles, their lights flashing but no sirens – no need. Drake marched over to the Mercedes. Martha Peel sat in the driver's seat. He yanked open the car door and she looked up at him defiantly.

'Martha Peel, I'm arresting you on suspicion of the murder of Jack Holt, Edward Murphy and your husband, Mervyn Peel.' She continued to stare at him unemotionally whilst he finished the standard caution.

Chapter 44

'Are you certain you'll be there on time?' Annie said.

Her voice sounded determined and definitely not to be challenged.

'I know it's been a busy couple of weeks.'

'Busy!'

After he had arrived home the previous evening, Annie had listened in stunned silence over dinner as he had explained he had been involved in a high-speed car chase along the M56. He had been late arriving home, having completed all the paperwork in anticipation of an interview with Martha Peel that morning.

'Whatever happens, I'll have finished by lunchtime. I've already told Sian I'll collect Helen and Megan after I've finished.'

Drake looked at the time. He was sitting on the side of their bed, having brought Annie a mug of tea. He finished his coffee and leaned over and kissed her.

'I'll be here on time.'

There was nothing to delay the start of his interview with Martha Peel. Her solicitor had been primed to be prompt.

He had enough time to drive at a steady pace to the area custody suite. He didn't want to be repeating his high-speed journeys any time soon. He found Sara sitting in a conference room sorting their papers.

'I'm going to call Gareth.' Drake said. He had allocated Luned and Winder to take a preliminary statement from Martin Swan first thing that morning. He had regained consciousness and the two detective constables were at his bedside.

Winder picked up after two rings. 'He's made a full confession, boss; he thought he was going to start a new life with Martha Peel in South Africa. She really took advantage of him. He helped with Jack Holt and staging Mervyn Peel's suicide.'

'Thanks, Gareth.'

'The medics think he's lucky to be alive.'

Drake rang off and turned to Sara. 'Swan has made a full confession. He was the one that helped Martha Peel with Jack Holt's body as well as the supposed suicide of her husband.'

'Let's hope we can rely on him.'

Drake nodded. 'I need to call forensics.' He found his mobile in his jacket pocket and called Mike Foulds.

He listened to the investigator confirm the information he had hoped for. 'I see, that's good, thank you,' Drake said.

He turned to Sara and nodded. 'It's her DNA on that hair follicle.'

Sara punched the air. 'Yes, we've got her.'

'Let's get started. I don't want any delay,' Drake said.

They walked through to the custody suite. After collecting the tapes, they settled into the interview room before Sara arranged for Martha Peel to be escorted in.

Drake dropped the tapes into the machine and once it was running looked over at Martha Peel and her solicitor, a man from a firm in Birkenhead he had never come across.

'You were arrested yesterday in relation to the murders of Jack Holt, Edward Murphy and Mervyn Peel. I want you to explain to me why you lied about where you were on the evening Jack Holt was killed.'

'Don't be absurd. I didn't lie.'

'We have an eyewitness from a member of staff at the Peel Foundation who confirms you were seen leaving in the Mercedes C-Class. It was clever using your husband's vehicle, believing that by doing so you might cast suspicion on him.'

'Who was it? Was it Katie or that Phoebe girl? They're completely flaky you know. You can't rely on a single word they say.' She shook her head as though she sympathised with Drake.

'And your vehicle was seen leaving on the evening

Edward Murphy was killed. Is that true?'

'Detective Inspector, you must know that my husband was responsible for killing Jack Holt and Edward Murphy.' Drake was well used to interview suspects patronising him. It wasn't going to work.

'How do you explain the croquet hoops?'

'It must have been his attempt to implicate David Ackland. After all, Ackland was tormented by Edward all those years ago at school. Mervyn knew about those punishment rituals.'

'Yes, of course. You told me about Murphy's schooling. So how do you explain the Mercedes being seen parked near to Edward Murphy's home on the night he was killed.'

She shook her head as though she pitied Drake and his questioning.

'If you ask anybody, and I mean anybody sensible in the Foundation who works for us, they'll tell you Mervyn and Edward hadn't seen eye to eye. There'd been a lot of arguments and Edward had threatened to go to the police about things he discovered which he thought weren't right about the finances.'

'And what were those?'

'I wasn't a party to that sort of information, Detective Inspector.'

'I understand a piece of development land owned by the Peel Foundation was transferred to the joint names of your husband and yourself quite recently.'

'Nothing wrong with that.'

'And following your husband's death you are likely to inherit that property automatically.'

'We were married, after all.'

'I'm not at all certain I understand where on earth you're going with all this questioning,' Peel's solicitor said.

Drake ignored him.

'You must have been aware of the financial situation of the Foundation.'

The solicitor piped up again. 'That's not a question, Detective Inspector. Do please move on.'

'How would you describe the financial position of the Foundation?'

'I'm not qualified to answer that question.'

'But if you were discussing things with your husband, surely he must have alluded to what was going on. For example, were there cash flow problems? Was the business able to pay its bills?'

'I'm not qualified to answer those sorts of questions.'

'That's not true is it, Mrs Peel. I understand from Leonard Ferrier, your agent in relation to the development of the commercial land, that you are intimately involved with all the day-to-day details of the proposed sale. He referred to you as having a confident grasp of all the details.'

Martha Peel smiled at Drake. It was cold and mechanical.

'Where were you going when we stopped you yesterday?'

'I was going to visit some relatives in South Africa. It had been planned some time ago.' Martha Peel made it sound like a holiday jaunt to Tenerife.

Drake found the details of the property in Cape Town Edward Murphy had stored secretly on his computer. He pushed a copy over at Martha Peel.

'Are you interested in buying this property?'

Peel lost that self-confident shine. She blinked and then frowned as she gazed at the paper in front of her.

'Did you want to reply to my question?'

'It's none of your business.'

'Murder is my business, Mrs Peel. We've spoken with the estate agent in South Africa who confirmed the transaction is proceeding and that you were expected on a flight yesterday.'

Now Martha Peel's stare turned anthracite-black.

'Would you please confirm your relationship with

Terence Willis?'

'How dare you interfere with my personal business.'

'He has posted a lot on his Facebook and Instagram pages and he's looking forward to a new life in the house you were buying. You've given authority for Leonard Ferrier to complete the deal for the sale of the land in Wales on your behalf. You had no intention of coming back from South Africa. You're expecting the land transaction to be completed so you could complete the purchase of this luxurious house near Cape Town.'

'It was all part of the Foundation's plans.'

'These property details were found secreted in a private folder on Edward Murphy's computer. It had nothing to do with the Foundation and you well know that.'

'I don't know how discussing the purchase of a property in South Africa is going to help you with your murder inquiry, Detective Inspector.'

'Did you kill Jack Holt?' Drake got straight to the point.

'It's absurd to think I would.'

'You must have been aware he had attended the same school as Edward Murphy. You told us yourself that we should be investigating Murphy's troubled childhood. By doing that you hoped it would throw us off the scent. And then when you killed your husband you thought everything was neatly tied off. You knew we suspected your husband of having killed Jack Holt and Edward Murphy. By staging a purported suicide you thought we would close both murder inquiries. And no doubt you thought of Ackland as some sort of insurance policy if we weren't prepared to believe your husband was responsible for killing Holt and Murphy.'

Peel chortled. 'This is absurd. Have you completely taken leave of your senses?'

'I'd like you to take a look at this,' Drake pushed over a copy of the suicide note. 'Your first mistake was to have typed out the note. But you couldn't have asked your husband to write it, could you? We could have checked your handwriting so you took a risk.'

'This is absurd.' Peel moved uncomfortably in her chair.

'We've had the wording of this suicide note examined by an expert who confirms that in his opinion it is simulated. It's a fake, Martha. It was written by you, wasn't it?'

Martha turned to her solicitor. 'Can't you stop this? This is madness.'

'This is all speculation and circumstantial, Detective Inspector,' the solicitor said.

Drake looked over at him. He wouldn't be reacting in the same way after the next section of the interview.

Drake pushed over an image of the lump hammer used to cave in Edward Murphy's head. 'This is the murder weapon used to kill Edward Murphy. Do you recognise it?'

'How on earth would I?'

'Because the crime scene investigators recovered a hair follicle from the hammer which contains your DNA. How do you explain that?'

Drake watched as a brief spasm of panic worked its way over Martha Peel's eyes. Then she blinked, several times.

'And finally, Mrs Peel, we have the evidence of your accomplice.'

'What the hell do you mean?'

'You left Martin Swan for dead at the property in Flint. But we arrived just in time to call an ambulance. He suffered a substantial head wound but the medics think he will pull through. Two of my officers spoke with him this morning when he provided evidence confirming he assisted you with the murders of Jack Holt and Edward Murphy, as well as staging the alleged suicide of your husband.'

Martha Peel suddenly stood up. 'This is madness… Martin Swan… I mean he, I thought.'

'You thought he was dead.'

She sat down. 'No, that's not what I meant. You're twisting everything.'

It took another hour for Drake to complete the

questioning of Martha Peel. With every answer she threw sand in his face, hoping she'd be able to explain away all the evidence. At the end Drake stared at her. She was a woman going to prison for a long time. No jury would acquit on the evidence they had. She'd get advice in the strongest possible terms to admit her guilt and limit her jail time.

He was pleased to leave Martha Peel walking back to her cell, complaining vociferously to her solicitor about Drake's conduct. He read the time on his watch. He was going to be late leaving and the requests from Superintendent Hobbs from an update could wait. He had more important things to do that afternoon.

Chapter 45

Drake indicated for Portmeirion and drove down for the parking area that he had used on previous occasions. It surprised him how quickly he had been able to put Martha Peel to the back of his mind. She had been charged with three murders and the attempted murder of Martin Swan before he had left the area custody suite, which meant she would begin the process of going to trial. Now he was having the afternoon and the rest of the weekend off.

Both his daughters were in good spirits, and they giggled in excitement at the prospect of visiting the venue where he and Annie were going to get married.

'We've still got enough time to have a leisurely walk around,' Drake said.

'I've been reading all about the history of the place,' Helen announced.

Both girls' jackets were buttoned up against the cold weather. Each had a patterned bobble hat in striking colours. It had amazed Drake how expensive each had been. He hadn't complained, his girls were worth every penny.

They walked down at a leisurely pace into the village, admiring the different buildings and their striking colours. The sheer beauty of the place never lessened its impact on Drake even though he had visited several times. They skirted around the lawned area in the middle and after a few moments found a café.

He ordered his usual Americano and a latte for Annie. Both Helen and Megan chose a complicated mixture of frothy milk and very little coffee, with bits of chocolate and marshmallow. Millionaire shortcakes and flapjacks accompanied the drinks. Drake realised how much he valued his family and regretted having spent too many hours in the past at his desk or in the Incident Room, or inside the area custody suite interviewing suspects.

They had enough time to wander down to the edge of the

estuary by the paved area outside the hotel itself. The last visit had been when Mair Drake had married Emlyn. Drake squeezed Annie's hand when they reached the spot overlooking the water where he had proposed. It had felt utterly natural and he recalled her smiling back and kissing him fondly. He remembered thinking, like a teenager, that he didn't want that moment to end.

Now in a few weeks' time, when the weather would be better, they'd be able to enjoy the view as husband and wife.

His daughters walked ahead. They had reached the quay and looked down at the pretend yacht. The Welsh Dragon, the national flag of Wales, fluttered weakly on a flagpole. A small swimming pool used by guests of the hotel was behind them and Drake resolved to book a weekend for Annie and himself at the hotel in the summer. They could enjoy the outdoor pool and all the luxury the hotel offered.

'We'd better walk up to the Town Hall.' Annie tapped on her watch.

Drake nodded. He called over to both girls and they joined Annie and him as they walked up to the building known as the Town Hall in which an ornate roof from a stately home had been rebuilt by Clough Williams-Ellis, the man behind Portmeirion.

They climbed the stairs to the inside of the building and memories of his mother's ceremony came flooding back. One of the venue's wedding planners greeted them.

'I'm Ian Drake and this is Annie, my fiancé,' Drake said. 'And this is Helen and Megan.'

'It's lovely to meet you all. I'm sure you're going to have a most wonderful day here. Let me explain how we can create fabulous memories for you as a family.'

Chapter 46

Drake drove over to the Crown Court building at Mold. Several weeks had elapsed since he had interviewed Martha Peel and the recollection of doing so had receded. He had been well accustomed to not allowing the memory of such interviews to play on his mind.

Martha Peel's attempts to betray Martin Swan as a deluded liar who was infatuated with her soon evaporated. At the initial hearing her lawyers vociferously argued her innocence and even made a bail application. The swiftness with which the judge dismissed their application entertained Drake and from the comments of Andy Thorsen who was sitting by his side it was clear that her lawyers were completely misguided. 'Bail application was stupid,' Thorsen had said at the time.

She soon changed her stance and pleaded guilty which meant that neither Drake nor any of the other detectives on his team would need to give evidence. There had never been any doubt Martin Swan would plead guilty to two charges of murder. He would be sentenced to life in prison, but his minimum term would reflect his involvement and the degree to which Martha Peel had manipulated him.

Drake parked and walked over to the building he had visited many times. He found Andy Thorsen sitting in the office reserved for the team of prosecution lawyers. Thorsen introduced Drake to the barrister prosecuting the case.

'This is Sean Thomas,' Thorsen said.

'I'm very pleased to meet you,' Thomas said, thrusting a hand at Drake. 'This has been a most difficult case and you and your team deserve a great deal of thanks.'

'Thank you. I'm pleased Martha has seen sense and pleaded guilty.'

'The barrister representing her is extremely experienced and she would have given her very clear unequivocal advice. She stands zero chance of securing an acquittal.'

'She planned everything so carefully, or thought she had.'

'I wanted to ask you about the Foundation. Tell me what happened?'

'Without Mervyn Peel and his wife, the organisation collapsed. There were debts owed to a bank and one of the properties was repossessed. Once Mr and Mrs Peel were out of the equation there was no one willing to take on their operation.'

'I'm amazed how many people were taken in by it.'

'They took advantage of people and once a vulnerable person had committed their capital and finances to the organisation they were stuck, like a fly in a trap.'

'It's all very sad.'

'Some of the people who were conned out of their money have started a group action against what remains of the Foundation's assets. They may get some of their money back.'

'That's a jolly good thing. At least, if the judge asks me, I can tell him.'

Drake wanted to share that one of his own detectives had a personal connection to the Foundation. Winder had told him that Phoebe's reconciliation with her parents had been an emotional affair. Tears had been shed but a flood of love had enveloped her. She had slept for hours on end and it had taken weeks for her to return to a semblance of normality.

Winder had beamed broadly when he had shared with Drake that Phoebe was talking about starting a legal career. He had even mentioned she was going to do work experience with a local firm of solicitors he knew.

A court clerk came into the room and announced the judge was ready. They filed down into the court room and Drake sat to one side. Andy Thorsen sat behind Sean Thomas. Martha Peel was brought up from the cells and she sat in the dock at the rear of the court. She looked straight ahead, making no attempt to look in Drake's direction.

Martin Swan joined her in the dock, looking tired and drawn.

She got to her feet as directed by the court clerk and entered a guilty plea to all the charges she faced. Martin got to his feet and entered the same plea. They both sat down.

Thomas took time to carefully explain to the judge everything that had happened. His presentation was articulate and comprehensive. The judge nodded but said nothing, occasionally scribbling a note on his pad.

As soon as Thomas had finished, the judge invited Martha Peel's barrister to address him. It didn't come as a surprise to Drake she tried to blame Mervyn Peel for everything. He had been a controlling, malign influence in her life for over twenty years. She had been unable to do anything without his say-so. She didn't have her own life and he controlled everything she did.

Drake didn't have any way to disprove anything the barrister said. It was no excuse for murder but perhaps it might lessen the minimum term. Martha Peel might be released from jail earlier than might otherwise be the case.

Martin Swan's defence barrister was on much firmer ground and referred to the various psychological reports prepared. Everything pointed to his client being a vulnerable individual who had been seduced by the Peel Foundation and its promise of personal fulfilment, as well as Martha Peel's offer of a new life in South Africa.

'Get up,' the judge said once the defence barristers had completed their pleas of mitigation. 'I have heard everything that has been said by learned counsel on your behalf. These were shocking and depraved murders and you, Martha Peel, will be sentenced to life imprisonment with a minimum term of thirty years. I have listened to everything that has been said of you and on your behalf, Martin Swan. I take into account everything said about your involvement with the Peel Foundation and Mrs Peel in particular. You will also be sentenced to life imprisonment, there is no other alternative sentence I can impose. However, taking everything into account the minimum term will be twelve years. Take them down.'

The judge left the court room and, once Peel and Swan had been taken down to the cells to start their life sentences, the sounds of chatter and people leaving filled the court room. Drake thanked Thorsen and Thomas. He made his way to the entrance lobby and watched as a civilian from the public relations department briefed members of the press. He didn't want her to spot him, he didn't want to do any interviews. He didn't want to think about Martha Peel and Martin Swan and Mervyn Peel or the Peel Foundation ever again.

He walked over to his car. The temperature was warming significantly now and next weekend he was getting married. There was nothing more important than that.

Printed in Great Britain
by Amazon

30476915R00167